The Path Forward

By

Hazel Goss

Other Books by Hazel Goss

Forced to Flee
A novel set in war-torn Kosovo in 1992. Follow the journeys of two doctors who make different choices when faced with Serbian hostility and atrocities.

The Pathway Back
The first book in the series of time travel adventures. Read some of the reviews.

Mitchell Ward
A moral dilemma
This story moved very quickly and believably through time. It was very thought provoking – the realisation of how much would alter if the past was changed. A really good read. I hope there will be a sequel.

R Dyer
An exciting adventure through time with romance and fantasy
I really enjoyed this book. It has time travel into two periods of history and gives the reader plenty of surprises.

A J Wagstaff
Cleverly planned time travel ripping yarn
The characters were believable, and I could empathise with them, coming as they did from the same world as me. These people drink tea, go for runs in the park, enjoy an occasional cruise and lead perfectly normal lives, apart, that is from the discovery of an old ship's timer and its effect on their family.

To my sister, Lesley, for reading my manuscript and my daughter, Amanda, for reading it twice.
Finally, to my husband, John, for his support, patience and encouragement, with love.

Chapter 1

2035

The spotlight from the drone caught the woman and the little girl in its glare. 'Danger, danger, go inside, underground. Danger, Danger, go inside…' the mantra repeated, chilling them with fear. Where could they go?

'Hey, come in here, quick!'

They followed the man through a front door and ran down the stairs to the basement. Just before the last step the woman stumbled and fell. She cried out and her daughter shouted, 'Mummy.' The man helped her up and pulled them into his basement flat and shut the door.

*

Xen struggled for handholds, hampered by narrow fissures and the dark. The way out had to be up. He felt with his right hand, gripped and pulled. A brick came away, tumbled down, hit his shoulder and covered him with loose debris.

His eyes were gritty. He blinked and blinked. For a moment he couldn't move. When his breathing calmed, he tried again. This time he touched concrete. When he pulled on it there was a feeling of solidity. He pushed up on his left leg, pulled with his right hand, and then he saw a glimmer of light.

Carefully he tested the next handhold. He just needed a ledge to push his foot against. The one he found was too high to be comfortable, but he put his foot on it, testing its strength. Now, thrusting upwards, his arms aching with effort, his head and shoulders were out.

Relief and joy diminished when he finally stood and surveyed what had once been his hometown, Harrogate. It was unrecognisable; flattened to heaps of rubble. Flames flickered from crevices and smoke mingled with the dust-laden air.

He had lived in a flat with a view of Parliament Street; opposite him should be Betty's Tea Room. There was still a slope down towards the Royal Baths, but no buildings left standing.

Xen wondered how long he'd been underground – hours, days? No, he was not really hungry, though the dust had made him very thirsty. Where were all the other people? Was he the lone survivor? What cataclysmic event had caused this devastation? He'd no memory of an explosion; they'd not been at war. A gas leak couldn't have destroyed everything.

Xen became aware of his bare feet; the toes were grazed and sore. Walking anywhere was not going to be easy but he couldn't stay where he was. If he could make his way down towards the Montpellier Quarter, where there had been cafes and wine bars, he might find an unbroken bottle. He would even be willing to drink the sulphurous spa water – if he could find some. Would there still be a little stream in Valley Gardens?

Stepping carefully on the largest chunks of concrete the toppling of masonry sounded loud in the eerie silence. The going was very slow. Xen found he was holding his breath to listen for any sounds of other people. There was nothing. The sun shone weakly through the dust haze but illuminated no living creature.

'Hello', he called, his voice sounding muffled, oddly dead. Louder, 'Hello, is anyone alive here?'

A response. 'We're trapped. Help us, please. We've a child and Joanna's injured. Can you call the fire brigade and ambulance?'

What could he say? How could he give them no hope?
'I'm getting closer to you. Keep talking; tell me your names.'

'I'm Andy and my wife's Isabelle. We're not hurt but we can't find a way out.'

'My name's Xen. You're right underneath me. I'll move some of the rubble. Shout if you want me to stop or see daylight.'

He picked up bricks and chunks of concrete, tossing them away as quickly as he could. Sweat soaked his pyjama top. His throat rasped from breathing the dust. One hefty piece of concrete was almost beyond his strength. He levered up a corner, heaved and as it rolled, he staggered and almost fell. Steady, he thought, I'll be no help to anyone if I injure myself.

'I can see light, Xen. We can help now. We'll move the rubble from our side – it'll be quicker.'

Two more slabs of concrete and they were grasping hands. As Xen pulled, Andy emerged, ghost-like with dust. They turned and helped Isabelle and then the rest of the group – an older man and a little girl with her mother. The mother, Joanna, had a broken arm, and everyone had small cuts, bruises and abrasions.

They thanked Xen, excitedly, all talking at once, but fell silent when they saw the state of the town. The sight was shocking. They sagged down onto the rubble, unable to comprehend what had happened. Xen sat too, but his need for a drink was pushing him into action. He looked at the group. The little girl and her mother Joanna were dressed and had shoes on, but the others were clad in pyjamas with nothing on their feet. Moving was going to be difficult, painful, but necessary.

'I'm very thirsty. You must be too. Shall we walk down the hill? Perhaps the blast missed the lower levels. As we go, we can shout to see if there are any other people who need help to get out.'

3

They were numb and barely managed a nod. Xen stood and picked up the little girl. Joanna stood quickly, seeing this stranger holding her child. She bit her lip, trying not to show her pain. Slowly everyone began to move, helping each other over the treacherous rubble. Morgan, the older man recovered enough to shout, 'Hello does anyone need help?' This prompted Isabelle and Andy to join in. They all listened between shouts as they picked their way slowly and carefully over the rubble, but there was no response.

'What's your name?' Xen asked the girl. She gave no reply but sucked her thumb like a baby. He thought she must be five or six.

'My name's Xen and we're going to look after you.' She closed her eyes and he felt her grow heavy and limp as she fell asleep. There were so many questions he wanted to ask, but his thirst seemed more important than answers.

They stopped when they found some buildings still standing. Andy tested the door of a wine bar and found it unlocked. 'Hello, anyone here?' He came out after a few moments. 'The people are all dead. I need some help to move them.' Isabelle took the child from Xen and waited outside with Joanna as the others went inside.

The dead had bulging eyes and their mouths were open in a silent scream. The three men tried not to look at them as they heaved and dragged the bodies into a small room off the main bar. They placed them neatly, side by side, moving furniture to make space. It felt wrong to pile bodies on top of each other, like sacks of compost.

'You can come in now,' said Andy. The women had been sitting on the rubble and got up stiffly. Inside the men had already opened bottles of cold beer. Xen played barman and asked what they wanted.

'I'll have a beer too – that looks great,' said Joanna and can you find an orange juice for Ruby?'

Xen searched the fridge, noticing the light was out. 'You have choices, orange, apple or blackcurrant.'

Joanna looked at Ruby, but she didn't respond. 'I think she'd prefer orange.'

They all sat and drank, relishing the cleansing of the dust from their throats. When most of his drink had gone, Morgan stood and began to search behind the bar. He found a first aid kit and brought it to where Joanna was sitting. 'Show me your arm.'

She laid it on the table, wincing and he saw that it was badly swollen just above the wrist. He looked inside the first aid kit and gave her two painkillers. 'These should take the edge off the pain, but your arm will need some splints. I'll see what I can find.'

'Thank you.'

Morgan looked for pieces of wood outside, but there was nothing suitable. He came back in, frowning and then saw some handheld order tablets. He hefted them, solid plastic, slim enough and brought them to the table. 'Right let's bandage these in place to support your wrist. Isabelle will you give me a hand?'

When they had finished Joanna was very pale but managed to whisper, 'Thank you.'

'I'm sorry if we hurt you, but it had to be done. Now we could do with a sling,' said Morgan.

'This will do,' Isabelle said, handing him a diaphanous scarf. 'It was on the back of that chair.' She folded it into a triangle and soon the wrist was cradled.

'It feels much more comfortable now,' said Joanna and managed a smile.

*

Xen was feeling anxious. The immediate problem of thirst had been solved. 'When we feel better, we'll need to move on,' he said.

'Yes,' said Morgan, 'but where do you suggest we go? There's shelter here and plenty of food. Everything in the freezer's still frozen. It might be better if we stay here for a day or two.'

Everyone agreed with Morgan. Sitting at tables, in a civilised way, made the disaster outside seem like a bad dream.

'Of course, we should stay until we feel better. But the toilets don't flush, there's no running water and no electricity. Those bodies in the other room will soon begin to decompose,' said Xen.

'Then there'll be disease,' said Isabelle. They nodded heads in agreement but there was no more discussion. They were exhausted and fell asleep, some in the chairs where they sat, and others curled up on the carpet.

Chapter 2

Xen woke up in his own bed. 'Maizy, what's the time?'
'It's seven thirty-five,' said the disembodied voice.
'Maizy, what's the date?'
'Monday, June 3rd, 2030.'
Living alone, Xen sometimes held longer conversations with Maizy, but it would soon be time to leave for work.

He got up, turned back to the bed to smooth the sheet and saw it was covered in grit. He looked at his hands, saw they were filthy and covered in grazes and cuts. He became aware of his sore feet. It was that shifting of rubble and concrete. I must have a shower and change that sheet, he thought. The bizarreness of that thought made him look out of the window at the street below. Everything outside was normal, no sign of a catastrophic event. The dream had seemed so real. It was real. He had the dirt and cuts on his hands to prove it.

He went into the bathroom and showered, recalling the dire state of the people in his dream, Isabelle, Andy, Morgan, Joanna and the little girl, Ruby. They wouldn't be able to enjoy the luxury of a hot shower.

Why was he thinking about them? They were characters in a dream; not real people, or were they?

Still in a state of confusion, Xen went into the kitchen, turned on the television and drank his coffee. Maizy was able to turn any appliance on, and he had programmed her to turn the drinks machine on, set for coffee, seven-thirty every morning. He put bread in the toaster, cradling the mug in his hand. The news was about China, Russia and America trying to settle their differences. The talks were taking place in Europe. It sounded positive. As long as they were talking, peace would reign throughout the world.

Xen ate his breakfast standing. It seemed he would be ready for work quicker if he didn't sit. He placed his used cup and tray in the dishwasher, 'Maizy, dishwasher on', and he heard the machine filling as he picked up his keys and briefcase.

His flat was on the third floor and he usually ran down the stairs, but today he used the lift. The efforts made the day before had exhausted him. He tried to jog to the station, but resorted to walking, his grazed feet rubbing on his shoes. He arrived, just in time to board the train to Leeds. Nodding to other commuters he recognised he then sat next to a smartly dressed woman. She was not inclined to chat, her eyes and fingers busy on a tablet. She was at work already and hadn't even got to the office.

When the train arrived, Xen got off and joined the press of people in Leeds, all hurrying purposefully heading for the row of taxis. There was a short queue. When it was his turn, he opened the door and keyed in his destination and then paid using his phone. Driverless taxis used to be called auto taxis but now the auto had been dropped. It was still possible to ask for a driver, but commuters rarely did.

At the college, his walk to the lecture theatre took just a few minutes. Xen organised everything he would need. His presentation, technology in the classroom, was stored on the tablet in his bag, and he felt confident having given the lecture several times before.

One or two students were in the room before him, chatting quietly, so he said good morning to them and then checked the Wi-Fi was working. It would be ironic if the technology were to fail.

When it was time to begin, he looked at the faces in front of him and was shocked to find Isabelle, from his dream. Seeing her stopped his thoughts in their tracks and transported him back to the night before. An awareness of rustling and impatient chatter dragged him back to the present.

'Are you unwell, Professor Baxter?'

'No, no, I'm fine. Just remembered something, that's all. Let's get started.'

The lecture lasted an hour and then Xen was free to have a drink in the refectory and check his notes for the lecture he had to give in the afternoon. It was considerably more interesting to him than the one he had given in the morning.

He was going to demonstrate a new phone that needed just daylight or artificial light to work. The technology was revolutionary and ideal for places in the world that lacked electricity. This phone did not rely on masts for its signal and never needed charging.

One of these would've been useful last night, he thought. They might have been able to locate people trapped underground or found out if the destruction extended throughout the whole country.

Xen was making a mental note to borrow one and then realised the events of the dream could not really have happened. Despite that, he couldn't explain how he had woken aching and with dirty, sore hands and feet, but now was not the time to dwell on it. He needed to concentrate on work.

When he left the lecture theatre at five o'clock, he heard his name being called and turned to see Sean hastening to catch up with him.

'Xen, glad I've caught you. Are you rushing home or have you time for a drink?'

'I'm not in a rush, Sean. Are we just being sociable or is there a problem?'

'A bit of both, really. What about that bar we all went to for Dave's birthday?'

'Fine. If you're ready, we can walk there now.' They strolled in the sunshine and Xen realised he was happy to be delaying his return home. While he was out, and with company, he could forget the dream. They sat on bar stools and Xen ordered the drinks, registering his fingerprint and then tapping the symbols.

They were served quickly, the beers cold and refreshing. For a moment they both drank without speaking, then Sean began. 'I've been looking forward to this all day. Sheer heaven. Just what I needed.'

'Why? What's happened?'

'Well, nothing specific really. I'm bored. The same old routine, teaching physics and cosmological theory. I want to do something that will make a difference.'

'Like what?' Xen saw Sean colour slightly. 'Come on, Sean. You've got to tell me now you've got so far.'

'OK, I've been accepted to work for the government.' Xen's eyebrows raised but he said nothing, so Sean continued. 'It's kind of hush-hush. I'm not allowed to talk about it.'

'Ha, you're going to be some kind of spy.' Xen laughed, looking with incredulity at his friend. Sean was athletic, Scandinavian looking. He would make an ideal James Bond. 'I think we should have something stronger than beer to toast your new job.'

'You got the last round. I'll get these. Wine, whisky?'

'A glass of red, thanks.' Xen watched Sean tapping his order, feeling pleased for his friend but regretting he would soon lose him. Friends made at work tended to talk about it. They discussed other members of staff or certain difficult, or brilliant students. It would be almost impossible to chat to Sean once he moved to his new job, especially if he was sworn to secrecy. They rarely discussed their private lives. Perhaps they should.

Xen knew that Sean was single but had been married briefly and miserably. He was not sure of any hobbies but, by his physique, he assumed he was sporty.

When Sean returned to his seat and the drinks came, along with a bottle to top them up, Xen asked, 'Will you have to move away from here – to London?'

'Not initially but I'll go away for training. Then, apparently, I can live anywhere I like. We can still have a drink together and you can moan about the state of the students, as usual. I'd like that.'

'So would I,' said Xen. They finished their drinks and topped them up. 'I'll have to have something to eat if you intend to finish that bottle. Another one of these and I'll not find my way to the station.'

'They do great steak and ale pies. Shall I order?'

'Yes, but you must let me pay for mine.'

'Definitely not; I'm celebrating, and the new job comes with a much higher salary.'

Xen thanked him with a rueful smile. He wished he had Sean's confidence to make more of his life.

*

That evening Xen arrived home late, still feeling the effects of the wine. As he entered the hall, he bumped into the little table that he usually put his keys and wallet on. The nautical sand timer, one of his few ornaments, wobbled dangerously but he caught it before it fell.

He went into the bathroom, and as he washed his hands, he looked at the bags under his eyes and noticed some grey hairs. That's the trouble with being dark haired, he thought, you go grey early, but at least I'm not going bald, like some men of thirty-two.

Going to the kitchen, he avoided the table in the hall, but seeing the sand timer reminded him of the day he found it.

*

Diving was a recreation he'd indulged in for years. The last dive he had gone on, during the Easter break, had been in the Indian Ocean. The wreck they had explored was the *Santa Monique*, a cargo ship which sank in 1895.

Whenever possible he booked diving trips with Racine. He had met her during their training, and they made a good team. They seemed to breathe at the same rate, so their air consumption matched. She was totally reliable, and he felt

11

safe with her. She said the same about him. They never met in between diving holidays and were not attracted to each other. Racine was happily married with teenage children. He envied her contentment.

On their last day, when they had explored all areas of the *Santa Monique*, Xen spotted the top of the timer sticking out of the sand. He brushed the sand away, thrilled with finding something that looked really old. He showed it to Racine, who looked impressed, then he placed it in his dive bag.

They surfaced soon after the find, and while still bobbing in the water, before getting back on board, Xen asked Racine not to mention his bounty to the organisers. The rules concerning finding artefacts were not well established by the Indian government and consequently some of the more unscrupulous dive companies were keen to claim any treasures found. There was quite a lucrative market for artefacts.

When he was back on shore, in his hotel room, Xen admired his find. It seemed unaffected by such a long sojourn buried under the sea. The glass was still intact and the sand inside still flowed. It had some tiny markings on the bottom which indicated that it was not from the *Santa Monique* but from a ship called the *Daphne*. This was surprising. He wondered if it had been sold on when the *Daphne* was no longer seaworthy. That would make it older than 1895.

He had tried to find information about it on his tablet, but the *Daphne* seemed elusive. He wrapped the timer in his dirty washing, hoping customs wouldn't stop him and search his luggage at the airport. The flight was overnight, and he had had a weird dream on the aircraft but dismissed it in the morning.

*

While cleaning his teeth, getting ready for bed, Xen wondered if he would return to that vivid dream he'd had.

He got up, went to his briefcase, and put the phone that he'd used in his lecture on his wrist. Even if he didn't dream there was no harm in wearing it until he had to give it back. Now he felt he could let himself relax and sleep.

Chapter 3

Xen opened his eyes reluctantly, aware of the bed feeling very hard.

'Morning, or should I say afternoon. Would you like some breakfast? We have rolls, butter and jam.'

'That sounds brilliant. Any tea or coffee to go with it?'

'Sorry,' said Isabelle. 'We're too scared of a possible gas explosion to make a fire. There's bottled water, beer or various soft drinks.'

'Then a soft drink it is, any flavour, thank you,' said Xen and sat up. He saw Joanna cradling her arm, her daughter half perched on her lap. He stood up feeling full of aches and went over to her. 'Is it very painful?'

'It could be worse. Morgan seems to find painkillers in the most unlikely places, so I'm dosed up.'

'And how's Ruby?'

At the sound of her name the girl squirmed and looked briefly up at Xen, but she said nothing.

Xen ate with enjoyment but missed hot coffee. The fizzy fruit drink was both too sweet and tasteless. When he'd finished, he took his plate to the kitchen with a view to washing it, but then remembered there was no running water. He put it on the pile with the other dirty plates and went to find Morgan or Andy.

They were outside, talking earnestly and quietly, but they stopped when Xen reached them. 'Sorry, am I interrupting something?'

Morgan smiled, 'Not at all. We were just discussing where to go after here. The bodies smell really bad now and I think we can only stay one more night before we must move. We were about to walk to Valley Gardens to see if there's anything left of the café, or any useful shops or houses on the way. Are you coming?'

Xen nodded. Andy went back into the bar to tell Isabelle, who said she would come with them, so the four of them set off as quickly as they could over the rough ground.

Isabelle walked beside Xen. 'I was looking at you when you were asleep – I think I've seen you before. Did you ever lecture at Leeds Uni?'

Xen nodded. 'Were you a student there?'

'Yes, five years ago – 2030.' She didn't notice the shock on his face because they were traversing rubble and she was looking down.

He wanted to ask her more about life since 2030, before the war or whatever it was, but Morgan and Andy, who were a little way ahead, started shouting excitedly. They stopped talking and caught them up.

The two men were looking at a shop that appeared to be intact. The window was not even cracked. Morgan tried the door, but it was locked. 'I suppose the destruction did happen at night, so it's not surprising. Perhaps we should knock or call out. There must be other people alive.'

It sounded shockingly loud when Morgan banged on the door and shouted to attract attention, but there was no response. They wasted no more time and put their shoulders to the door, which failed to budge.

'It looks easy when you see police do it on television,' said Isabelle. 'Perhaps we could just lob a stone through the glass panel of the door.'

The men looked sheepish as they did as she suggested. They opened the door, careful not to tread on the shards of glass. It was a treasure house for hikers, filled with rucksacks, boots, socks, waterproof coats, picnic blankets and hampers. They each found their own size in socks and boots and put them on. Then they decided to take five large rucksacks and a small one for Ruby.

'Let's put a sleeping bag in each so we have a more comfortable night,' said Isabelle.

Xen nodded, 'We can stock up on food and water tonight, and if we begin our travels in this direction, we can take waterproofs and as many picnic blankets as we can carry. We might have to sleep rough,' said Xen.

'You know it's possible to carry two rucksacks at a time. I've seen people do it. They have a small one on their front and a large one on their back,' said Andy, so they took extra rucksacks, including two for Joanna.

When they entered the bar the stench of the dead was appalling. Joanna and Ruby stood up, smiling a welcome. They smiled even more when they heard the wealth of things in the shop.

'That's great news,' said Joanna, 'but I'm not sure we should sleep here tonight. There's enough daylight left for us to fill the rucksacks and go down to the shop. We can find space to sleep in there, can't we? The smell here is awful now.'

'Mummy is that little pink one mine?' Everyone smiled as she gave Ruby her rucksack. They'd all worried that the shock had made her mute.

The rucksacks were filled with tinned and dried food at the bottom and bottled water at the top. Xen thought the most vital need, longer term, would be unpolluted water, but he accepted they were doing the best they could at the moment.

The group carried their heavy loads down to the shop where they rested and slept that night. As Xen shut his eyes, he hoped he would be back home in his own bed when he woke.

*

He was disappointed when he woke, to find he was still there, in the future. Dreams could cram a lot into a short time, but this seemed the longest dream ever. Perhaps it wasn't a dream. How could any dream seem so real? Had he moved permanently forward five years? The others were still asleep, so he went outside to look at his phone. He realised it would be old technology now, but he had to try. There was no signal, but the phone was not supposed to need a battery and connected directly to the satellite network for information. He stood in the early morning sunshine, looking at the device balefully when he saw it light up with a news flash.

China's death ray indiscriminately annihilates western towns. 'This is the greatest threat to civilisation since the nuclear bomb,' said the Prime Minister. 'China's actions are condemned by all nations of the world. What response will Russia and America make? Is this now a world war?'

Xen went back inside, and when the others woke, he shared the news with them.

'I suppose I should've figured that for myself,' said Morgan.

'Yea,' agreed Andy. 'With all the media hype and panic, before we woke up to all this, I suppose we should.'

'Well I didn't. I still can't understand why a town like this, with such beautiful buildings, full of ordinary people, should be destroyed. It makes no sense to me at all.' Isabelle's voice rose to a squeak as she finished speaking. She began to cry, and Joanna hugged her with her good arm. Ruby, sensing something bad began to wail in sympathy.

The men looked at each other and nodded.

'Right, we've no time to feel sorry for ourselves. Somewhere in the countryside there must be people who can help us. There must be smaller towns like Ripon, or Boroughbridge that have survived intact. I suggest we have a drink, open some of the cans of fruit we bought and then move on. Come on, up you get.' Andy was in organiser mode again.

The women sniffed, wiped their eyes on their sleeves and stood. The simple breakfast was soon over, and they collected their rucksacks and left the shop. Once outside they all looked at Andy. He'd given the order to move so they were ready to follow. Andy was tall, brown haired and solidly built. He looked dependable. But at that moment he was uncertain of which way to go. Xen used the Iridium sat-nav on his prototype solar phone and they began to walk the ten miles that would lead, they hoped, to civilisation. Progress was very slow. Even the wider roads were strewn with rubble, but at least they had good footwear.

'We could do with an army vehicle, something with caterpillar tracks. That would trundle over this terrain effortlessly,' said Morgan.

'It should be easier when we clear Harrogate and get onto country roads,' said Andy. He was holding Isabelle's hand, both to comfort and to steady her. Joanna was holding Ruby's hand and Xen wondered where her husband or partner was. She'd not said anything, and he was reluctant to ask.

After three hours they walked down the hill to the River Nidd at Knaresborough. The car park by the river looked normal, except there were no cars, and there were buildings standing beside the river but those further up the hill were destroyed in the same way as Harrogate. Xen led the group into the car park where they rested and had something to eat. He wondered if the river was clean enough to fill their water bottles and took a closer look. Bodies, human and animal floated along, turning as the currant took them, languorous flotsam in no hurry to reach the sea. He turned away quickly, almost overcome by the macabre scene.

As they ate their picnic Xen said, 'I don't understand why I'm the only one with a phone. What's happened to yours?'

'I have to wear this. I call it my badge of shame.' Joanna pulled up the sleeve on her good arm to show what looked like a watch with a yellow wristband. Everyone looked with interest as she went on to explain. 'It looks like a phone, but

I can't make calls or use the internet. I couldn't find a job that let me work only in school hours. This device is supplied by Social Services to people out of work. They top it up once a month so I can pay my bills. When it's empty Ruby and I go hungry.

'And does that happen often?' asked Isabelle. She saw Joanna nod and felt moved to touch her hand. 'I'm so sorry.'

There was a short silence and Morgan said, 'I had a solafone, similar to yours but smaller. I took it off at night. Lost it when we got buried.'

Everyone looked at Andy, prompting him to say, 'We both decided that our lives, and everyone else's, were being wasted staring at screens. People seem to have lost the ability to communicate unless it's by an electronic device. Solafones are essential but, like Morgan, we took ours off at night. They would've been useful as a torch when the building collapsed, but we couldn't find them. I was wondering if I could use yours to see if our relatives are alive. I only have a Mum, but Izzy, Isabelle, has both parents.'

Xen took his off and handed it to him.

Chapter 4

Isabelle's parents, Jason and Catherine Brownlow, were sailing in the Mediterranean. They were both retired and had sold their house in Harrogate not long after Izzy got married. They had spent most of the money on a second-hand, ocean-going yacht. They were both dinghy sailors but had enjoyed flotilla holidays in the Greek Islands and longed for the freedom to explore the world with their own boat.

They went on navigation courses and Jason studied for his Yacht master's certificate. When they felt they could learn no more theory but needed to put their knowledge to the test, they ventured across the Channel. On that first cruise they'd been blessed with light winds and sunshine. It had been idyllic, and they made plans to explore further afield, preferably somewhere warm. The decision to follow the sun resulted in them sailing down the coast of France, stopping at various ports along the way.

They had done the same along the coast of Portugal then Spain and finally Gibraltar. Neither of them could speak Spanish or Portuguese, so they had been looking forward to being able to speak English again. They were moored in the yacht harbour when the attack began.

Initially it was difficult for Jason and Catherine to understand the extent of the destruction. They consulted their solafones and discovered the news with horror. No capital cities had been hit and none in Third World countries. One small town in America had been razed, two in Russia, one in Spain and one in Britain, Harrogate. Once they read that Catherine began to cry and Jason fought down his fear so as to ring their daughter.

There was no reply, so he rang Andy. He left messages with both. They clung to each other in despair. What chance was there of Izzy being alive if the reports were true? *There had been a total annihilation of everyone and every building in Harrogate.*

'Our old house will have gone too. If we hadn't bought this yacht we would have died,' said Jason.

'I don't care about our old house. I can't believe she's gone. Jason, I want to go back. We must search for her.'

'We need to find out if this weapon leaves any fall out. It could leave poisoned air, like Chernobyl.'

'God! You're so damned sensible. Let's leave anyway, today. I want to be in England. I really want to be there now. Could we leave the boat here and fly?'

Jason stood up abruptly, walked away from her with his hands over his face. 'Catherine stop, please; I need to think.'

While he thought Catherine looked for flights. Most of them went to London, but on a Wednesday, there was a flight to Manchester. Her phone showed her it was Tuesday. They could pack and catch that flight if Jason agreed.

She went into the tiny galley, made tea then cut two slices of honey cake. She carried the tray back on deck. Jason gave her a wan smile. 'Tea and cake, the British panacea for all ills, thank you. I'm sorry about my outburst. I really don't know what to do.'

'I do. We're going to book two seats on the Manchester flight tomorrow, at 10am. We'll hire a car and drive to Harrogate.' Catherine waited for objections to come but he just nodded. He seemed to be happy to let her take control. As they ate the cake and drank the tea, in silence, Catherine booked the flights.

There was then an active time where they shared tasks. Jason went to pay the Harbour Master two month's mooring fees while Catherine packed clothes and other

21

essentials. When Jason returned, she asked him to take their non-perishable food to the food bank in town. By the time he came back all their tasks were completed.

They ate in the town that night in a café they had visited before but if felt very different. All the other diners were subdued. Jason wondered how many had friends or relatives in a devastated town. Perhaps they were frightened of the possibility of another world war.

The television was on and it showed the destruction of the towns in America, Spain and then Harrogate. It was so total; nothing could be recognised. Catherine cried uncontrollably when it showed Harrogate, broadcasting images from a low flying drone. Jason paid for their meal and led her out of the café and back to the marina.

The following morning, they barely spoke, both wrapped in misery, devoid of hope. They locked the boat, gave the key to the Harbour Master and got into the waiting taxi. When they reached the airport and checked in their luggage, there was an announcement. Flights were proceeding as usual, but passengers should be aware of the possible danger of more attacks.

'What shall we do? I'm prepared to risk it. The airline wouldn't send up planes if they believed they were in danger.' Jason saw Catherine nod her agreement and continued, 'It's a show of power by China. A threat saying don't mess with us because we have the ultimate weapon.'

'I'm worried about reprisals. Any similar horror, like a nuclear bomb, would trigger a full-scale war. I suppose it's possible the other powers may also have some kind of death ray.' Their gloomy conversation was halted because it was time to get on the plane.

The journey seemed endless and neither of them could lose themselves in the films on offer. They tried to sleep but it was impossible.

'I should've tried Phil and Jenny's numbers, Sonia's or any of our sailing friends. I could only think of Izzy.'

22

'We can still contact them when we arrive at Manchester,' said Catherine, covering his hand with hers. 'They haven't contacted us either. We know why that could be.' Her voice tailed off to nothing. It was too hard to say they could be dead. She wondered, how anyone could face the death of all of their friends and family?

It was a relief when the plane touched down and they had something practical to do. The queue at the car hire was not long and, when it was Jason's turn, he explained they wanted an auto car but with an over-ride so it could be driven if there was no signal available. This was an unusual request and the booking assistant called a supervisor.

'We are going close to Harrogate and I have no idea if the auto car signal there was destroyed along with the town.'

'I understand sir, but I must point out it'll cost an additional £100 per week. How long do you want it for?'

'I'm not sure, but I'll pay for two weeks.' The deal was done, and the car brought itself to meet them just outside the office. The luggage was loaded, and they set off, having set the destination for Wetherby, south of Harrogate.

There seemed to be nothing to say. They sat quiet with their own thoughts, such that Jason jumped when Catherine moved suddenly. She said, 'I'm trying Sonia.' He could hear the ring tone and grinned with delight when Sonia answered.

'I'm so pleased you're OK,' said Catherine. 'I assume you were not at home when it happened.'

'No, thank goodness. Roger and I were having a short break in London. I expect to find our house destroyed but we're going there now to see.'

'Where are you, exactly, because we're just coming up to the Wetherby services?'

'That's amazing. We're in the café there, rather scared about going the rest of the way.'

'Stay there and we'll meet up.'

23

'That's wonderful,' said Sonia. 'See you soon.'

Catherine closed down the phone and gave a sigh of relief. 'I had the terrifying fear we'd lost all the people we love. I just want to contact Izzy and I can come to terms with everything else.'

The car parked itself. They hugged each other before going to the café to meet their closest friends.

As they walked towards the entrance Catherine's phone rang. She didn't recognize the number but listened and then squealed with delight.

Chapter 5

'My mum and dad are alive and in Wetherby. I've told them where we are, and they've asked us to stay here. My aunty Sonia's coming too with her husband Roger. I can't believe it.' Isabelle's joy was infectious. Everyone hugged everyone else. It was wonderful to share good news. 'We should all stay here because they've got two cars. There'll be room for all of us.'

'I wonder if I could use the solafone now, if we're not rushing on. I have a daughter and grandchildren, hopefully still alive in Leeds,' said Morgan. 'They'll be worried about me.' Isabelle looked at Xen for confirmation.

'No problem, Morgan. By the way Andy, did you manage to reach your Mum?'

'No, but I'm trying to keep positive. She's another hater of everything tech, so probably hasn't even switched her solafone on.' Morgan went off to make his call and everyone settled as comfortably as they could to wait for the cars.

'I don't understand why we seem to be the only people to survive this. Harrogate was a large town so there must be other survivors,' said Andy.

'We were buried so there could be many others alive but unable to get out. I just hope rescuers arrive soon.' Isabelle sighed and Andy put his arm around her. It was mid-afternoon, the sun was clearer, it was warm, and Xen fell asleep.

*

He opened his eyes and felt around in the dark. He was in his bed at home. He was relieved but wondered why he'd woken in the middle of the night. 'Maizy, what's the time?'

'It is 3.45 am.' Something must have woken him, but what? He went into the bathroom, and as he washed his hands, he realised his prototype solafone was not on his arm. He'd lent it to Isabelle, and she'd given it to Morgan.

Sweat filmed his body. How could he explain that he'd left it in the future? How could he guarantee to go back there to retrieve it? He felt so agitated he asked Maizy to get him some hot milk. When his drink was ready Xen added a tot of whiskey. It was too hot to drink but he cradled the mug, the warmth comforting. He felt confused and unable to sit so he paced as he tried to think. What had he done before each dream? He remembered coming home, bumping into the hall table and catching the sand timer. What about the dream before that? The timer had still been in the bedroom from when he'd unpacked it weeks ago. He'd given it a clean and moved it into the hall that day.

Xen was beginning to feel excited. He sat down with his laced milk, drank it slowly and thought about the day he had brought the timer to his hotel room. Did he dream? It came back to him vividly.

He was scared, running. There were loud hailers saying,
'It may not happen but just in case stay indoors. Shut all the windows. If you have a cellar use it.'
He'd gone into the cellar of his flat, where they kept the rubbish bins and unwanted furniture. He was alone, terrified and then there had been a sound like a train coming through a tunnel, overwhelmingly loud. He'd curled up like a foetus.

When he woke from that dream, still curled, he'd blamed it on a film he'd watched on television. Now it seemed possible the sand timer was sending him into the future. If he touched it again would he be able to get his solafone back? It seemed likely. Xen, feeling calmer, went back to bed and woke at ten o'clock, grateful there was no work that day.

The realisation he could return to the future made Xen feel in control. It was a while since he'd felt that, so he celebrated by making a cooked breakfast. When he'd eaten,

26

he sipped his coffee and toyed with a fiendish crossword puzzle. As he pondered over 23 down, 'pay back' it occurred to him he might not have to touch the timer at night. Would it work during the day? Xen counted the letters in 'retribution', but they didn't fit. Could it be 'reimbursement'? Yes, he was on a roll. He decided to finish his meal, clear up and touch the timer. The worse that could happen was nothing.

Xen stood in the hallway, looking at the timer, feeling nervous. He thought of the solafone left in the future and knew he had to try. But if he arrived fully clothed, they'd ask questions so he must get into his pyjamas. Once he was suitably clad, he picked up the sand timer, turned it over and put it down.

*

Xen didn't have time to watch the sand run. He saw whirring images, felt disorientated then, standing unsteadily on his feet, he felt sick. He grabbed the doorframe and stood for a moment watching Morgan and Andy chatting. The timer had sent him back to the wrong time – they'd done this before. He knew they were going to walk down into the town and find a shop. Isabelle was going to tell him he was in the future. There was no way he could go back to his own time, so he would have to live the scenes again.

Xen wondered what he'd done wrong. Perhaps sleeping was important. Was the timer punishing him for trying to take control? The day in the future seemed interminable, but eventually they all went to sleep in the camping shop. Xen closed his eyes but found it difficult to relax. It seemed sleep was impossible, essential though it was. He had to go back to his own time, turn the timer over and go to sleep. Then, if he got it right, he could retrieve the solafone.

It did not happen. There was no sleep for him that night. He went for a walk but stumbled in the dark and fell cutting his hands and knees. Events were not happening as before.

He went back inside the shop in a state of panic. It would be dawn soon and he should show his companions the news. Izzy wouldn't be able to contact her parents. What was going to happen now?

Everyone woke up and gradually organised themselves to move on. This time there was no sat-nav to guide them. They used the hazy sun and tried to walk in a roughly northern direction. It was difficult to even find the roads at times, with rubble everywhere. They found, and recognised, the long, green area, known as the Stray. The trees had been beheaded but an expanse of dusty grass remained.

They halted for lunch and tried to orientate themselves so as to take the road to Starbeck and then Knaresborough. They had no idea how widespread the devastation was. Xen knew that it did not extend to the whole country, and that Izzy's parents and aunt were fine, but he couldn't tell them.

It occurred to Xen that he believed everything that had happened the last time he had lived through this day, but perhaps the future depended on the choices made. In that case he might not get his solafone back. His companions might not contact their relatives or meet them. He might not return to his own time.

These thoughts began to give him a headache, or perhaps it was the lack of sleep. Either way he wanted to move on. He stood up and put on his rucksacks.

'Going, are we?' asked Morgan, smiling. He stood too and the others followed.

The walk to Knaresborough would be long under any circumstances, but there was still rubble everywhere until they left the town. The last few miles were easy in comparison, but they were all exhausted.

Ruby, normally so quiet, whined to be carried. Xen and Andy took it in turns while Morgan carried their smaller rucksacks. Eventually they arrived at the river bridge. The car park, an empty expanse of concrete, seemed unwelcoming. It was late and they needed food and somewhere to sleep.

'I've been here before,' said Andy, 'and had lunch in a café by the water's edge. It's worth a look. It might be undamaged. Shall I let you rest and do a recce?'

'No let's all go,' said Izzy.

As they walked along the river Morgan said, 'I don't understand why there're still no people about. Some of the buildings here look in perfect order. That ice-cream stall's still standing.'

'They're all shops, cafés and pubs so they would've been closed when it happened. If the people lived higher up and didn't have a basement, they'll be dead. Anyway, are we breaking into this café or not?' Andy seemed irritable and they wasted no more time talking. The door was mainly glass, so they smashed it and entered the café. The two women and Morgan sat on the hard chairs, exhausted, but Xen and Andy opened doors and cupboards looking for food.

'There's a toilet here and it works,' shouted Andy over the noise of flushing water. 'It's sheer heaven to wash your hands.' The women brightened up and took it in turns to use the facility.

'There's no kitchen or food, unless you count tomato sauce,' said Xen. 'I hoped we'd be able to cook something hot tonight.'

'When I came here before, I had to queue at a kiosk across the paved area to order and pay. I think the kitchen must be there too.' As he spoke Andy left the café to explore and Xen followed him.

They broke into the kiosk and found a freezer, cooker and store cupboard. 'This is great, the cooker runs on bottled gas,' said Xen. In a few minutes they were grilling partially defrosted burgers and sausages. The smell wafted outside, drawing the others to see what was happening.

Everyone squeezed into the small kitchen. Isabelle buttered bread buns, Joanna found some tomatoes and little Ruby opened a tin and discovered a chocolate cake.

They feasted, then settled down to sleep. Only Xen and Joanna seemed unable to settle.

'I don't know what's up with me. I can usually sleep really easily, but last night I didn't sleep at all and I thought I'd be exhausted tonight, but I still feel wide awake,' said Xen.

'I saw you go out last night and nearly went after you but felt I couldn't leave Ruby. I trust everyone, but if she woke up, she'd be frightened.'

'You didn't miss much. It was so dark I slipped, fell, and cut my knees and my hands. You seemed asleep when I came back.'

'Yes, but tonight I just can't settle. I keep thinking of everything that's happened. All my friends are probably dead. I'm an orphan and my friends mean....... meant a lot to me.'

Xen could hear she was crying. He got up, sat beside her and put his arms around her. Her head was tucked into his shoulder and he could feel her shaking with quiet sobs. She's far too thin, he thought feeling her elbows digging into him.

Joanna's tears stopped and her breathing slowed as she fell asleep. Xen felt he couldn't move without disturbing her, so he wriggled to get more comfortable and closed his eyes. If I go to sleep and return to my own time she'll probably fall over and wake, he thought. I mustn't sleep. This poor woman needs me. The truth was he was finding comfort in holding her in his arms. Eventually he did sleep.

Chapter 6

June 5th, 2030

The alarm woke Xen. It was Wednesday and he had to go to work. He lay for a few moments thinking about his timetable and smelling the coffee brewing. Suddenly he remembered he was having lunch with the rep for solar phones. He was supposed to report on any enthusiasm shown by the students and return the prototype.

Perhaps he could ring in sick and ask the college secretary to cancel the meeting. That was not the sort of thing he usually condoned, so he wondered if he could find a reason to hang on to the solafone for longer. Could he say he would like to show it to another group of students later in the week? Yes, he would do that. It was only a white lie.

*

Lunchtime arrived and Xen walked quickly to the cafe close to the college. He was on first name terms with the owner, Marnie, and had asked her to save him a table for one o'clock. She made excellent sandwiches, homemade soup and a fabulous selection of scones and cakes. She smiled broadly at him when he arrived and pointed to his reserved table. He gave her a thumbs up and sat down to wait for Mike. While he was waiting Marnie asked if he wanted to order anything.

'Just a jug of iced water please. I can't order anything else until Mike arrives.'

'OK, oh is that him coming in now?'

'Yes. We won't be long ordering; I have to get back to college.' Xen stood up and shook hands with Mike and they both sat down. Xen offered him the menu.

'So, what do you recommend then, Xen?'

'The soup is always excellent and it's spicy parsnip today. It's served with chunky bread that's usually delicious.'

'Right, I'll go with that.' He put the menu down and Marnie came over to take their orders.

'This place is a little gem. I just love being waited on by real people. So many bars have robots. This is lovely. But, while we're waiting, how did our gadget go over with the students?'

'They were very impressed. I'm certain it will be the phone of the future.'

'Really? Well that's great.'

Before they could say anymore the food arrived and they ate with relish. When Mike had finished, he sighed. 'You were right, really excellent soup and bread. So how are the cakes?'

Xen smiled. 'They are just as good. I'm full but go for it if you've room.'

He looked around for Marnie and she came over, smiling. As she picked up their empty dishes she asked if they wanted anything else.

'I have to say I've really enjoyed that. A chocolate brownie will finish my meal perfectly.' Marnie nodded and looked at Xen.

'No more for me, thanks, and can you bring the bill when you bring the cake please?' Marnie walked away and Xen realised he had to ask to keep the prototype solar phone.

'Mike, has your company thought of a name for this gadget? If not, I'd like to keep it till this time next week and offer students a chance to name it. Perhaps your company would offer a small prize for the name you like the best. What do you think?'

'Just a minute I'll text my boss.' He did so, simultaneously beginning to demolish the cake that had just arrived.

Xen was in an agony of suspense, wanting to cross his fingers like a child.

'Mmm, truly scrummy.' His phone pinged with a message. 'Right, my boss likes the idea and I like the idea of meeting you back here next week. So, let's shake on it.' They shook hands, stood up and Mike payed the bill.

As he walked back to college Xen wondered how to touch the timer correctly to return himself to Knaresborough at the right point in the future. Touching it once had got him to the wrong day – perhaps touching it twice would work? Perhaps he just needed to sleep.

*

As Xen opened his front door, he saw the timer. Later, when he was ready for bed, he would turn it twice before he went to sleep.

He asked Maisy to make a cup of tea and then the phone rang. It was Sean.

'Fancy a drink or a meal tonight? I'm getting anxious about my move and could do with some company.'

'I'm home, in Harrogate, now Sean. Shall we meet halfway?'

They agreed to meet in a pub they both knew in an hour. This gave Xen time to relax with his cup of tea. He thought about holding Joanna in his arms, her long, brown hair tickling his face. He'd not felt the need for female company for months. Not since his last girlfriend left him for someone else. It had hurt and he'd been reluctant to put himself in that position again. Now he realised how lonely he'd been. It would be good to see Sean and have a chat.

*

They met in the car park and walked into the pub together. Sean accessed the touch pad and ordered two lagers. They sat, silent, and considered the menu.

'As you've got the beers and paid for the food last time I'll pay for our meals,' said Xen.

'Great. I fancy a pepperoni pizza.'

'I'll order, then we can relax and chat.' He'd just finished doing that when their drinks arrived. 'Here's to your new career,' said Xen and they clinked glasses. It had been a mild day and the pub was a little too warm. The contrast of the cold beer was delicious.

The pub was not crowded but there were enough people to make it lively with conversation. They could chat easily without being overheard. Xen told him about the students having a competition to name the new phone.

'That's a great invention. When will it be in the shops?' asked Sean.

'I'm not sure when it goes into production but if they want to keep ahead of the competition it should be soon.'

'Well I'll be one of their first customers. Anyway, change of subject, how's your love life? Anything to report?' Sean grinned, raising his eyebrows.

Xen frowned as he said, 'Not exactly but I'm interested.'

'Good. What's her name? How old is she? Does she come with baggage? Come on, give.'

'Her name is Joanna and she's in her early thirties. She's attractive, slim, shorter than me with brown hair and beautiful big brown eyes.'

'I think you're smitten. Baggage?'

'She has a lovely daughter called Ruby; five years old.'

'Where did you meet her, then? My experience of single mums is they don't get out much and can't afford a sitter.'

'Enough questions, Sean, I met her in Harrogate, and we haven't even had a date. Let's leave it there. Time for you to share.'

'Ah, well I've decided not to date anyone so close to starting my new job. I have to go away for training, as I said, and then I'm really not sure where I'll be.'

'I thought you said you'd be able to live anywhere once you were trained so you could stay put in Leeds.' Xen was worried now that he might not see much more of his friend.

'I'll certainly keep my house, but I'm not sure what the job entails. I may have to travel abroad. One thing is sure. I'll keep in touch. My new life could be quite solitary, and I'll need to meet up with proper friends, like you, to keep sane.'

They laughed, and then their food arrived, and they began to eat with great enjoyment.

'So, what do you think about China's rise to power? It's been quite meteoric hasn't it,' said Xen. 'I've been having a strange, recurring nightmare where China has devastated Harrogate with a death ray.'

'That's bizarre. You've been watching too much sci-fi. But, having said that, there are rumours of new weapons. Didn't you hear the news last night? The on-going peace talks got a bit heated and China's delegate hinted they had a super weapon.'

'That's really worrying. Perhaps I'm becoming clairvoyant or something.'

'Unlikely, you've just got a vivid imagination. Want another drink?'

'Yes, why not?' Sean ordered and when the drinks arrived Xen suggested another toast. 'I was thinking of the political situation and I want to toast the future. They raised their glasses and said together, 'The future.'

'When do you actually go away for training? I was wondering if you'd like a game of tennis next week. I know you'll thrash me, but I'll still enjoy it.'

'Yes, we could have a game. Term ends on Friday and I have a week at home before I leave. I'll book it and let you know details.' They finished their drinks and Xen said he really hadn't room for another. They left the pub together then separated in the car park. Xen felt the effects of the alcohol and was grateful for cars driving themselves. He could remember when the prototypes were demonstrated and were not very successful, but the problems were quickly solved and now they were the only cars on the market.

When Xen arrived home, he got ready for bed and then turned the timer over, twice.

Chapter 7

2035

The object of his dream, Joanna, was beside him when he opened his eyes. He could hear the river and knew, without sitting up, he was in Knaresborough. He smiled happily, knowing he'd arrived at the correct time in the future, and Joanna smiled back.

'Things are looking better,' she said. 'Morgan's been in touch with his daughter and she's coming to get him. The only people without relatives or friends are you and me.'

Xen sat up, concerned for her. 'Is there no one you want to contact?'

She shook her head and he saw tears brimming in her eyes. He put out his arms and she shifted close to him and snuggled in. 'Sorry, I'm such a wimp. I shouldn't feel sorry for myself. I have Ruby and she means everything to me, but...' she didn't finish her sentence.

'It's OK. I know what it's like to feel lonely. I had a girlfriend for several years. She left me for someone else. I was so hurt I was scared to have another relationship. I still am.'

'Me too, my partner left when he found out I was pregnant. He hadn't told me he didn't want children and I was expecting him to be pleased. I had a well-paid job in advertising and a lovely house. When the baby came, I took my full maternity leave, but when I was due to return to work, I found they'd replaced me, and I no longer had a job.'

'That was a horrible thing for them to do. It must be illegal.'

'Yes, and I tried to take them to court over it. But they stopped paying me, the legal team was too expensive, and, in the end, I had to sell my house to pay the fees. Until the destruction I was renting a tiny flat and, as you know, had to claim benefit.'

'Perhaps this situation we're in will be the beginning of something better for you. Anyway, I'm enjoying this cuddle, but really need to stand up now.'

'Please do it quietly so you don't wake Ruby. That walk exhausted her.'

Xen stood and left Joanna to talk to Morgan, Andy and Isabelle. He wanted his solafone back on his wrist and to see what the timescale for lifts was going to be. Wetherby wasn't far by car to Knaresborough and he would've expected to see someone by now. They were all looking miserable when he got closer, as if something had gone wrong.

'Hello, Xen,' said Isabelle. 'The police are not letting anyone drive close to Harrogate. They're waiting for scientists to investigate to see if the blast left any dangerous chemicals behind. They didn't believe my dad when he said we'd phoned. The police have already announced, apparently, that there were no survivors. Dad said we could have to wait several days and was worried about food and water. I said we could manage for at least one more day.'

Morgan added that his daughter had been amazed and delighted when he phoned, but she had been turned back too. He then gave Xen the solafone.

'I think I know where we can spend the night and possibly have some cooked food,' said Andy.

They gathered their rucksacks while Xen went back to tell Joanna the news and to see if Ruby was awake. She was rubbing her eyes, got grit in them and started to cry.

'Come on Ruby, I know where you can wash the grit off your hands, and we might be able to find you some cake.'

She sniffed and tried to smile. 'I like chocolate cake best.'

'I'll see what we can find.' Xen let Andy lead them to the riverside café, and they repeated the finding of food and cooking. He knew they'd done it before, and he had to be careful not to appear too knowledgeable. His patience was rewarded when Ruby found the chocolate cake. She was so pleased with herself.

They settled down to sleep and Xen hoped he would wake up at home, vowing to keep the solafone on his wrist from now on.

*

He woke in his own bed, and once again Joanna was in his thoughts. He couldn't be falling for a woman who lived in the future, could he? Perhaps the timer could transport people back in time? Perhaps if they fell asleep entwined it could work. But if Joanna went back five years Ruby would be a baby. A stupid, impossible thought. It made Xen feel irritable as he got out of his bed to start the day.

As he cleaned his teeth he wondered if he had aged when he'd gone forward five years. Had he? There had been no opportunity to examine his features and he hadn't thought of it then. There was also, he realised, no reason to return to the future. He had his solafone. That reminded him of the competition he'd promised to organise.

Xen focused on the seminars he was going to do on the journey to work and for a while Joanna receded into the back of his mind.

At lunchtime he bought a sandwich and ate it in the refectory. He looked at the names the students had suggested for the prototype phone, and not one had chosen solafone. Someone had to do it this week or he might have to propose it himself.

He went to his lecture in the afternoon and looked at the latest name suggestions on the train home, but still no solafone. He sighed and looked forward to a quiet night and to sleep in his own bed without dreaming.

When he entered his front door, Xen gave the small table a wide berth. There was to be no accidental touching of the timer tonight.

*

2035

A tin lid clattered to the floor and Joanna opened her eyes to see Ruby holding the cake tin. Her eyes were huge with guilt and Joanna struggled not to laugh. Morgan sat up followed by Andy and Isabelle.

'So, is it chocolate cake all round for breakfast, Ruby?' said Morgan, laughing.

Everyone else, including Mum, was smiling, so Ruby relaxed and nodded her head. 'I like chocolate cake.'

'We gathered that last night,' said Morgan. He wriggled out of his sleeping bag and went over to her. 'Shall I find a plate and cut you a piece? Sorry Joanna is that OK with you?'

'Yes, of course, I think I'd rather have toast myself.'

Everyone got up, went over to the kitchen area and breakfast was soon ready. Ruby managed toast as well as her cake. With her mouth full she said suddenly, 'Where's Xen?'

There was silence as they looked with raised eyebrows at each other.

'Perhaps he couldn't sleep and has gone for a walk. I know he has trouble sleeping sometimes,' said Joanna. 'He'll come back when he gets hungry.'

Isabelle frowned. 'We do need him to come back because we can't communicate with the outside world without him.' The others nodded.

'Let's clear up breakfast and, if he's not back, I'm happy to go and look for him. I think he'll have gone on the road to Starbeck in the hope of finding the roadblock and people to talk to. That's what I would've done,' said Andy.

40

Joanna and Ruby left the others to clear up and wash the dishes. Her broken arm was a nuisance and Ruby would be in the way. They went to look at the river, but it had a rank smell and they saw dead fish being washed along.

'It pongs,' said Ruby. 'Let's go in the café and play with the toys.'

The café had a small box of toys to keep little children amused while their parents chatted. There were some colouring sheets with pictures of river creatures and a couple of boxes of crayons. There was also a box of dominoes and Joanna knew Ruby wanted to play that.

While Ruby tipped out the contents and turned all the tiles face down Joanna wondered about Xen. He'd been such a comfort when she was upset. He was kind and made her feel safe. She also sensed that he liked her. It was difficult not to keep looking towards the door in the hope of seeing him.

When the door did open it was Morgan. 'Isabelle's gone with Andy to look for Xen. Can we make a threesome?'

'Yes,' said Ruby and turned the tiles face down again. They each took seven and the game began.

'I used to play threes and fives when I was a lad. Is Ruby too young for that?'

'Yes, you have to be able to divide by three or five and she hasn't learnt that at school yet,' said Joanna.

'I can count in fives, Mum, listen five, ten, fifteen, twenty, twenty-five, thirty….' She continued chanting until she reached a hundred and Morgan and Joanna gave her a clap.

'When am I going back to school, Mum?'

'Not for a while, Ruby, and it will have to be a different school. Your old one got broken, like our flat.' She looked at Morgan. 'We were so lucky to have been invited into Andy and Isabelle's basement flat. I haven't really thanked them. There was so much to cope with.'

41

'I haven't either but I'm sure they don't expect formal thanks. It's still hard to believe that we've lost everything. I just hope, when we get out of here, the banks will believe who we are. We've no proof.'

'I hadn't thought of that but, if you can give personal details, surely they'll have to give you access to your own money? Not that I had anything in a bank account, but I still have my wrist band, so they should give me what I'm owed. That will be a pittance, so I have no idea where we'll live when all this is over.'

'There must be a system to house people after a disaster,' said Morgan.

'Are we going to play dominoes?' Ruby had her hands on her hips. The adults both laughed and played the game.

Later they went for a walk around the car park area and discovered it went into an overflow car park further along the river. There was a solitary car there and Morgan went closer to have a look. The windows had condensation on them and, when he peered through the mist, he saw the bloated bodies of a couple. He turned away and gestured to Joanna not to go any closer.

Ruby had found a wall to climb on and Morgan said, 'They were a courting couple. Seeing them, so unsuspecting, makes me even more grateful I'm alive.'

Joanna nodded. Morgan went over to Ruby to hold her hand as she balanced along the wall. Joanna watched, pleased that someone else was giving her daughter some attention.

They returned to the café for lunch when Ruby said she was hungry. As they ate Morgan noted that the others were being a long time. He hoped they'd come back soon. He was finding it difficult having no means of communication.

The afternoon dragged and Joanna started to worry, especially when it began to rain heavily. Ruby screamed with the first gigantic clap of thunder and after that she continued to quiver with fear. Joanna cuddled her while

Morgan cooked a meal. When he entered with laden plates he said, 'The burgers and sausages were completely defrosted so wouldn't be safe to eat much longer.'

'If they don't come back tonight, we'll have to move on. We may find them en route, and even if we don't there have to be people within walking distance.'

'Yes, we'll pack up in the morning and head in the general direction of Boroughbridge. It's a low-lying town by the river and, hopefully, far enough from the blast to be in one piece.'

Ruby settled down to sleep and Morgan and Joanna talked quietly. Joanna said she felt it was bleak without Isabelle, Andy and Xen and she was worried.

'That storm was horrendous and it's still pouring with rain, so I suspect they've taken shelter somewhere,' said Morgan. 'They know where we are so if they do meet the authorities tomorrow, they'll be able to rescue us.'

Joanna stood up and paced around the café. 'I know we should be grateful, but I do want to get out of here.' She turned to Morgan, who had been watching her. 'When we do get rescued what will you go back to? I know you have a daughter but do you, did you, have a job?'

'I was a soldier, retired now, sort of.'

Joanna stayed silent so he felt obliged to elaborate. He took a deep breath. 'My rank is General. General Morgan Ashbourne at your service.'

'Phew, I feel I should bob a curtsey or something.' She saw him give a wry smile. 'Why did you say retired, sort of?' She sensed he was struggling, unwilling to talk about himself, but she was curious.

'I've been overseeing training, inspecting various camps throughout the country. My stay in Harrogate was due to come to an end soon. I'm based at Whitehall when not elsewhere.'

'So, you've still got a home in London?'

'Yes, but since my wife died nowhere is a real home. It's been five years since she died, and I still miss her.'

'I'm sorry,' said Joanna. I know what it's like to feel lonely. I don't miss Ruby's dad. He was not as nice a man as I thought. But I do miss having someone in my life, other than Ruby, of course.'

'She's a credit to you. I'm not sure my daughter would've coped with the experience Ruby's going through, especially all the walking. Do you fancy a game of threes and fives to pass the time?'

They played, Joanna keeping a tally and eventually, when they were both yawning, she said, 'Let's stop now. I can hardly keep my eyes open and I've won by just fifteen points.'

Morgan smiled. 'I can accept defeat graciously. Thank you for making this evening so pleasant.'

Chapter 8

Isabelle and Andy set off up the hill. A high retaining wall had collapsed, filling the road with soil and shrubs.

'I'm glad the weather's fine or this would be impossible to walk on. It would be a quagmire. As it is, I'm quite enjoying the soft soil, as opposed to rubble that threatens to twist your ankle with every step,' said Isabelle.

'Well make the most of it because I can see an almost impenetrable wall of rubble at the top of the hill.'

Isabelle stopped and looked up to where he was pointing. 'Perhaps we can find a way around it when we get closer.' Andy nodded and they set off again.

'I should've brought some water, she said. 'I'm thirsty already.'

'Just be glad you're married to an ex-boy scout. Let's wait until we get to that heap of rubble.' Andy grinned and they pushed on until they reached the top of the hill. They stopped and Andy took off his rucksack and gave Isabelle her water and opened a bottle for himself. 'Don't be too greedy, that's all I brought.'

She reluctantly put the cap back on and surveyed the scene. 'It's more of a mountain than a hill; too dangerous to clamber over all that. So, shall we try left, or right?' Isabelle gestured as she spoke, and Andy followed with his eyes.

'It's Hobson's choice, whoever he was. Let's go left and try to turn right when we can. At this point I can't predict which way Xen would've gone so I don't think we've much hope of finding him. I just hope he didn't attempt to scale that monster hill.' Just as he said that Isabelle caught her foot on chunk of concrete and lost her balance. Andy grabbed her arm, pulling her upright.

'Whoa, thanks, I nearly fell.' She laughed as she clambered more carefully over the rubble. They became quiet because progress was slow and hard going. After half an hour they came to an area which had had less buildings. They could see the road and even grass verges. The pace picked up and they swung their arms, enjoying the freedom to look around instead of at their feet. The landscape was desolate, no standing trees, just torn shards sticking up. The grass was grey with dust.

'I think somewhere along this road there's a right turn that takes you back in a northerly direction, but I'm not sure how far we should go today. I'm hungry, are you? The sun's high so it must be about lunch time.'

'I'd be happy to stop. I've been imagining the luscious taste of a bar of chocolate for some time.

Andy and Isabelle sat on the grass and shared the food. It was eerily quiet, no birds, no rustling, no breeze. It felt stiflingly hot. Then a black cloud obliterated the sun's rays and before the first drops fell, they felt chill. When the first heavy drops of rain fell, they scrambled to their feet.

'We need to find shelter. I think it's going to pour.' Andy's words were lost in a streak of lightning so close they could feel the heat. It was followed instantly by a thunderclap that shook them, rumbling and reverberating. Before the sound died away there was another flash of lightning. On high ground, in the open, they were dangerously exposed. Andy grabbed her hand and they ran back towards the mountain of rubble. The lightening zigzagged as if aiming for them and they dashed under an overhanging slab of concrete, safe for the moment.

Their chests were heaving with fear and the effort of running. Speech was impossible with the constant thunderclaps and drumming rain. They huddled together, soaked and exhausted.

Hours later, when it was dark, Isabelle woke Andy to ask him to move so she could get out of their tiny shelter and relieve herself. He grumbled about being disturbed but moved into the drizzle to let her come out. She was fumbling with her trouser zip when she tripped and fell. Her head crashed onto bricks and blood spurted from her wound.

Andy, properly awake now, stretched his aching limbs and wondered what the time was. He thought there was a glimmer in the east and hoped daylight would come soon. They'd missed their evening meal and he felt hungry, damp and miserable. When Isabelle seemed to have been gone for a long time he began to worry. Where was she? It didn't take that long to have a pee.

'Izzy? Izzy what're you doing?' He peered into the darkness, moved a few metres further away and trod on something soft. He groped to feel what it was and found her outstretched hand, limp, lifeless. 'Izzy, wake up Izzy, please.' He felt along her body trying to find where she was hurt and reached her head. Her beautiful auburn hair was sticky with blood. Andy took off his shirt and tried to wrap it around her head to stem the flow. Did she have a pulse? He held her wrist but there was no rhythmic movement. Isabelle was dead.

Andy was holding her in his arms, sobbing when the sun came up, revealing the extent of the injury to her head. She couldn't be dead, he thought, but her white face and staring eyes told him she was. He closed her eyes tenderly with shaking fingers.

He thought of Izzy's parents. They'd been told she was alive and now they had to hear she was dead – cruel, too cruel. He crushed her lifeless body to him in an agony of loss.

*

2030
Xen went to work and ran the competition for a name for the solafone again. He looked at the entry slips on the train

47

home and was pleased to find two entrants offering the same name. The company will have to give two prizes, he thought, but they were going to make a fortune out of the invention. He felt free to let his mind wander because there was just one more day before the long summer break. Most of the students had gone already and he had no lectures tomorrow, just a lunch date with Mike, the rep.

Xen arrived home, had a cup of tea and felt an overwhelming desire to meet Joanna again. He tried to resist touching the timer but was drawn to it. He stood beside the table looking at it. 'What are you trying to tell me? I feel you have something you want me to do.' There was no reply, no vibration, nothing. He rang for a pizza to be delivered and then rang Sean to see if he'd booked the tennis court for the next week.

'Hi, Xen. Only one day left, thank God. Are you ringing about the tennis? I've booked it for Monday morning at 10.30. Is that OK?' Xen agreed it was fine and made a note of the details.

'I wondered if you'd like to do lunch afterwards. If so, I'll book us a table at the Tavern, next to the tennis club.' Xen liked that idea and there was really nothing more to say so he rang off. It would've been good to share his time travel adventure, but Sean was unlikely to understand. Scientists tended to be practical, but then again cosmology was very theoretical. He could, perhaps, ask if Sean thought time travel could be possible. There would be no need to go into personal details. Xen decided to see if an opportunity arose after their game.

It was nearly time for his pizza to arrive, but he was drawn again to the sand-timer. He was standing in the hall looking at it, when the courier arrived. He opened a can of lager and went into his small lounge to watch television as he ate.

Ten minutes later Xen was almost too full to eat any more. He went into the kitchen to get another beer from the fridge but found it impossible to move past the table in the hall. He turned the timer over twice and went back into the living room. Sitting down he felt full, warm and drowsy. His eyes closed and he thought, I mustn't sleep, fully clothed it'll look odd to the others in the future. But sleep overwhelmed his resolve.

Chapter 9

2035

Ruby woke early, as usual but was surprised to find Mum and Morgan already up, drinking tea.

'Where's everyone else? Where's Xen?'

'They didn't come back last night, Ruby, so we're going to find them today, as soon as you've had breakfast, 'said Joanna. Ruby wriggled out of her sleeping bag and put on her clothes while Joanna organised her breakfast.

'I think this will be our last day of trying to find civilisation,' said Morgan. 'I'm sure the others haven't returned because they've been rescued already.' He rolled up sleeping bags and packed them into their rucksacks.

They set off up the hill but within minutes were struggling walking on mud. The torrential rain, and possibly the force of the blast, had put too much pressure on a retaining wall. It had collapsed, filling the road with sticky mud.

'I think I preferred rubble to this,' grumbled Morgan and then he, unexpectedly, began to laugh. It reminds me of when I was a small boy, living in London and my parents took me on a day out to Epping Forest. My dad had a book of walks and we were following it. I remember him reading, 'You will now find in front of you a fine, wide track.' But what we were facing was a sea of mud like this. I got about halfway across and then tried to lift my foot, but my welly stayed in the mud and my foot came out of my welly. I teetered, calling for help, but Dad couldn't reach me quick enough and I fell, splat.' Joanna and Ruby laughed with him.

A little while later they all heard a strange wailing sound. They moved quicker and saw, Andy rocking, crying, with his arms around Isabelle's lifeless body.

*

Xen woke on the floor of the café. He opened his eyes, looking at the ceiling and listening for sounds from the others. It was silent. It felt wrong. He sat up and then stood as he realised everyone had gone. There were some rucksacks, but Ruby's distinctive little one had gone, as had two of the large ones.

I mustn't be hasty, he thought. Perhaps they've run out of food. He went into the kitchen and opened the freezer. The smell was rank. Everything was liquefying.

Xen looked around for anything he could eat and found two tins of pears. He opened one, ate from the tin, drained the last of the juice and then wondered if there was any bottled water left. He searched everywhere and could find none. It was clear why they'd left, but also clear that he had a problem. If he was to go in search of them, he had to have something to drink. He retrieved his rucksacks and stuffed his sleeping bag in the big one. His little rucksack still held some dried food – rice and pasta so he took all of it out and replaced it with the tin of pears.

The original plan had been to go north, so he turned in that direction and went slowly up the hill. The ground was saturated with water and a landslide meant he was soon struggling through deep mud. It clung to his shoes making his feet leaden, his pace slow.

Xen thought about time and wondered if he had been gone more than a day. Was time moving at the same rate five years on? Had they had a few hours start on him or several days? He realised there was no choice. He wanted to find them, he was in the future, so he could only press on.

Xen paused to rest and felt his solafone vibrate. It was a text from Isabelle's parents.

We are at the northern barrier between Knaresborough and Boroughbridge. Make your way there if you can. You might even meet the scientists. They look like spacemen. If they find nothing you will be allowed out, or they will let us in. Love you, M &D

He saw it had been sent just a few minutes ago, so the others might not be far ahead. He sent a short reply.
This is Xen, Isabelle was using my solafone. We should all be able to meet today.

'Joanna, Morgan, Andy?' he shouted several times. There was no reply, so he moved on, feeling more hopeful. He looked up, when he needed another breather, and saw movement ahead. He could also hear weird sounds – shrieking, crying. He hurried now, worried. Something was seriously wrong. He shouted again and Ruby heard him.

'Mummy, Xen's coming.'

Joanna wiped the tears from her eyes and shouted at him, 'It's your fault she's dead. They went looking for you.'

Morgan put his hand on her shoulder. 'Oh, Joanna, that's not fair. He didn't make the storm or push her over. It was an accident.'

That set her tears flowing again, and it was Ruby who put her arms up for a hug when Xen reached them. He held her to him as he took in the scene.

Andy was cradling Isabelle's body, rocking. Morgan still had an arm around Joanna. Her face was streaked with dirty tears. Xen felt a wave of sorrow mixed with anger. Joanna was right. If he had come back yesterday none of this tragedy would have happened. He was just wondering if he could touch the timer once and arrive earlier, like he had before when Ruby shouted, 'Drone, it's a drone.' She bounced up and down with excitement in Xen's arms, pointing. Everybody looked up, except Andy. He was so deep in misery he was numb to everything around him.

Joanna felt Ruby's excitement and said, 'This means we could be rescued soon.'

'It's going to be very hard meeting Isabelle's parents. I had a text from them,' said Xen.

They both read it and Morgan said, 'Let's hope the drone's camera's taken clear pictures. It'll prepare them for the worst when we meet them.'

Their silence was broken by the throb of a helicopter engine. It hovered over them and then moved away to find somewhere to land. It was so loud Andy looked up. He tried to stand but was so stiff he needed help. Xen put Ruby down, went over and gently took the weight of Isabelle off him. Andy awkwardly got to his feet. Joanna went to give him a hug, but he turned away from her. His face was drained of colour. His clothes and hands were filthy, stained with Isabelle's blood.

'I'm sorry, Andy. I should've stayed with you. Joanna's right. It was my fault,' said Xen.

'No, no ones' fault, an accident. She slipped in the dark. Everywhere was wet from the storm,' said Andy.

'So where were you then?' asked Joanna, turning to Xen. He looked at her, not knowing what to say, when there was a shout. Three men were walking towards them, in protective suits, one carrying a medical bag and another a stretcher.

*

The helicopter couldn't take all of them in one trip, so Andy, Isabelle's body, Joanna and Ruby went first. Morgan and Xen stood watching them go. The silence felt oppressive.

'There's something not right about you, Xen. You disappear, and when you turn up you've had a shave and your clothes are different and clean. Did you get to the barrier and have some TLC before coming back to us? Did you know the helicopter was coming?'

'No, I woke up in the café this morning and you were all gone, so I walked north and found you.'

Morgan looked at him with suspicion. 'You haven't answered the question. You were absent for twenty-four hours, not one night. I need a better explanation. You've also got the oldest solafone in the world, but Isabelle told me you used to lecture in technology. No technophile would ever be seen dead with something like that on his wrist.'

'It's of sentimental value, an original prototype. I'm sorry Morgan...' His voice was drowned by the helicopter's return and they rode in silence. As they came into land Xen could see an ambulance and television cameras.

The paramedics, enveloped in protective suits, hustled the two men into the ambulance without giving them any opportunity to speak to the excited reporters. There were a lot of flashes as they got what pictures they could.

Morgan and Xen both said they were not in need of medical attention but were ignored. It seemed there was still great anxiety about the effect of the blast. They were the only people to appear, so far, who had been in Harrogate and survived. Tests had to be made. The ambulance took them into Leeds, where an isolation unit had been prepared at one of the city's hospitals, Seacroft.

On the way there they were told by the paramedics that the scientists investigating had not found any harmful chemicals in the town. This was good news, increasing the chances that there would be nothing wrong with the survivors other than any injuries they had sustained. It prompted Morgan to borrow the solafone again to text his daughter. He was looking forward to seeing her again, even if it had to be through glass for the time being. He wanted to arrange to stay with her for a few days when he was discharged, before going back to work.

Xen realised that, if he woke in his own bed in the morning, he would have to give the solafone back, but it probably wouldn't matter now they were in civilisation. Everyone could buy new ones, when they left hospital, except Joanna. He thought about her and wondered if they had scanned her arm. He hoped it was healing and wouldn't need resetting. He dearly wanted to talk to her and feel that bond he'd felt before.

*

The hospital staff were well organised. Everyone had to strip off, have a shower and put on clean gowns. Morgan, Xen and Andy were sharing a room, and they presumed Joanna and Ruby would be close by. Andy was quiet, but eventually told them about meeting Catherine and Jason, Isabelle's parents.

'They saw the drone pictures but hoped she was injured, unconscious. It was almost as bad as when I found Izzy. They reacted like me and I lived it all over again. I'm glad Sonia and Roger were with them because I was useless.'

'I'm so sorry, Andy,' said Xen.

'Sonia said she'll come and visit us because she wants to hear what happened. Not Izzy's accident, I already told them about that. They want to know how we survived and how we got out.'

'I suspect we'll have to tell our story many times over,' said Morgan. 'The reporters were like baying dogs when we got into the ambulance. Soldiers and police were holding them back with difficulty. It's going to be particularly hard for you, Andy, because they'll be there at the funeral. I can almost see the headlines now.'

'That's enough Morgan,' said Xen, tersely. 'Andy needs to take one day at a time.'

'Sorry, Andy, I wasn't thinking.' Their conversation halted as meals were brought. In any other circumstances they would have enjoyed the food, but the loss of Isabelle and Andy's grief pressed hard upon them.

After the food the tests began, blood, urine, swabs, and finally whole-body scans. They were told that if the results were clear they could leave the hospital in the morning.

Xen wondered if he would ever see any of them again. If they dispersed around the country, even if he came back to the future it would be hard to find them. Why had this happened? The last time he'd touched the timer – he'd felt compelled to do so – he'd achieved nothing.

'Morgan I've been thinking it might be good to keep in touch after this. Perhaps we could exchange names, addresses, e-mails – anything?'

There was a long pause before Morgan replied. Finally, he said, 'I could give you my details, but not really sure if we'll feel a need to contact each other. What about you Andy?'

'I'm happy to share mine but I don't have an address anymore. I've no idea what's going to happen after this, but you are the only people who've shared my experience. Let's do it.'

Normally such information would have been shared onto solafones. As this was not possible, they asked a nurse if she could find some paper and a pen. The same nurse took their information to Joanna and returned with hers. Xen pocketed it, feeling pleased. Now if he woke in his own time, he might seek them out. Perhaps he could warn them of what was going to happen, though it would take some explaining.

Later they settled to sleep, looking forward to possible freedom in the morning.

Chapter 10

2030

Xen awoke in his own time, in his own bed and lay for a moment trying to think what day it was and what had to be done. He remembered, without resorting to Maizy, knower of all things. It was the last day of term and he was meeting the solafone rep, Mike. It was going to be an easy day, no lectures, just writing a few notes and clearing up. He should be able to come home straight after lunch.

Those thoughts made it easy to leave the comfort of the bed, shower, dress and eat a quick breakfast. He ran down the stairs and all the way to the station. He felt lively and fit, hardly out of breath when he entered the train. Perhaps it was all the long and difficult walking he'd been doing in the future. It had made him fitter. He might even give Sean a better game of tennis on Monday if he felt this good.

*

Mike had arrived at the café before Xen and ordered himself a coffee. He stood up when he saw Xen and they shook hands.

'I've been looking forward to this lunch since last time. I love talking to real people, and I've noticed they've changed the menu. When everything is done robotically that rarely happens.'

Xen picked up the menu and smiled. Marnie arrived to take their order and Xen added a beer to his meal. 'I'm not going back to work for two months after this, so I can indulge a little. That reminds me.' He felt in his pocket and brought out the solafone. He held it out in the case it had arrived in. On the train he had noted numbers belonging to Catherine

57

and Morgan's daughter and then erased the memory. 'I've had some great name suggestions, but two students, chose the same one. I've got all the entries here for you, but I reckon "solafone" will be the winner.'

Mike took all the papers and read them while they waited for their order. Xen was patient, knowing the decision had already been made. Finally, he looked up and said, 'I agree, solafone is an excellent name. I quite liked "lightwork" but it's not so easy to say; solafone just trips off the tongue. I see the students have put a contact number down. Obviously, I must run it past the boss but I'm sure they'll agree to send both of them a voucher. Ah, here comes our lunch.'

They enjoyed their lunch and Xen, feeling a glow of contentment, offered to pay.

'No, definitely not, your idea for the competition has solved a problem for us – the company will pay. Would you like a coffee to finish up?'

'Thanks, Mike, but I'm full. You have one if you want one. I'm not in a hurry today.'

Mike looked at his watch. 'The only downside of a lovely, old-fashioned café is that everything takes longer, and this time I'm in a rush. I'm not sure when we'll meet next but, if you're amenable, I'd like to use you again to trial a new gadget.'

'No problem, I've enjoyed putting the phone through its paces, and thanks for the lunch.' They stood and shook hands before leaving.

Xen walked to the station thinking about Joanna. She would have left hospital by now and he wouldn't know how to find her. He sighed and then had an idea. He would walk to the flat she lived in before the blast. When they'd exchanged details, Joanna had given her old address, even though it had been destroyed. It shouldn't be difficult to find. He got off the train in Harrogate and walked there. He looked up to the top flat, where she'd been and thought about the time scale. Five years earlier Ruby would be a baby. Much as he wanted to see her, he knew he couldn't explain they'd met in the future. Xen walked away, grinning ruefully at his own stupidity.

When he got back to his flat, he sat at his computer and googled, General Morgan Ashbourne. It found him, 'General Morgan Ashbourne, a man at the peak of his career,' Xen read and marvelled at how normal he had seemed. He would never have guessed Morgan was so eminent although he had shown himself resourceful and intelligent. His career made impressive reading.

In his twenties he had been sent to Afghanistan, and in the years that followed he was awarded the DSO for leadership. He went up in rank and in 2014 served in Iraq, receiving the Victoria Cross for extreme bravery under fire. He was now retired from active service but still serving the military.

He thought about contacting Morgan, but it would sound so trite to say, you don't know me but in five years' time we'll meet. It was impossible. He really wished he could find someone to talk to who would not think him crazy. Xen realised his thoughts were unproductive so on impulse, and with a free summer ahead of him, he decided to improve his fitness and rang a local gym.

At the gym he was assessed by a trainer then given a programme of activities. He paid for a three-month subscription that would allow him to come as often as he liked in that time. The package included one class a week – he chose spinning. It would strengthen his legs and increase his overall fitness.

Later, at home, Xen was in his sitting room watching television, when his computer pinged a message.

I missed you this morning to say goodbye but wanted to say I was sorry I accused you of Isabelle's death. I was too upset to think straight. My arm is now in a pot and not painful anymore. Ruby keeps asking when we'll see you again and I said I would try to arrange something.

Joanna

That was surreal. Was it possible to communicate with someone living five years ahead? It seemed it was. He messaged back.

I'd really like to meet you both. What are you doing tomorrow? Where are you living?
Xen

She replied that they were free tomorrow, living in Leeds not far from the hospital. If he didn't know Leeds, they could meet in the foyer of the hospital. He said he would be there at 11am.

If only he could tell her how hard the meeting was going to be for him, but it would sound like he was making excuses because he didn't want to see her. He did. He really did want to see her.

Xen picked up the sand timer, turned it over watching the sand fall. He made himself a gin and tonic then stood in the hall and turned the timer over again. He took his drink and laid on the bed fully clothed.

*

Saturday 16 June 2035
It worked. Xen woke up slumped in a seat in the waiting room just outside the quarantine area at the hospital. He moved to sit upright, and his neck ached as if he had been there all night. How did the timer work out time? Then he became fully awake as he realised it might not be Saturday, here in the future. It might be the day they were discharged. He wished the whole, time travel thing was easier to control.

His phone showed him the date. It had worked, hooray. There was a water dispenser close by, so he went to it and filled a compostable cup. The cold, clean taste cleansed his mouth and focussed his mind. Was the card or fingerprint system still being used? He had his phone and cards but could hardly take Joanna for a coffee or even lunch if he couldn't pay. Five years into the future any cards would be out of date but perhaps his phone would be acceptable. He decided to have breakfast at the hospital café or restaurant and find out.

Xen followed the signs to the exit so he would know where to meet Joanna. When he got there, he saw a coffee shop and a map showing the location of the hospital's restaurant. The coffee shop was automated, and everything looked similar to those in his time. He took a deep breath, ordered a black coffee and a croissant and touched his phone. Alarms did not go off. His phone payment was accepted, and he wondered how his statement would show a charge from five years ahead. Perhaps computers would think this less odd than people might.

He sat at a vacant table and waited for his croissant to be warmed. The machine flashed a number and he went to collect it.

The hospital was very busy and Xen people watched. He realised his own style of clothes, jeans, short-sleeved shirt and trainers, were still being worn – by middle-aged men. Young men wore baggy lightweight trousers and close-fitting vest tops with sandals. They looked cool and comfortable.

He wondered how Joanna was going to react when they met. He looked at his watch to see if he had time to buy a new outfit. It would mean using a bus or taxi into town. Could he achieve that in an hour and a half?

Xen decided to try and went out onto the street and used the app on his phone to call a taxi. It arrived quickly and accepted his phone. A bus would have been cheaper but slower.

Although Xen was not familiar with the inside of the hospital, he knew the town centre well, so it was a shock to find several shops he had enjoyed browsing around, no longer in existence and one shopping area transformed into offices. Despite feeling disorientated he searched the shops until he saw one displaying mannequins dressed in modern clothes. He ran into the shop and in fifteen minutes emerged, transformed, carrying his old clothes in a carrier bag. There was just enough time to get back to the hospital.

*

Joanna was waiting in the foyer, with Ruby. When Ruby saw him, she left her mum and ran. Xen opened his arms and he lifted her up and swung her round.

'That's a super welcome, Ruby.' They were both smiling happily as they walked towards Joanna. She was not quite so effusive as her daughter, but when he bent to kiss her cheek, she turned so that he kissed her lips.

'You look lovely she said, those baggies suit you.' He realised she was referring to his trousers and thanked her. She went on, 'I couldn't dress up for you. We haven't received any extra money, even though we lost everything, so I have to wash our clothes every night. The charity shops are good, though, so Ruby has a new summer dress.'

'Give me a twirl, Ruby.' Ruby did and he told her she looked pretty.

'What do you want to do now, Joanna, stay here and have a coffee or go into town?'

Let's have a coffee now, here, and I'll tell you what's happening afterwards. I hope you can stay all day.'

Xen thought he'd like to stay all day and all night, but just nodded and followed her to the café.

They sat, sipping their frothy coffees, each waiting for the other to speak. Xen spoke first. 'You sent me a message, but I wondered how you did it. I thought your wristband couldn't act as any kind of phone.'

'It can't but look what I've got.' She proudly showed her other arm sporting a solafone. 'Before you ask, Morgan gave me his. Apparently, while we were trying to get out of Harrogate, it was his birthday. When his daughter, Kathy,

62

collected him she gave him his present, a new solafone. He just turned straight around and said I could have his old one. He transferred all his data to his new phone, reset this one and just left me with the contact numbers of all us survivors. It was kind of him, wasn't it?'

Xen nodded, thinking how lovely it was to see her smiling and happy. He saw her smile fade as she said, 'I've been keeping in touch with Jason and Catherine and they are going to the undertakers soon to organise Isabelle's funeral. I don't know when it will be, but I'd feel much better about going if you could come.'

'It's college holidays so I'll do my best. Talking about holidays have you found a new school for Ruby yet?' Ruby looked up hearing her name.

'No, I've decided to wait until September. She's had a shock, as we all have, and now she's having to cope with a new flat in a different town. We're not sleeping well either. It really is too soon for her and me.'

Xen nodded. 'So, what are we going to do with the rest of our day? Do you have a plan?'

'Mummy wants to go into Leeds and have lunch, if you can treat us.' Xen laughed and Joanna looked embarrassed. 'Ruby, you're not supposed to ask someone to pay for lunch.'

'That's what you said, Mum.'

'Oh dear, it serves me right for talking to you as if you're fifteen, not five.'

'I really don't mind. I'll happily pay for lunch and I think I could run to a few clothes for you, Joanna. As you said there will be a funeral to go to and you must have a suitable outfit and some day-clothes too. Come on, let's go on a shopping spree.'

63

Chapter 11

2035

Jason and Catherine left the undertakers and walked slowly, aimlessly, along the street.

'I still find it hard to accept she's dead, even though we've just made the arrangements for her cremation,' said Catherine.

'I feel the same, a kind of strange blankness. We didn't see much of her, travelling around in our yacht, but we kept in touch. If she needed us, we would've come running. She knew that.' Jason looked at his solafone. 'It's only 10.30. I don't want to go back to our flat. What shall we do now? Would you like to meet up with Sonia and Roger?'

'That would be lovely if they're free.' Jason rang Sonia and after a few minutes of conversation he said, 'We're meeting them at their hotel in half an hour. Let's walk to the end of the road and catch a bus.'

*

Sonia rose to greet them, and Roger hung back while she hugged Jason and Catherine for ages. When they separated both women were crying so Roger came forward with tissues and there were more hugs.

They sat in the lounge and a waiter came and asked them if they would like anything. Sonia ordered coffee for everyone and added four brandies. Catherine's eyes widened at that, but she said nothing. While they waited for the drinks Sonia said, gently, 'Have you made all the arrangements?'

Jason nodded. 'The funeral is on Tuesday, the 26th June, 11 o'clock at the Rawdon Crematorium. We haven't done anything about a wake. We don't know where to have it, or if to have anything at all. What do you think?'

'I think you should let us organise that for you,' said Roger. 'It could be here. I'll go and ask.'

'Sonia, we can't afford to have it here,' said Jason, when Roger had walked away.

'This will be on us. That's what Roger meant when he said he'd organise it. You have enough to cope with.'

'That's the awful thing about kindness, it just sets me off again.' Catherine scrabbled for another tissue and said, 'I also feel guilty that we're making all these arrangements without Andy, but he's in a worse state than us. His father died a few years ago, his Mum died in the blast and he has to organise her funeral and now Izzy. On top of all that, the company where he worked has been destroyed so he's no job and no home. He's a total wreck, so depressed he's had to go to the doctor's for help. I worry he might even be suicidal. I want to help him but don't know how.'

'Well you're taking some weight off him now by organising the funeral. I expect he'll be grateful for that,' said Sonia.

'I don't need him to be grateful. I just wish I could help him cope with all this.'

Roger returned, smiling. 'I've booked a simple finger buffet, for twenty people, in a private meeting room, from one o'clock onwards on that Tuesday. That will give everyone time to get here from the crematorium.'

'Thanks, Roger. We really appreciate it,' Jason said. They sipped their drinks in silence for a while.

'What are you going to do about finding somewhere to live, Sonia? Did you try to get to your house?'

'Yes, we tried but the whole area is completely flattened, and nothing can be salvaged. We've been talking about renting somewhere less frantic than Leeds. I wondered about Northallerton; Roger was living there when we met. A cottage in a village sounds idyllic but I think, as we're getting old, we need facilities like doctors and hospitals nearby. What about you? Will you go back to your boat?'

Catherine looked at Jason, but he was not reacting, so she said, 'We're not sure. We'll have to go back to it, of course, but the idea of sailing about on a perpetual holiday seems, well… pointless now. Also, we're worried about Andy, as you know, and want to be here for him.'

'Where's he staying at the moment?' asked Roger.

'The same lodgings as us, but he didn't want to come to make the funeral arrangements. He said he would meet us for lunch at that little café by the hospital.' Catherine looked at her solafone. 'Talking about that we should be going there now.'

Everyone stood, Roger giving Sonia a helping hand as she grumbled about her arthritis. They went out of the hotel and called a taxi to take them across the city.

*

When they arrived, Andy was already sitting at a table cradling a cup of tea as if he were cold. His face looked drawn and he had dark bags under his eyes, but he smiled with pleasure at seeing everyone.

'This is lovely,' he said standing up, 'I thought it was going to be just three of us.' There were hugs and handshakes and then Jason said, 'We felt a bit bleak after going to the undertakers so phoned Sonia, had coffee together and invited them to join us for lunch.'

'What's that your drinking?' asked Roger.

'Lukewarm tea.'

'Let's see if they can do anything stronger, I think we all need fortification.'

'I'd rather not have wine or spirits. Could I have a lager, please? I fancy something long and cold.

'Right-oh, what about everyone else?' They all opted for Rosé wine, so Roger ordered a bottle. While they waited for the drinks, they studied the menu, and then Sonia keyed their choices into the pad.

'Now will you tell me what you've arranged for Isabelle?' asked Andy.

Catherine gave him all the details and she saw tears glistening in his eyes when she said Roger and Sonia were paying for the wake.

'Thank you both so much. I've no income, nothing so I'm really grateful. Isabelle deserves a decent funeral.' Before anymore could be said the drinks arrived, swiftly followed by their food. It was good to see Andy eating. He had lost so much weight.

'We have a week before the funeral,' said Catherine. 'What do you think about inviting all the survivors to have a lunch meal before then. We can tell them about the funeral arrangements and ask them to come. It also means they can talk about what's happened to them since or whatever....' She tailed off, uncertain if this was a good idea or not.

'I think that's a great idea, Catherine,' said Andy. 'I'm going to apply for jobs tomorrow, but the days seem far too long. I really need something to look forward to. When?'

'What about Thursday, this week?' said Roger, his solafone in his hand. Everyone agreed and entered the details into their solafones then Andy offered to text everyone. He seemed so much brighter than when they had all met.

Chapter 12

June 2030

Leading two lives was confusing and Xen woke feeling anxious. What day was it? Had he missed his tennis game? He asked Maizy and was told it was 9am on Monday. Monday, he was meeting Sean just before 10.30, so it was time to get up.

Half an hour later he'd packed his sports bag, left it by the front door and sat down to eat breakfast. The freedom of the long summer break seemed less exciting than usual. Normally, by now, he would be on the computer looking for last minute, cheap holidays. He had no interest in a holiday now. His greatest need was to see Joanna as often as possible, but he couldn't control what happened with the sand timer.

He heard his phone ping and got up to look at it. He sat back down abruptly when he read it.

Hi, Xen, we're going to have a reunion lunch this Thursday, the 21st and hope that everyone who went through the Harrogate disaster can come. I'm inviting Izzy's parents and their friends, Sonia and Roger, Morgan and his daughter. The time is 12.30 at the 'Deli' near the hospital.

Let me know if you can come, Andy.

Xen messaged back.

That sounds great, I'll look forward to meeting everyone again. Thanks for arranging it, Xen.

*

Sean won, as expected, but Xen had put up sufficient opposition to make the game satisfying. They came off the court smiling and went into the changing rooms to shower and change before lunch.

'When do you go away Sean? I'd like to do this again.'

'Wednesday. I'm packing tomorrow and I have to go to the doctor for a malaria shot. I've already had several other shots, and after this one I'll be safe to go just about everywhere in the world. Unless we fit an early game in tomorrow morning, I can't do it until I come back.'

'No, that's fine. I'm working at my fitness though. I've joined a gym and have a spinning class on Thursday. You've made such a huge change of direction in your life I felt I should make more effort.'

'I'm glad I've had some influence,' said Sean, grinning, as he zipped his sports bag. 'Come on, I'm starving.'

The Tavern was cool and welcoming. It was not an old building but had been built in the style of a traditional pub, with a long, polished bar and draught beer on tap. There were various objects decorating the walls, all relating to sport; baseball bats, fencing swords and masks and every type of racquet Xen could think of.

Sean announced his name and they were shown to a table with a reserved card on it. They were each given a menu tablet and they ordered drinks. Xen really didn't care what he ate because he was trying to think of a way to talk about time travel. Finally, he decided just to launch right into it.

'I've been watching an old set of *Outlander*. Have you seen them, or read the books?'

'Yes, I love science fiction and time travel,' said Sean.

'So, do you, as a scientist, think that travelling through time could be possible?'

'Interesting question, and the simple answer is yes, though the explanation is more complicated.'

69

'Can you tell me the theory?'

'OK, it's based on Einstein's theory of relativity, E equals MC squared, usually referred to as space-time. Basically, if you can move at a terrific rate, time will go slower for you than for everyone else.'

'When you say a terrific rate, are you talking some impossible amount?'

'Oh yes, close to the speed of light, 186,000 miles per second, totally impossible.'

'So, if it *was* possible then a person who does that sort of incredible speed and returns will hardly have aged, but the people he knew could be dead or very old?'

'That's it. Our food's coming, so here endeth the lesson.'

Talking ceased as they began to eat, but after a while, as he slowed down, feeling full, Sean spoke. 'Have you thought about chucking it all in and joining me?'

'It did cross my mind, but I don't think I've got what it takes to be a…' Xen paused, looked dramatically around, and then whispered, '…spy.' I'm sure you need to be very fit, able to think on your feet and be good at self-defence.'

'You've been watching far too many films. My understanding is that there are people who travel and do what you've described but they have a huge back–up team. When I applied, they asked for IT skills and I had to put, 'sufficient for everyday use.'

'Yes, but I'd have to put that phrase next to the fitness question.'

'You'd be surprised at the pay, so think about it. In fact, I have the contact details here. He handed Xen a card. 'Ring them and have a chat.'

'I think you've set me up. The whole tennis game and lunch was all leading to you recruiting me. Do you get a bonus or something if you introduce a friend?' Sean held up his hands to protest but laughed instead. They chatted about other things after that and when they parted agreed to keep in touch.

Xen went home with his brain buzzing. He had come from university straight into teaching and then became a lecturer. He had never worked in any other sort of environment. Could he change his whole lifestyle? There wouldn't be long holidays, but Sean kept talking about the money, and that would be useful.

He came to the conclusion he had little to lose, and sent an e-mail requesting information and an application form. He asked Maizy to make him a coffee and before he had drunk it a reply came.

The form was daunting, twelve pages long, but he read it through and began to feel excited. It took him two hours to fill it in, checking and changing details until he was satisfied. He sent it, along with his CV and stretched, feeling tired, but satisfied.

Xen changed into his 2035 clothes and turned the timer over twice before going to bed. He assumed, if it worked, he would find himself in the hospital again.

*

Xen woke up in the hospital, as he'd predicted, and met Joanna and Ruby there for a coffee. Joanna said she was looking forward to meeting all the survivors on Thursday. Neither of them knew where the 'Deli' café was so they decided to find it. They asked directions and it was only a hundred metres from the hospital entrance but before they got to it, they found a park, with swings.

'Look, swings. Can we go in there, Mummy?'

'Yes. We've plenty of time.'

Once in the playground Xen found he was Ruby's favourite. He had to push her on the swing and then pull the roundabout round while she held on tight shouting, 'Faster, Xen, faster.' After that he was dragged by the hand to the climbing frame to watch her climb. It seemed Ruby's enthusiasm for the playground was unlikely to stop so, when Joanna and Xen had had enough, Joanna suggested they got a bus into town.

71

'Are we going shopping again?' asked Ruby.

'We'll have some lunch first and then, if there's a suitable film, we could go to the cinema,' said Xen.

'I've never been to the cinema, but I've seen films on television.'

'The cinema is like an enormous television. You pay to have a seat and watch it with lots of other people. When the film's going to start, they turn the lights out so you can see the screen better and then you have to be really quiet,' said Joanna. 'It's ages since I've been to one. Great idea Xen.'

The rest of the day went well. They all enjoyed the children's adventure film but Ruby most of all. She came out of the cinema jumping with excitement. 'Can we go again? I really want to see that one about the baby elephant that they said was coming soon.'

'I'm sure we can, Ruby, but it's expensive so we can't do it too often,' said Joanna.

They used the bus to the hospital because Joanna and Ruby lived close by so Xen offered to walk home with them.

'That's really kind but it's not dark and we can manage from the bus stop.'

'Oh, I'd hoped to stay longer,'

'I'd like that too, Xen, but not tonight. I'm sorry. Perhaps after the lunch with the others?' They hugged and kissed, Joanna's kiss lingering with a promise he'd hoped to fulfil that evening. Xen watched as they walked away feeling lonely and disappointed.

What was he going to do now? He didn't know how to return to his own time. It usually happened when he was asleep, but he had nowhere to sleep and it wasn't even very late. He could fill some time by having a meal but what could he do after that? Perhaps a hotel? That seemed better than trying to sleep on a hard chair in the hospital.

The decision was made. He found a modest hotel, checked in and payed in advance, hoping he would have disappeared before morning. The hotel restaurant had room for him, so he ate there too. He went to sleep thinking about Joanna and Ruby and woke, as he'd hoped, in his own bed and time.

Thursday 21ˢᵗ June 2035

Xen had looked at the calendar on his phone, to work out how to be sure he arrived in the future on the Thursday of the lunch date. It seemed the future was ahead by one day. So, he needed to arrive on what was actually Wednesday, in his time. That was good because it meant he could still go to his spinning class.

*

Once again Xen arrived at the hospital and marvelled that no-one saw him materialise. He supposed they were all so busy and by the crick in his neck he must have arrived, still sleeping, in the middle of the night. How did he sleep upright without falling off the chair?

He stood up, gingerly, feeling in need of cleaning his teeth and having a shower. He made do with a wash and then headed off to the coffee shop.

Fortified with caffeine and carbohydrate, with just a twinge of guilt for the new healthy living man he was trying to be, Xen settled back in his chair and texted Joanna.

I'm in Leeds already, really keen to see you both, Xen. X

He was pleased to get a text back quickly.

'You can come round to us now, if you like. Ruby's still in her pyjamas but that won't matter. Our address is, Flat B, 17 Oakfield Road, LS14 6UG. Go out of the hospital, turn right then first on the left. I'll put the kettle on. X

Xen set off straight away and was there in five minutes. There was a call button for each flat, so he pressed B and heard Joanna, 'Hi Xen, I'll let you in.' He could hear Ruby squealing with delight in the background. Joanna hadn't told her he was coming.

He climbed the stairs and the door to their flat was open with Ruby waiting for him. He gave her a cuddle and went inside. The flat was clean, and had recently been painted, but the furniture was shabby. Ruby led him through the living room into the kitchen where Joanna was pouring hot water into two mugs. She turned just as Xen reached her and she fitted into his arms. Her 'hello' was stopped by his kiss that lingered. It was hard to let her go but he managed it, mainly because Ruby was pushing to get between them.

'That was lovely. I was about to say, hello and welcome to our little home. Here's a coffee and do you want anything to eat?'

'No, thanks, I've had a croissant and I suspect we'll be eating well at lunch time.'

'Let's take the drinks into the living room and when we've had them Ruby can show you the rest of the flat.'

'It's nicer than our last one, Xen. I'm glad it got knocked down and we came here,' said Ruby. Xen wasn't sure quite how to answer that, so he just nodded.

'Ruby I've put your clothes on the bed so will you go and get dressed now?' Ruby seemed to struggle with herself, reluctant to leave the room when Xen was there, pouted and then went into her bedroom. They both reached for their cups and drank, looking at each other, then Joanna said, 'I'm looking forward to seeing everyone, but it'll be hard knowing there'll be a funeral soon. What can we say to Andy or Isabelle's parents?'

'Let's just say it's lovely to see you,' suggested Xen. We can talk about where everybody is living now and if they've had any difficulty accessing bank accounts and so on.

74

Don't forget Morgan's daughter. What was her name? Yes, Kathy, will be there. I think she's got children so you can talk to her about that. It'll be fine.'

'I'm ready. Is it time to go now?' Ruby had not only her clothes on but her shoes and light coat.

'Yes, if we walk slowly,' said Joanna. They, decided, it was warm enough to leave coats at home and set off for the café.

When they arrived, Andy was there and stood up smiling. They all hugged, and he said, 'It's great to see you again. I thought I'd better come early as I'd sent out invitations. How have you been coping?'

Joanna was surprised by his friendliness. She had expected to see him still red eyed with grief and morose. She smiled back and said, 'I think I've fallen on my feet. The flat we've been given is so much better than the one we had in Harrogate. Ruby hasn't found any children around to play with yet, but she'll make friends when she begins school in September.'

'What about you, Xen.'

'Oh yes, thanks it's fine and I work in Leeds so it's actually easier for me to get there.'

'The company I worked for was destroyed so I have no job, but my flat is next door to Catherine and Jason's which means we have been supporting each other,' said Andy. Joanna was anxious not to dwell on the tragedy and changed the subject. 'Have you had much media attention? They've left Ruby and me alone since the first day.'

'They found our flats, so Jason talked to them and they went away happy. It seems we were only newsworthy for a day or so. Apparently, there were more survivors in other countries that were attacked. Russia, America and Britain are having talks now. If they decide to retaliate this could lead to another world war. It's a very serious situation.'

'I don't understand why it got to this point in the first place,' said Xen.

'Well what planet have you been on in the last twelve months?' asked Joanna. 'The talks collapsed years ago and there've been all those threats, sanctions, nuclear bombs stockpiled, despite the earlier agreements. We've all been living on a knife edge....'

Xen was glad she stopped in mid flow as Morgan arrived with a young woman. Immediately behind them came Jason, Catherine, Sonia and Roger. A flurry of hugs ensued, and Morgan introduced his daughter, Kathy.

'I'm so glad to meet you all,' she said. 'Dad's been talking about how you escaped from the basement and the awful accident. It's been a nightmare.' Kathy stopped, and for a moment there was an awkward silence, and everyone took refuge in the menu. The menu was a smart one, you could swipe your card or use your solafone then touch what you wanted to eat or drink.

Kathy sat next to Joanna and began to talk about her children. 'In the school holidays they like to be taken out and about, parks, swimming or museums if it's raining,' said Kathy.

'Yes, but I don't really know Leeds, and we haven't any money to pay entrance fees.'

'I know your situation. Dad told me. I wondered if you and Ruby would like to come with us on some of our trips. My children like to have others along. I like it too because they bicker less. It won't be for a couple of weeks because they haven't broken up yet. If you like the idea, I could phone you.'

'That would be kind and we'd love it, thank you.' The food arrived and the conversations dwindled as everyone began to eat. There were plenty of appreciative noises particularly from Ruby, who loved everything.

When everyone had finished eating Jason told them about the funeral arrangements, ending, 'It doesn't matter what you wear just come, please.'

Joanna glanced at him to see if this remark was pointed at her, but he was actually looking at Andy. She wasn't the only person that had lost everything. Ruby suddenly said, 'Can I come?'

'We'd like you to, Ruby. Funerals are not fun, but afterwards Roger's ordered us a feast at his hotel,' said Catherine.

'Will there be chocolate cake?' Everyone smiled and Xen said, 'I'm with you on that one, Ruby. We're both chocoholics.'

*

When the lunch was over Catherine, Jason and Andy went back to their lodgings. Sonia and Roger said they were going to look for flats or houses in Northallerton, and Morgan and Kathy went back to Kathy's house. Joanna, Xen and Ruby stayed for a few moments discussing what they were going to do.

'Well we could go back to your place, or mine or we could take Ruby to a park,' said Joanna.

'Park, park, park, please Mummy.' Ruby bounced up and down in her seat.

'Fresh air and a walk in a park sounds great,' said Xen, smiling at Ruby's delight. They left the café and caught a bus to the park. It was huge, but Xen knew where the playground was. As they were walking Xen's phone pinged. He stopped to read it letting Joanna and Ruby go on ahead.

Hi, Xen, Andy gave me your number. I'd like to talk to you after the funeral, on our own, please,
Sonia

Xen messaged back.

Very cloak and dagger, Sonia, but I'm happy to talk to you, Xen.

He caught them up just as they opened the gate to the swings. Ruby ran towards him, shouting, "Xen will you push me?' He pushed. Joanna stood close enough to chat and said, 'I'm not a brilliant cook and don't have fancy machines to do it for me, but if you'd like to come back to our little flat, you're welcome. Can you cook?'

'As a matter of a fact I can, and I like cooking. I'll come if you let me buy the ingredients and a bottle of wine. Do you prefer white or red?'

'I'm not being difficult, but I actually prefer rosé. It would just be for us two because Ruby eats early and will just have something simple like a sandwich.'

They both knew this was more than just a meal. It was a date, perhaps the start of a proper relationship, and Xen worried he shouldn't be doing it. If he stayed the night, he might disappear back to his own time. How could he explain that? It was a dilemma, but he knew he wanted to be with Joanna.

*

Ruby had a bath and was in bed by half past seven and while Joanna read her a story Xen began to prepare their meal. They ate it at the kitchen table.

'That was delicious, Xen, what did you add to the omelette to give it that gorgeous tang?'

'Blue cheese.'

'I don't like blue cheese,' said Joanna and giggled. 'I think this wine has gone to my head. Is it very strong?'

Xen picked up the bottle and read the label. 'It's not especially strong, but I expect you're not used to drinking alcohol.'

'You're right there. If I have any more, I might not be responsible for my actions.' They both laughed and Xen made a show of filling their glasses again. Before half of it had gone, she was in his arms, and they kissed gently then more urgently. Joanna pulled away from him and held out her hand, 'Bedroom?'

Xen threw caution away and when they were in the bedroom, he undressed her, partly because she still had a pot on her arm and partly because it was such an exciting thing to do. He shed his own hastily. Their need was strong and there was little finesse. It was over too soon and left both of them panting for breath.

'I really needed that, thank you. It's been a long, long time,' said Joanna.

Xen stroked the length of her arm and ran his hand lightly over her breasts. He felt her wriggle and wondered if they would play again, later. 'It's been a long time for me too.'

'Ruby wakes really early, about 6.30, so we should probably get some sleep now.' She yawned and Xen was unable to resist doing the same, but he remembered to say. 'I have to leave early tomorrow so I might not be here if she sleeps in. If so, I'll see you at the funeral.' Joanna nodded and fell asleep almost immediately.

Xen did not sleep immediately and felt restless. He got up and finished his glass of wine, and Joanna's as well, hoping that would help. Within a few moments of slipping back into the bed he slept.

Chapter 13

Tuesday 26th June 2035

Xen had worried about what to wear to the funeral. The new trendy trousers would be fine, but he needed a more sober top. He went to his wardrobe and surveyed the choices. Finally, he took a dark blue, plain T-shirt that had a slight sheen. He'd noticed that other people wore shiny tops in 2035 so hoped that would be suitable. On top of that he added a black jacket. He could always carry it if other people didn't wear one and it did seem suitable for a funeral. If he was going to keep going into the future, he really would need to buy more clothes.

He'd changed into these clothes before going to sleep in his own time, having turned the timer over twice. Now he opened his eyes and saw he was not in the hospital but on Joanna's sofa. Ruby discovered him there, forgot to be quiet when Mummy was still asleep, and shouted, 'Xen.'

'Hello Ruby, give me a minute, I've just woken up and don't feel all that brilliant.'

'Do you feel sick?'

'No, I'll be fine in a minute and then I'll make us a drink.' He looked at his phone. 'Don't wake Mummy, it's still early.' Ruby put her finger across her lips and nodded. She snuggled up beside him and he put his arm around her. Xen felt very protective and began to understand what it must be like to be a father. When his queasiness had gone, he moved gently away from her and said, 'I'll make a drink now. What would you like?'

'Tea please with lots of milk, and Mummy likes coffee.' While he was making the drinks, Ruby went back into her bedroom and picked up her doll and tea set. She arranged the cups on the coffee table and sat her doll beside them.

In the kitchen Xen thought of taking Joanna breakfast in bed, but when he looked in the fridge and cupboards, he was shocked to find them nearly empty. He took Ruby her tea and she said, 'Kirsty's having a drink too. Then she's having breakfast of bread with strawberry jam.'

'That sounds good. I'll take Mum's coffee in and give her a surprise. I don't suppose she gets coffee in bed often.'

Ruby pretended to give Kirsty a drink and listened to her Mum's delight at seeing Xen. 'I think Mummy loves Xen, Kirsty. She's so happy when he's here. I'd like him to be my Daddy,' she said.

*

While Joanna was getting dressed, Xen walked to the corner shop and bought bread, milk, strawberry jam, coffee, tea and some other useful items to help fill her fridge. When he got back, they enjoyed breakfast together and Xen was glad Joanna didn't think to ask how he had got into her house that morning. He must ask her for the combination to the front door.

'I think Ruby needs some exercise before the funeral. She'll find it easier to sit through the service if she's tired,' said Joanna.

'What would you like to do, bearing in mind we need to be there just before eleven?'

'Let's get the bus to the crematorium and see if there's a park nearby.' Xen googled the area and saw that there was. 'It's a bit of a trek, but we can do it if we leave now,' he said. They got ready quickly and were soon running down to the main road to catch the bus. They arrived just in time, boarded it and stood breathing hard while Joanna used her pass. Xen used his phone and they all sat down, Ruby with Joanna, Xen a few rows back. They couldn't chat so Xen relaxed and watched the city streets, noticing changes when he went through areas he knew.

81

*

Sonia and Roger left their hotel in good time to pick up Jason, Catherine and Andy. Once they were all in the car the atmosphere was of silent apprehension. The crematorium car park had a few places left and their car parked itself. It was a short walk under a grey sky, almost as if the weather felt it had to be in tune with the sadness of the day. Sonia and Roger let the others go ahead, aware of their huge loss and not wanting to intrude on their thoughts.

They reached the building at the same time as Morgan and Kathy and it seemed some formality was needed so they all shook hands. Xen, Joanna and Ruby arrived soon after and Ruby, not understanding any need to be subdued, chatted to everyone about their trip to the park.

Catherine cried, smiling as Ruby reminded her of Izzy as a little girl; her happiness and innocence. A few friends arrived who lived in the area but there were a lot of sailing friends missing, who had lived in Harrogate and were now dead. Jason thought of them all at the sailing club, during Izzy's 18th birthday celebration at the clubhouse. He was fighting back his own tears when his memories were interrupted by the arrival of the hearse.

Everyone went into the building, the three family members sitting on the front row and the others gathered behind them. The coffin was rolled in on a gurney to organ music, 'Jesu, Joy of Man's Desiring'.

There was a welcome from the minister, who spoke in celebration of Isabelle's life. Sonia was then invited to speak.

'I have known Izzy since she was born and have been privileged to be her godmother and adopted aunty. She was a lively, pretty child and grew into a beautiful woman and a lovely wife to Andy.' Andy nodded, tears rolling unchecked down his cheeks. 'Izzy went to university and studied to become a teacher, like her dad. Up until the destruction of Harrogate she worked as a primary school

82

teacher in the town. Her school was destroyed, and all of the pupils and teachers died in the blast.

Izzy was a keen dinghy sailor and many of her sailing friends would have been here today if they had not lived in Harrogate. It seems impossible to mourn Izzy's death without mourning the deaths of other people, those we knew, and those we didn't.

This is a time of great sadness for everyone in Yorkshire, but today we are especially remembering our own, wonderful, Isabelle.' Sonia, pale but dry-eyed stepped away from the lectern and went back to her seat. Roger held her hand and found it shaking. He handed her a tissue as she allowed the tears to fall.

There were no hymns and the minister said some prayers and mentioned a collection for all those who had died.

They left the crematorium and gathered, briefly, outside. The fresh air was a welcome relief from the sadness inside. Ruby held her mum's hand and whispered, 'Is it time for lunch now? I'm hungry.'

It will be soon, but we must get to the hotel first,' said Joanna.

She looked around for Xen and saw him talking to Morgan and Kathy. He waved for her to join them. They walked over and Xen said, 'Kathy's going to give us a lift to the hotel.'

'That's very kind, thank you,' said Joanna.

'Thank you,' echoed Ruby, making them smile.

*

The Rose Suite in the hotel was elegant with pale pink, plush chairs and long, swagged curtains. The small group of mourners were offered drinks as they entered. They sipped them and gravitated towards the finger buffet. Ruby could barely contain herself.

'Can we start Mummy?' Joanna nodded and collected a plate to load for her. Everyone else joined in except Andy, Catherine and Jason.

'I can hardly bear this, Catherine. I keep thinking of Izzy and then muddling her funeral with yours. I couldn't eat or drink anything then and I'm not sure I can now. If only we still had the sand timer.' Catherine was too emotional to speak. Jason put his arms around her and held her tight. After a while she opened her eyes and pulled away from him. 'Where's Andy? We must look after him. He's feeling just like us.'

Andy was standing, his drink untouched in his hand, looking at the food. Catherine and Jason came up to him.

'If you could eat something you might feel better, Andy,' said Catherine. He looked at her and smiled, wanly. 'I will if you will.'

Sonia bustled up to them. 'All three of you go and sit down and I'll bring you some plates and you must try to eat some of it. The salmon sandwiches are really delicious.' They did as they were told and eventually managed to eat something.

When Sonia was satisfied her friends were as comfortable as they could be, she looked around for Xen, knowing he would be with Joanna and Ruby. She went to them and asked Xen if she could have a quick word with him. He got up and they went into the reception area.

'What did you want to ask me?'

Sonia hesitated and then said, 'I can sometimes see an aura around people… and I can see yours. Most people have a steady light, but yours is flashing on and off. It's happened every time I've seen you, as if you are only half here and half somewhere else. I'm not sure what it signifies, but I wondered if you were from a different time.'

Xen's reaction was to sit down abruptly, his eyes wide with surprise.

Chapter 14

2030

Xen had fallen asleep in Joanna's bed and woken up in his own, feeling pleased he'd managed to obtain the code to enter her flat. He lay there thinking. Why do I have to return to my own time? I'd be happy to make a new life, somehow, in 2035. It's really annoying having very little control over the leaps forward and backward in time.

Then he remembered his talk with Sonia. She knew about the sand timer. She even knew it came from the *Daphne*, so it had to be the same one. Unfortunately, she was unable to tell him how she knew about it because Jason and Catherine had come to find her. She had just quickly said, 'We must talk again, but you have a mission and I think it's to prevent Isabelle's death.'

He wondered, why specifically Isabelle? Why not prevent the deaths of the thousands all over the world that died in the attacks? He would ask her when they met again but he wasn't sure when that would be. He sat up in bed and texted Sonia.

Hi Sonia, So many things to ask you! Why must I save Isabelle when so many others died? I'm back in my own time but would really like to meet again soon.
Xen

When his text had gone, he checked his e-mails – there was one from the government department. Probably a direct rejection, or he had forgotten to fill in a box, he thought.

His negative thoughts gave way to a frisson of fear as he read that they wanted him to come for an interview on Friday, if he could do so at such short notice. He was advised to bring an overnight bag, and sport's clothes because, if he had a successful interview, he would be required to have an intense medical.

What day was it now? Wednesday; enough time to buy a suit and think about the questions he might be asked. Perhaps Sean could give him some pointers, though he was leaving today.

He got up, drank his coffee and sent a text to Sean. By the time he'd finished his breakfast a reply had arrived.

There were no difficult questions, all straightforward. I got the impression they were looking for a high standard of education, self-confidence and initiative. You'll be fine. Glad you took up my suggestion.

S.

Xen frowned when he read the mention of self-confidence and initiative. He was confident to stand in front of students and present a lecture, but in other ways he knew he was a wimp. He really hated confrontations and violence. If they asked him about martial arts, he would have to admit he'd no experience at all. Negative thoughts again.

He stood up, annoyed with himself, and checked the time and place of the interview. It was 15.00 in London, so he would need to buy a train ticket.

*

Xen bought his ticket online, so now there was no going back. Then he went to several men's clothing shops until he found suits. As he pulled the jackets to one side looking for his size, he wished he were buying clothes for 2035. This suit would be out-dated in five years' time, and he might be fatter with a middle-aged paunch. That thought made him determined to have a session at the gym that afternoon,

By lunchtime he was carrying a large bag back home. It contained a suit and a shirt. His mood was lighter and more confident than earlier. He ate a healthy lunch realising it was easier to eat properly when he felt in control.

An hour later he was in the gym following his programme of exercises. It felt easier than the first time he had done it, so perhaps he was already feeling the benefit. He hoped so. When he had finished his workout, he thought that perhaps he should run home, but by the time he had showered he'd changed his mind and walked. While he was walking his phone vibrated and he stopped to read Sonia's text.

Can you come tomorrow? Have lunch with me at my hotel. Roger will be out revisiting a house we've seen, measuring for curtains etc. 1ish if poss.
Sonia

Xen had been unsure what to do on Thursday but the idea of seeing Joanna again was delightful. He replied, quickly that he would see Sonia then. Only when he got home did he wonder how he was going to arrive at Joanna's flat in the morning and then excuse himself for lunch.

It was still worrying him when he turned the timer over twice before going to bed, dressed in the clothes he had worn for the funeral. Sonia will think I've only one set of clothes, he thought, and she'd be right. Perhaps after the lunch I might shop for some more. Living in two different times was proving expensive.

*

2035
Xen woke up sprawled on a settee in the foyer of Sonia's hotel. Why was he there? He'd thought the timer always

returned him back to where he was previously when he fell asleep, which should mean Joanna's flat. He looked at his watch and realised it was only 6.55am, ridiculously early for lunch, and he felt hungry. Breakfast in the hotel was not a good idea. It would be too expensive and if he met Roger, it would be hard to explain.

Xen stood up, carefully, aware of some lingering vertigo, and went out into the cool morning. The air revived him, and he started to walk briskly, enjoying the exercise. Half an hour later he arrived at a coffee shop. It was busy, but he managed to find an empty table and used the electronic menu to select iced water, coffee and a croissant. Just before pressing the order button he went back, deleted the croissant and opted for porridge with blueberries instead. Making a healthy choice pleased him. He looked around and spotted a rack of newspapers and fetched one back to his table.

Russia and America Threaten Reprisals for China's Atrocity

Russia and America have demanded the destruction of China's Death Ray and have asked China to sign an agreement that no matter what the provocation such a weapon should never be used again. In return they would agree not to use their own, 'next generation', master weapon in retaliation.

If China's, President Chow, refuses then two of his cities will be destroyed and all trading would continue to cease indefinitely.

It made frightening reading. Somehow, from his own time, the situation must be prevented, but how could an obscure university lecturer do it? Who would listen to him? Travelling into the future? They'd think he was mad.

His breakfast arrived and he ate it without much interest, being overwhelmed by the responsibility of his knowledge. Perhaps Sonia would have some ideas. Thinking of Sonia made him look at his watch. There was still plenty of time, but he ought to move on and buy some new clothes. He imagined himself carrying armfuls of bags and wondered if it was possible to transport objects back with him to his own time; or forwards into this time. So far, he had only brought with him what he was wearing. The sensible thing would be to buy a holdall and keep it at Joanna's.

*

The shopping trip proved enjoyable. Xen bought a washing kit, pyjamas, a bath towel, two pairs of baggy trousers and three tops. After removing all the labels, he put everything into his new holdall.

Was there time for a coffee? He decided to have one in the department store, when he realised, he'd bought no underwear. He almost ran back to the underwear section and bought three pairs of pants. Now there was no time for a drink. He had to keep his appointment with Sonia.

Xen arrived at the hotel with twenty minutes to spare and ordered a coffee to sip while he waited. He saw Sonia walking towards him; slim, with short white hair, beautifully cut. She was wearing a flowing summer dress and the bangles on her wrist made him think of an elegant gypsy.

He stood up to greet her. Sonia gave him a hug and they sat down together.

'Can I buy you a coffee, or something stronger?' he asked.

'No, I'm fine thank you, Xen. I'll have a glass of wine with lunch, but there's no rush. We couldn't talk easily at the funeral, but we can now. I'm going to tell you how I know about time travel. I've not done it myself, but Jason, Catherine and Izzy have all gone back into the past.'

'Did they have strange auras?'

'No, well actually I don't know because I never saw them when they travelled. I just waited, very anxiously, for them to come back. Catherine was killed in a road accident. The sand timer enabled Jason to go back and stop it happening. Then he stayed in that time never returning to his own. I knew what he was doing, and, because of that, I also went back in time, just a few months and stayed in that time.

'I believe you, but I don't understand why I, who only met Isabelle for a day or two, should be involved.'

'It doesn't seem to have anything to do with who you are. It's who has the timer. The timer seems to want to specifically protect the women in Catherine's family.' Sonia looked at her solafone. 'Let's continue this over lunch. I booked a table in the bistro, follow me.'

Once they were settled in the bistro Sonia sipped her wine while they waited for their order and then asked, 'What's your normal era?'

'2030. Sonia, I don't understand what I can do to prevent Isabelle's accident. I can't seem to control the timer.'

'Have you tried turning it over more than once?'

'Yes, last night I turned it twice and arrived here, but I expected to be in Joanna's flat. There's no obvious logic.'

'In that case I think you'll have to trust the timer. It seems to take you to where you need to be.'

Xen's forehead creased into a frown. 'Are you going to tell Catherine and Jason?'

'Not if it worries you. They would understand….'

'Yes, but they'd put pressure on me to solve this mess. I don't know how to do it. I might let them down.'

Before Sonia could reply their order arrived. They both sat for a moment, not eating, not talking, just thinking. Sonia picked up her nearly empty wine glass. 'Let's have a toast, Xen, to a successful mission.'

They clinked glasses and Xen felt the tension easing. He was going to offer her another glass of Chardonnay, but the waiter anticipated her need and topped it up without anyone speaking. She nodded her thanks and picked up her knife and fork. 'Eat up Xen, this is too good to waste.'

*

They parted after lunch and Xen went to see Joanna and Ruby, but when he got to their flat, they were out. He sat on the step, in the sunshine, to wait. He felt calmer about everything now he had someone who understood, but he still needed to know what he had to do.

He wondered if the timer would transport his friends back five years. If it could, would they want to go? Catherine, Jason and Andy obviously would, but what about Joanna and Ruby? If they went back would Ruby be as she was now, or would she be a baby?

His head was beginning to ache with the 'what ifs', and he was pleased to have his thoughts interrupted by Ruby's squeal of delight. He got up just in time to field her exuberant leap into his arms, her legs wrapping around his waist.

'Hello, Ruby, lovely to see you too. How are you, Joanna?'

'We're both fine, and we've got some news. Come in and I'll make us some tea. I've bought Ruby's favourite chocolate cake to celebrate.'

When they were all sat around the kitchen table with the kettle noisily coming to the boil Xen looked at Joanna with his eyebrows raised.

'OK, this is our news. I went for an interview today and I got the job. They have a crèche and Ruby loved it.'

'That's brilliant, well done.' He got up and gave her a hug. 'What will you be doing in this job?'

'Mummy's going to work at the university, Xen. So, she'll be able to see you every day.'

Xen frowned.

'What's the matter?' asked Joanna. 'I didn't get the job just to be near you, if that's a problem.'

Xen heard the hard edge to her voice and held up his hands. 'That wouldn't be a problem, but there is one. I'm

91

going for an interview tomorrow, in London, and if I get the job, I won't be at the university anymore. I might have to work in London, I'm not sure.'

'Oh, so we might not see so much of you. The trains are fast but commuting every day would be expensive. I don't know whether to hope you get it or not. I suppose I'm being selfish.'

'I'll make the tea, and I will say, if I get it, the money will be quite a lot more.' Xen made the tea and Joanna cut up the cake. It was delicious and Ruby managed to get chocolate cream all over her face and hands.

Later, when she had been helped to wash it off, they went to a park and Ruby played on the swings and demanded that Xen, not her Mummy, push her. Xen obliged and then he tried to teach her how to go higher on her own.

She began to get the idea but then stopped. 'If I can do it myself you and Mummy won't push me anymore.'

'Yes, we will, if you want us to,' said Joanna, laughing.

*

Later, when Ruby was asleep Xen asked Joanna when her job started.

'The first Monday in August,' she said. 'At first I'm to help sort out those who failed to get their first choice and have opted to come to Leeds. After that it's more ordinary admin. It means I won't be relying on government charity. No more going hungry for us. I'm so pleased, Xen.' He hugged her and told her he was proud of her turning her life around.

As they were getting ready for bed, Xen asked if he could leave his bag with her – he would be seeing her again but was not sure when. It all depended on his interview. He also said he would be leaving early in the morning and would probably go before she woke up.

'That's fine, Xen, but please text me to tell me how you got on. You're part of our lives now.'

Chapter 15

2030

Xen sat up in bed, relieved to find himself in his own home and time but anxious about the interview. There was no rush to get up, but he couldn't stay in bed. He pulled on tracksuit bottoms and a T-shirt and went for a run. It was easy at first, going downhill towards Valley Gardens and then in through the gate, but then it was uphill, and that slowed him down.

His breathing was harsh by the time he reached the children's play area, so he stopped for it to calm. Ruby would love this place, he thought. I wish we lived in the same time.

When he felt ready Xen tackled the steep hill that would take him out of the park and through an area of woods. It proved too much for him without having to stop for a breather again. He could make the run circular, but that meant a lot of running on pavement, so he retraced his steps, reaching his flat feeling energised and ready for breakfast. Whilst eating, he thought about the interview, calmer now than when he woke. Sean had said he had nothing to lose and he was right. He packed an overnight case as suggested and hoped he would need it.

*

Xen arrived at Kings Cross station and queued for a taxi. When it was his turn he got in the vehicle, keyed in the address and paid with his phone. The journey took a long time, cost a great deal, and he decided to try getting back by bus.

The entrance was not imposing and there was no sign on the door, just a number. It was not surprising, thought Xen, but slightly disconcerting. He rang the bell and waited. An intercom crackled and he had to state his name before the door clicked open. A voice told him to go upstairs and enter the first door on the right. There was no sign on that door either, but when he opened it there was, at least, a reception area with a computer. It asked him to please sign in, and then it took a photograph of him. The last instruction it gave him was to sit and wait to be called.

It was unnerving to be greeted without any human interaction. He even wondered, idly, if he was going to be interviewed by a robot. This fear increased when a grey, metallic, robotic humanoid glided in on wheels. It said, 'Welcome Mr Xenaphon Baxter. Please follow me.'

It was a relief to be shown into a medium-sized, normal looking office with a real person standing up to greet him, hand outstretched. Except, this was someone he knew, Morgan Ashbourne. He paled and stood irresolute for a moment, before shaking the offered hand.

'Are you feeling unwell, Mr Baxter? You went very pale at the sight of me.'

'I'm so sorry. You look very like a friend, a friend who died. It was a shock.'

'I think you should sit down. May I call you Xenaphon?' He pointed to a comfortable armchair and Xen sank gratefully into it.

'I prefer Xen; my whole name's such a mouthful.'

'Fine, I'll join you in the other armchair, then we can both be comfortable. Talking about names I assume your father chose yours, being a classics scholar.'

'Yes, he was disappointed when I chose tech.'

'Well that leads me nicely into asking about your technological abilities. I know your qualifications. What I want to know is your experience in hacking. Your school records show you hacked into the school system and altered all your year group's exam results, passing them all with top grades.' His lips were twitching with the beginning of a smile.

'It was not my finest moment. I was lucky not to be expelled. I was only twelve and did it for a joke.' Xen felt uncomfortable and anticipated what was coming next. 'If you know that then you also know I was fired from my first job for exposing fraudulent dealings. Money was being creamed off to multiple companies, a complex trail of illegal laundering. That's what made me decide to become a college lecturer.'

'Yes, I was coming to that. I'm not surprised they fired you. They had to pay an enormous fine, their chairman had to resign, and the company only just survived.'

Xen was unsure whether Morgan approved of his actions or not. He'd never been accused of disloyalty before. He decided to say nothing.

'Right, before we get down to more important things would you like some coffee, tea or one of those awful fruity infusions?'

'I'd like a flat, white coffee, no sugar, thank you.'

'So would I. I'll just give Robby our order.' He tapped a tablet and then looked back at Xen. 'This job means working on the edge of legality. If we employed you it would mean signing the Official Secrets Act, and even your closest relatives and friends must be unaware of what you're doing. If this worries you then we need to stop here, after you've had your coffee, of course.'

As Morgan said that, Robby appeared with a tray carrying two mugs of coffee and a plate of cakes. It bent at the waist and placed the tray on the coffee table by the chairs.

'Thanks, Robby.' The next few moments were filled with the business of refreshments. Morgan ate cake with relish, but Xen refused it, saying he was on a healthy living programme.

95

'I approve of that, but you must forgive me indulging myself.' He sat back in his chair and crossed one leg loosely over the other, mug in hand. 'So, does it worry you to be, as I said before, working close to the edge of illegality.'

Xen shook his head and then said, 'That, doesn't worry me but I'm not a violent person and I could never physically hurt anyone. If that's required, then count me out.'

'No, Xen, that's not part of the job description, I assure you. Now, tell me why you want to work for us?'

'I had a friend who applied to you and gave me your card. He wanted a complete change of lifestyle. It made me realise I'm also stuck in a rut. I hope, by working for you, I can make a difference in Britain, by using my expertise and my contacts.'

Morgan nodded. He finished his coffee, uncrossed his legs and sat forward. 'I'm satisfied with our chat today so I'm going to suggest, if you're happy, we organise the medical. If you pass that you will be asked to attend a physical training course.' He stood up and raised an eyebrow at Xen who realised he had to agree.

'That's fine, I'm happy, thank you.'

'Your medical will be here, tomorrow, at nine o'clock.' Morgan stood, went to his desk and tapped his tablet. 'OK, a hotel has been booked for you, including evening meal and breakfast. The details have been sent to your phone. We will, of course, pay all your expenses.' He held out his hand, indicating that the interview was over. Xen stood, shook it and left, his brain buzzing.

The directions on his phone showed the hotel was only a few hundred yards away and he strode out enjoying the fresh air. When he'd checked in, Xen went to the bar and ordered a cold beer. He took it to a quiet corner and sat in an armchair. As he began to relax a little, he thought about the interview. It had gone well, once he'd recovered from the surprise of meeting Morgan.

Morgan! Why didn't Morgan recognise me when we met in the future? Isabelle had only been to one of his lectures, but she knew she'd seen him before. His name alone was enough for people to remember him and comment on it. Perhaps it was something to do with the Official Secrets Act?

Xen remembered the times they'd been together. He'd rescued Morgan from the basement after the destruction of Harrogate. They'd met again in hospital in Leeds. Later they'd all met socially, and Morgan had brought his daughter Kathy. Then there was Isabelle's funeral. All occasions when Morgan could have revealed that they'd met before. Did he realise Xen had been time travelling? It seemed unlikely.

Xen finished his beer, dined in the hotel's restaurant and went to bed early, after setting the alarm on his phone. Before he settled to sleep, he sent Joanna a message.

The interview went well, and I've had to stay overnight to have a medical in the morning. Tell you more when I see you,
Xen x

*

In the morning Xen turned his alarm off and got up. The small, sparse room was clean and functional, but no more than that. There were no pictures on the walls and the tiny window overlooked a car park that was deep in shadow despite the sunshine. He would be glad to get home to the green spaces of Yorkshire.

He ate breakfast in the hotel and tried to make healthy choices. He was drinking his second cup of coffee when his phone vibrated.

I'm glad the interview went well. Good luck with the medical, I'm sure you'll pass.
Joanna x

*

Entering the building was the same as before but he was asked to go into a different room. Once there a disembodied voice requested him to remove his clothes and don a gown and then wait to be called.

It started as a normal medical, the doctor asking questions and taking vital signs, and then he was told he was to change so he could use the gym equipment in the next room. For the next hour Xen cycled, rowed, stepped and jogged until he was exhausted. He was offered a shower before leaving, which he accepted gratefully.

Back out on the street Xen walked to a main road and paused at a bus stop. He was studying the timetable when he heard,

'Do you want some help?'

He smiled at the elderly woman who'd spoken. 'Yes, please. I want to get to King's Cross station.'

'If you get this bus coming it stops at several stations including King's Cross.'

Xen thanked her and used the bus. Once he'd reached the mainline station and was on his way to Yorkshire, he was able to relax and enjoy the ride. He thought about Morgan and Joanna. He wanted to see her and wondered how he could stay more than one night in the future.

Chapter 16

2035

Xen was delighted to find he was in Joanna's flat when he woke. Ruby was still asleep. It was 7 o'clock so that was surprising. He recovered quickly from the usual disorientation and went quietly into the kitchen to make some coffee. He checked the fridge for milk and food – it was almost empty. It would be black coffee unless he went shopping.

Xen felt something was wrong. It was too silent. He peeped into Ruby's bedroom and saw that the bed was empty, neatly made. Not caring about being quiet now, he strode into Joanna's bedroom and that was empty too.

They must have gone away. Why didn't she tell me?

He messaged her and drank a cup of black coffee, waiting for an answer. When it pinged, he grabbed his phone.

Sorry. You made it sound like you'd not be coming for a while, so I accepted an offer from Sonia to go up to Northumberland for a few days. She's buying a house in the area. Andy's here too. I'll be back on Tuesday, hospital appointment re my wrist. Did you pass the medical?

Andy's there too. It made Xen feel jealous even though he knew Andy was grieving. His reaction was selfish, but he'd looked forward to seeing Joanna, telling her about his interview, making love to her. The day was going to be long and boring now. At least he could shop for non-perishable food to fill her cupboard.

He couldn't even see Sonia, but he could try Morgan. Whatever the outcome of the interview, talking to him five years later would make no difference.

Xen went shopping, had some breakfast and then sent Morgan a text. The reply came back almost immediately.

Happy to meet. You suggest venue, any time today. M.A

Xen arranged to be at a bar in town at 11.30. This gave him time to go for a walk. The medical workout in the gym yesterday had made him ache and his muscles needed to move. He did some stretching exercises and then walked briskly for an hour. When he returned to Joanna's flat, he had a drink of water and called a taxi to take him to the pub.

Morgan was already there, waiting in a secluded booth. Xen made his way towards him feeling nervous but smiled and tried to look casual. Morgan stood as he got closer and said, 'Good to see you, Xen, what would you like to drink?'

'I'll have a pint of lager, thanks.' They sat down and Morgan ordered on the tablet.

While they waited Xen told him he'd called to see Joanna, but she was away, having a short holiday in Northumberland. Morgan said it was a lovely part of the country and he was sure Ruby would enjoy going to the beach. The drinks arrived and Xen saw Morgan was drinking whiskey. He thought it a bit early for spirits and Morgan caught the disapproving look.

'I thought I might need a bit of support. You didn't come to see me to chat about Joanna, did you.'

Xen had worried about how to broach the subject, and Morgan was making it easy for him. He breathed deeply and said, 'We met five years ago, when I went for an interview, but you didn't acknowledge me when we met again in what was left of Harrogate. Why?'

'I might say the same to you.'

This was awkward – in his own time he had only just met Morgan. So, he said nothing and drank his beer.

'I did recognise you, Xen, although it took me a while. But I knew it couldn't actually be you because you were dead. You'd died five years ago, or so I thought.' Xen was shocked. He was going to die very soon.

'Are you feeling ill? You've gone really pale, Xen?'

Morgan's voice seemed far away, and everything began to revolve.

'I'm going to the toilet,' Xen said and stumbled away. He thought he was fainting and closed his eyes. There was a rush of wind that sucked him into a vortex, and when he opened his eyes, he was on the bathroom floor, in his own flat. After he'd been sick, the sense of movement ceased. When he stood up, he felt tired but well enough to go into the living room and sink into his favourite chair.

'Maizy can I have a large mug of tea please?'

'Good afternoon, Xen, your tea will be ready in four minutes.'

Morgan had said Xen was going to die imminently. If only he'd said how it happened then, perhaps, he could prevent it. The timer brought him back, abruptly, before he had told Morgan about the time travel. Why? Morgan was a powerful man, working for the Secret Service, but was he a patriot? Could he be a spy for China? Xen stood up, surprised at his own thoughts. Morgan had been really kind to Joanna.

He picked up his tablet to scroll through his messages and stopped to read one from Morgan.

I'm pleased to inform you that you have passed the medical and I am able to offer you a post in our technical department...

The message went on to give a date for training and a salary scale. The latter made his eyes open wide. He had

101

been asked to reply within one week and decided to think about it for a while.

He sent texts to Joanna and Sean telling them he'd been offered a job. Then realised he was hungry. He'd had no lunch and the violent trip back to his own time had temporarily quelled his appetite.

He looked in his freezer for a ready meal. While the microwave was doing its job, he found his contract of employment to see what notice he had to give. It was two months, so, with the summer vacation he had time to make a decision before sending in his notice.

Sean replied:

Congrats! Currently doing the physical training. Exhausting and challenging! I hope you'll accept the offer. I'll be back in a few days. We can meet then and catch up.

Joanna replied while Xen was reading Sean's message.

I'm really pleased for you. I hope you take it, even if it means we can't meet so often. By the way I'm coming home tomorrow, can you come over?

Xen thought about Joanna, remembering her and Ruby playing in the park, and he wanted to see her now, not wait until tomorrow. The evening seemed endless. Television just irritated him. He was too anxious to settle. Should he take the job? When was he going to die? How was he going to die? His greatest desire was to see Joanna. He showered, changed into his 2035 clothes, made sure he had his wallet in a pocket, turned the timer over twice and went to bed.

*

Catherine and Jason were pleased when Andy was invited to go to Northumberland. It gave them time to themselves and a chance to talk about their future. They had all their assets tied up in their boat but the fun of living on it and sailing around Europe or the world was now less enticing. It was difficult to understand why, but Catherine voiced one idea. 'I think, if I'm honest, I was passing the time until Izzy…' She took a deep breath trying to fight back tears and tried again, '…until we had a grandchild. Then I wanted to buy a house or flat somewhere near so I could help. And now it'll never happen.'

Jason held her close, as she sobbed, murmuring, 'I know, I know, my darling. you don't have to say any more. It hurts so much.'

He held her until her shoulders stopped heaving and she buried her face in a tissue. 'Do you think we should have one more trip, perhaps taking Andy, before we make a decision?'

Catherine managed a weak smile. 'If I remember, when Izzy tried to teach him to sail a dinghy, he was not impressed. He tried really hard to please her and understood all the theory, but he just couldn't really enjoy it.'

'Yes, I can remember him coming dripping into the clubhouse having capsized and saying he failed to see the pleasure in getting wet and cold every Sunday. I just thought it might give him time to decide what to do with his life. His company, in Harrogate, was destroyed, so he has no job. Many of his friends and colleagues have died. We're his only family now. I'm not sure what to do.'

'I think we need to suggest it to him. But if he refuses, do we go back to the boat, cruise for two weeks and then make a decision? That would leave him alone. No, Jason, we can't do that.' There was silence for a while as they considered the options.

It was Jason who said, 'We will offer him a cruise. If he says no you stay here, and I will go and put the boat up for sale. I might even be able to ring the harbour master and see if he'll do that for us, but we'd need to research its value.'

'You'd still have to go there to collect all our personal things, but that would take just a few days. If we did that where should we live? I can't bear this poky place much longer.'

Catherine looked like she was going to cry again so Jason said, 'Shall we go and be decadent and treat ourselves to a meal out?'

She nodded adding, 'A lovely idea. What about that Thai restaurant? I'll need to wash my face and change.'

'You don't need to change, just some lipstick and you'll be fine. I'll ring the restaurant and check it has a table.'

'OK, ready in five.'

Jason booked the table for eight o'clock and when Catherine was ready, he suggested a walk beforehand to chase way their blues.

Chapter 17

2035

Xen woke, as he'd hoped, on Joanna's sofa. It was 7am and Ruby was having a lay in, unless they hadn't returned yet. He got up and peeked into her room. She was sprawled on top of the duvet, one arm behind her head the other thrown out sideways, sound asleep. Her holiday at the seaside must have tired her out. It might have been the first time she'd seen the sea. He wished he'd been there with her. He pulled the door closed very quietly and went into the kitchen to make a cup of tea. He was sipping it, sitting at the table when Ruby entered and shouted his name with delight. He gave her a hug and poured her a drink of milky tea as she chattered, excitedly about her holiday.

Joanna joined them looking tousled and sleepy but pleased to see Xen. She kissed him, sat down and let Ruby carry on.

'The sea went on forever to the, err.... horizon. That's a line where the sea seems to a stop but doesn't. You should've heard the seagulls squawking and when we had fish and chips – they tried to steal our chips from our hands. I built sandcastles with Andy and then he made me a car to sit in with shells for the buttons.'

Xen found it hard to keep his smile at the mention of Andy, but Ruby's enthusiasm was delightful, and he didn't want to spoil it. 'What happened when the tide came in?' he asked her.

'We watched it get closer and closer and then I had to get out of the car, or I'd have got wet. My sandcastles fell down but when we left a little bit of car was still there. Will you come with us next time Xen?'

'I'd like to, Ruby. It sounds like you had lots of fun. Did you see the house Sonia and Roger want to buy?'

Ruby nodded but Joanna replied. 'It's a beautiful stone cottage, but it wasn't how I imagined, small and quaint. It was really big and modern inside. Roger said it was the garden that sold it to him. It has roses around the front porch that smell gorgeous. There's lawn at the back and flowerbeds with crazy paving running around them. At the bottom a trellis hides the shed and vegetable garden. They must have a lot of money to lose their house and possessions and still be able to buy one like that.'

'Sonia said when they move in properly, and have enough furniture, we can come again. I hope it's soon,' said Ruby.

'I think we should have some tea and breakfast and then let Xen tell us about his new job.' Joanna bustled around producing toast for the adults and cereal for Ruby. 'Thanks for stocking us up again, Xen. I'm looking forward to earning a wage soon, and then you won't have to help us anymore. Anyway, tell us about your interview.'

Xen recounted the bleakness of disembodied voices when he arrived and said he'd felt better when he saw a real human. He was not sure why, but he decided not to mention the human was Morgan. He also glossed over the actual questions he was asked but said he had to stay in London to have a medical. They both laughed when he exaggerated his exhaustion during the work out.

'So, what will you actually be doing?' This was a difficult question to answer.

'Well it will be all technical stuff with state-of-the-art equipment. Just up my street. But I haven't accepted it yet. I'm still making up my mind. It will mean working in London and I'll only be able to see you on weekends.'

'Well we can cope with that because I start my new job in August, and in September Ruby will be going to her new school. Our weeks will be busy too. It just might be harder for you with all that travelling.'

Xen dearly wanted to tell her it was easy, just a couple of turns of the sand timer before he went to bed but knew she would think him crazy. Joanna then threw him into a turmoil by saying, 'We've visited Sonia and Roger's new house, but we've never been to your lodgings. Can we visit after I've been to the hospital?'

'I won't have time today. I'll come with you to the hospital, but I need to leave for an appointment after that.' Lies and omissions were necessary, but he hated lying and wanted, really wanted, to stay with her for the night. He'd been dreaming of making love and now, because of his panicked answer it was not going to be.

'What, something to do with your new job?'

'No, oh hell. I'm lying, Joanna. There's no appointment. My lodgings consist of a tiny bedsit in a rough part of town. I don't want to take you both to sit in squalor. Sorry,' He whispered the apology and hung his head in real shame. Another lie.

Joanna folded her arms around him. 'I don't know why you felt you had to lie. The truth is always best. We won't ask again, but if you decide not to take the job you must find yourself somewhere better. Then we can visit.'

*

The hospital confirmed that Joanna's bones were knitting well and her next visit, in three weeks, would be to remove the pot. They returned to Joanna's flat after that and eventually Xen had his deep wish to make love to her again fulfilled. They took it slowly and Xen knew this was not just sex for him. He hoped she felt the same but was scared to ask.

The following morning Xen woke up beside her. He had a moment of panic, feeling out of control. Why wasn't he at home in his own bed? He texted Sonia and said he needed to talk to her. She was the only one he could tell about meeting Morgan at the interview. When a reply came quickly, he thought she must be an early riser.

Don't panic, Xen! We were coming to do some shopping in Leeds today and could meet for coffee. Not sure how to get rid of Roger, Joanna and Ruby but perhaps you can think of something? Shall we say 11 at the café in the park?
Sonia x

Xen thought Roger could take Joanna and Ruby to the lake to feed the ducks, or he could push Ruby on the swings, but how could he suggest it without it looking odd? He hoped inspiration would come to him before they got there.

*

They sat outside under umbrellas to shield them from the sun. Joanna and Ruby chatted about their stay in Northumberland and how lovely their house was while Xen sat silent. Joanna, noticing this, mentioned his interview. Xen told Sonia and Roger a potted version and said he'd yet to make up his mind. Eventually the conversation slowed, they finished their drinks and Ruby began to get restless. 'Can we go to the swings now please, please?' she said.

Everyone smiled and they stood up together to walk to the playground. When they got there Sonia said, 'Oh I had a cardigan when I arrived at the café. I must've left it there.'

'I'll go back for it,' said Xen. 'I need the exercise.'

'I'll come with you, forgot to use the loo. Will you push Ruby on the swing Roger?'

'No problem, see you later.'

As they walked back towards the café Sonia said, 'So what's the problem?'

Xen explained how he'd not returned to his own time and then told her about meeting Morgan at the interview.

She stood still and looked at him intently when he added that Morgan said he'd died five years ago.

'I can see why you needed to talk about this, Xen. Let's think about them in the order you said. The fact that you're still here means the timer has another task for you now. It must be something to do with Morgan, or just for you to tell me. If you could stay in this time you could avoid your early death and be with Joanna permanently, but first you must save Isabelle.'

'I'd have done that already if I knew how. Any ideas?'

'It might be to do with your new job. You didn't say what you'll be actually doing.'

'Working for the government but I'm not allowed to talk about it.'

Sonia blew out a low whistle. She said nothing as she recovered her cardigan that was still draped over the back of the seat in which she'd been sitting. 'I think I will go to the loo and think about how I'm to react to that last bombshell. You're full of surprises, Xen.'

Xen loitered around the café for a while and then bought some sweets for Ruby to have later. Sonia came up to him smiling. They began walking towards the playground as she said, 'I think your mission is not just to save Izzy but to stop the use of that new weapon the Chinese have. You've five years to discover what they're inventing and take an action that will make sure they can't use it.'

Now it was Xen's turn to stop with shock. 'Who do you think I am, James Bond?' Their talk had to end as they arrived just as Ruby got off the swing and ran up to them. She grabbed Xen's hand, 'Will you pull me round on the roundabout, ever so fast. Roger says he's too old to do that?' Xen let her lead him. Roger grinned. 'I'm glad you're doing that; far too energetic for me.'

Joanna and Sonia stood watching, both smiling.

'Can we treat you to lunch?' asked Sonia.

'You've done so much for us already,' said Joanna.

'It would be our pleasure. We can have it here. The café does a variety of lunches – quiche and salad, jacket potatoes with various fillings. They also do sandwiches. What do you think Ruby would like?'

'I think you know, after having us stay, that Ruby will eat almost anything. Thank you for asking us, we'd love to.'

When Ruby started to say she was hungry they left the playground and returned to the café. It was getting busy, but they found a table and ordered. Roger paid for all of them although Xen offered.

'I hope you're all enjoying your meals as much as I am,' said Sonia. Everyone nodded their appreciation. 'By the way, I heard from Catherine yesterday. When Andy got back, they offered him a trip on their boat. They're thinking of selling it and settling back in England. I'm hoping they'll buy somewhere near us if they do. Anyway, Andy said he would like to go, but wasn't sure about being seasick. They're flying out to Gibraltar tomorrow.'

'Everyone's having holidays. I'm feeling left out,' said Xen, smiling.

'You teachers have oodles of holidays, but I suppose you mean going away somewhere. Sonia and I would be happy for you to join us any time, after we've moved in.' Roger grinned as he said this, adding. 'You could all come. What about the last week in July, just before you start your new job, Joanna?'

'How long's that Mummy?'

Joanna said, 'About four weeks. I'll have my pot off then and we could go swimming in the sea.'

Ruby jumped about in her seat with excitement, but Xen didn't know what to say. It would be difficult to stay at Roger and Sonia's and to keep disappearing during the night.

'Thanks Roger, Sonia, I'd enjoy that, but I've decided to accept the job. There is a period of training to undergo so I

110

can't make any definite arrangements. Perhaps I might come up for a day, even if I can't stay over.'

*

When it was time for them to go to bed Xen said, 'I'll be up early tomorrow and will go home to work on my resignation letter and job acceptance. Now I've decided, I'm keen to do it and I need to keep up my fitness and go to the gym. If there's no quick response I hope to be back the day after.'

Then he told Joanna that he loved her. She hugged him with delight but didn't say she loved him too.

Chapter 18

2030

Xen woke up in his own bed, for which he was deeply grateful. It had worried him when the timer failed to bring him home before, but it seemed obvious, now, that it meant for him to talk to Sonia first. He was being controlled, manipulated and it was not comfortable.

When he was dressed, he read his messages.

Hi, Xen. I'm back from my training and have a few days off before starting the job. Can we meet for a drink, tonight? You suggest a pub.
Sean

It was good to see you, Xen. I was wondering if I should contact Morgan and try and find out the details of your death. Not sure how I'd tackle it. What do you think?
Sonia

I'm sorry I didn't say I love you last night. You really surprised me and it's a bit quick. We've only known each other a month. I really, really like you and Ruby does too but let's not rush things. Joanna xx

Xen answered the last one first, telling Joanna that he was happy to take things slowly, though he doubted his feelings would change. To Sean he wrote he'd see him at The Duck at 7pm.

Sonia's text was worrying. He had a feeling of uncertainty about Morgan. He was a high-ranking officer.

Would Sonia be putting herself in danger if she spoke to Morgan about him? Eventually he wrote:

Thanks for offering to talk to Morgan. I really do want to know how and when I died but not sure I fully trust him. Please be careful. Xen

His next tasks were to accept the new job and to write a letter of resignation to the university. They were difficult to write, especially the resignation, but eventually he was happy with both and sent them off.

Now he had the rest of the day to fill and his thoughts turned to Joanna. He was glad she'd written and knew she was worth waiting for. There was just the difficulty of a relationship with a five-year time gap. If he could stay in the future he wouldn't die prematurely, and he could be with her. But then he wouldn't have saved Isabelle, or prevented the devastation caused by China's new weapon.

The thoughts were depressing him, so he packed his gym gear and went out. The day was overcast but muggy, as if a storm was brewing. He jogged steadily to the gym, pleased that he was getting fitter.

*

When Xen got home, having missed lunch, he decided to have an early evening meal. Before preparing it, he read his e-mails. There was one from Morgan.

It is with pleasure I received your acceptance of the cyber technician post. Your training data is attached. You will be required to take up your position on August 1st, 9am, reporting to Michelle Symonds at the address below. Accommodation will be arranged, the cost of which will be deducted from your salary.

There was a second attachment with details of his salary, and even when his accommodation was deducted it was still considerably more than he had been earning. It was exciting, and scary.

Xen opened the training document and found his physical training would last for five days, starting on Monday at an army barracks. That was to be followed by two days of job training beginning on the first of August, so he would be learning while being paid for it. He stood up, suddenly full of energy, and went into the kitchen to make something to eat.

'Play some loud dance music, Maizy.' Maizy obliged and Xen danced around the kitchen as he retrieved plates and cutlery from the dishwasher and returned them to their cupboards and drawers. A microwave meal pinged and by the time he was ready to eat it he was ravenous. He craved something sweet after it but restrained himself, knowing he would soon be drinking a pint or two with Sean.

*

The Duck was a short bus journey away, or a long walk. Xen opted for the bus, knowing he'd had plenty of exercise. Sean was already there, looking handsome, fit and happy.

'Great to see you Xen.' He lowered his voice to a whisper, 'I needed you to arrive because those two women standing by the bar have been giving me the, what's that old phrase? 'The come-hither look'. I think they want to eat me.'

'I can see why. You're toned and radiating confidence. It's a remarkable change, Sean. If that's what a new job does for you, I can't wait. Oh, I think they're coming to see you, us. Are you interested?'

Xen saw Sean shake his head, so he said, 'I'll get rid of them.'

'Hi, are you two handsome guys looking for company? My names Cheryl and this is Lorraine.'

'I'm sorry Cheryl, but we're a couple; not interested in girls.'

'Oh, well that's a shame. Bye boys.'

They watched the women as they teetered back to the bar in their four-inch heels.

'I can't believe you said that,' laughed Sean. 'You know, I think you've changed too. You'd never have done that a month or so ago. By the time you've been through the physical training you'll be fitter too, or dead. One or the other.' He was laughing and Xen laughed too, but mentioning his death made Xen feel scared.

'So, seriously, do you think I'll cope with the training?'

'Yes, though they push you hard. There were soldiers there, younger than me, collapsing, but the sergeant gave them time to recover. I know there are programmes on TV showing a lot of bullying aimed at new recruits, but if you really try hard, they're OK.'

'Thanks Sean, I feel a bit more confident now. I've sent in my resignation to the university, and I have to say I feel excited about this new life. The only downside is seeing less of Joanna and Ruby.'

'What, you've got two girls on the go. You really have changed.'

'No, nothing like that, Ruby is Joanna's daughter, five years old.' Xen went on to tell Sean more about Joanna, her relationship going wrong and being left with no job and going onto benefits.

'So, you've come into her life, like a knight in shining armour.' Sean saw Xen frown and added, quickly, 'I'm not being critical, just a bit worried that she's so needy.'

'Not for much longer. She's just got a job at the Uni in admin. They provide a crèche so Ruby can be looked after during school holidays. Would you like another drink?'

'A not so subtle change of subject, but yes please, same again.' When the drinks arrived, Sean took a swig and then said he'd found out that he'd have to live in London and would be going abroad sometimes with a multilingual partner.

'Do you know where yet? I'm based in London too, as from the first of August. I don't know where.'

Sean shook his head and yawned. 'It's time for me to call it a night.' He quickly finished his drink and stood up. 'It's been great seeing you and I'd like to do this again in London when we're both settled.'

'So would I.' Xen raised his glass, 'See you then, Sean, bye.' Xen watched him walk away, feeling pleased that their friendship was growing and could continue in London.

Chapter 19

2035

Jason took the helm as the sky got darker and the wind freshened.

'Andy, would you take down the jib. Catherine, reef the mainsail.'

'Aye Aye, Captain,' said Andy, smiling, though the smile left his face as he clipped his safety harness onto the rail and staggered to the prow of the yacht.

He had already released the sheet and the jib was flapping wildly. He turned his face from the whipping fabric and hauled it down. The rolling of the deck seemed to lessen as he pushed the sail through the hatch, but he realised Catherine, behind him, was reefing the mainsail and that was helping too.

They had both finished when there was a flash of lightening and rain began to fall. Jason fixed the autopilot towards the nearest port and went inside.

'I always thought the Med didn't get rough, but I was wrong there,' said Andy. 'I'm beginning to feel a bit queasy.'

'Even experienced sailors can feel seasick in certain conditions. Here take this.' Catherine handed him a pill and a cup of water. 'I'd offer to make a cup of tea, but I think it's probably too dangerous. We're bound to spill it.'

She took a pill herself and offered one to Jason. He hesitated and then took it.

Jason was just about to say something when Andy rushed to the toilet and was sick. Catherine went after him and Jason could hear their voices but not what they were saying because the wind was roaring too loudly. He put on his waterproofs and went back to lower the mainsail and start the engine. The wind took his breath away and the waves, green and huge looked like rolling hills flecked with snow. When the sail was completely furled and the engine working, the yacht was easier to control. Jason released the autopilot and took the wheel himself. Now it was more important to face each wave than just run for the shelter of a harbour. In any case, Gibraltar was several hours away, and he hoped the storm might pass before then.

Down below Catherine had found a bucket, worried that Andy might not make it to the toilet the next time. She heard a shout from Jason and opened the door. 'I can't hear what you're saying.'

'Sorry, I'm getting hungry. Are there any chocolate bars left?' She nodded, shut the door and went down the steps again to look in a cupboard. As she grabbed the nearest chocolate bar, Andy was making use of the bucket and groaning. 'I'm retching and retching, but there's nothing left to come up. I think I'm dying.'

'You'd feel better laying down, Andy.'

'What did Jason want?'

'A bar of chocolate.'

'Oh, God, just the thought…' He reached for the bucket but tipped it up, so the noxious contents slithered on to the floor. His hands flailed and he managed to grab it this time, apologising to Catherine who grimaced and went to find some disinfectant and wipes.

By the time the mess was cleared up she was beginning to feel queasy herself. She needed fresh air and put on her waterproofs and life vest. Andy had fallen asleep, so she wedged his bucket in place before opening the door.

The air blasted at her, wet and chill. The sea looked evil, trying its best to capsize them. She went up to Jason and shouted, 'Do you want a break? Shall I take the helm? He didn't bother to shout back, just nodded and indicated the course she should take, if possible.

They swapped places and Catherine wrestled to keep pointing the prow to ride the wave and not let it swipe them broadside. As she did so she made up her mind that this was an omen. They were being shown that it was time to sell the boat, and begin a new life ashore, even if there were not to be any grandchildren. That thought made her cry again, but her tears mingled with the rain and she didn't even try to brush them away. Grief could hit her at any time, and at least she was on her own so felt no need to be brave.

It seemed so dark Catherine wondered if the afternoon had turned to evening, but when she looked at her solafone it was only 3.15. She was no longer feeling queasy and the tears had helped her overcome her misery, at least for now.

Jason came out again and reported that Andy was still asleep and asked her if she wanted a sandwich. She shook her head but said she'd like some water, so he fetched it for her and braced himself near enough to her to talk, albeit shouting.

'This had made up my mind for me. I think, assuming we get to a harbour without damage, we must go ahead and sell her.'

Catherine smiled. 'I thought the same thing. I'm sure Andy will be really anxious to get onto dry land and put this down to experience. So, where do you want to live?'

'Leeds is too big and bustling, so perhaps a smaller town like Boroughbridge. What about you?'

'I'd like to go further north, closer to Sonia and Roger. I know Roger still knows nothing about the sand timer and the adventures we all shared with it, but I miss not getting my dose of Sonia's wisdom.'

Jason nodded and there was silence as Catherine continued to haul on the wheel, both of them drenched in spray and rain, thinking their own thoughts.

It was nearly an hour later that the rain eased, and the waves became less threatening. Jason had taken the helm again and Catherine braved the fug of the cabin to make some sandwiches. Andy lay awake looking wan and sorry for himself.

'The storm seems to be easing so I'm making sandwiches. Could you eat one?'

'No thanks, Catherine, I'm giving up food, at least until I can get onto dry land.'

'OK but you must keep drinking, or you'll get dehydrated. Ginger ale is good for settling tummies; I'll get you a can.'

Andy sipped it slowly, waiting for any repercussions and trying not to look at Catherine as she put cheese into the buttered bread, adding pickles. She took the sandwiches outside, preferring a possible dousing to eating near a sick bucket.

*

Three hours later they were back in the safety of the harbour at Gibraltar. Andy had scrambled to get off as soon as they were tied up, mumbling something about going to the nearest bar. Catherine hoped he would not have alcohol on a totally empty stomach.

'It'll be too late to see the harbour authorities about selling it now. I don't know about you but, I'd like to go ashore anyway and have a meal,' said Jason.

'Yes, I think we've earned it. And we should find Andy and see how he is.'

*

Main Street had shops and cafés with outside seating, and they found him eating a huge beef burger and chips with a pint of beer at his side. He waved cheerfully and they came and sat with him. 'I can't believe how much better I feel, a new man. I'm really sorry about the trouble I caused you.'

'Don't worry about it, Andy, we've all been there,' said Catherine. A waiter came up, so they ordered drinks and looked at the menu. When they'd chosen and were waiting for their meals to arrive, Jason said, 'Catherine and I talked about the future and we've decided to put the yacht up for sale. I don't suppose you'll mind, having experienced the storm.'

'It's your yacht and I know I'm never going to be a sailor. In fact, I was thinking of packing up my stuff and seeing if I can fly back. It's time I stopped moping, got a job and a place to live of my own.'

'That's great, but I wonder if you would give us a hand before you do – to get everything shipshape aboard? We're going to leave as well, but we can't put her up for sale until tomorrow. We'll understand if you want to stay in a hotel or something, rather than sleep on board.'

'Sorry,' said Andy. 'I was being selfish. I'll come back, help you and we can then fly back together when you've got everything arranged.'

*

The following day was very busy. The official they spoke to offered to give them a slight discount on mooring fees, saying the harbour would berth the yacht until it was sold. They paid for a month in advance and then went to the chandlers, he recommended. They asked them to value the yacht and advertise it.

Andy, anxious to make up for his seasickness, booked three seats on a flight to Heathrow, and helped with packing and cleaning. By the evening everything was tidy and gleaming. They walked back along Main Street for a meal, packed and ready for their flight early the following morning.

'I can't believe the agents were so close in their estimates,' said Jason. They both seemed confident that it would sell quickly, and I don't think they've undervalued it.'

121

'Well I'm not complaining. It's more than we paid for it and we've used it for over a year,' said Catherine. I just hope it sells soon so we can get on with buying a house and settling somewhere.' She turned to Andy. 'Where will you look for work, Leeds?'

'The sort of research I was doing means I have to go wherever the work is. I'm a free agent, so anywhere in the country or even America would be fine. I'm going to look online when we get back and see what there is. I tried a while ago to apply for jobs, but my heart wasn't in it and I never sent any of them off. This trip has done more for me than confirming I'm no sailor.' He grinned, 'It's given me back my zest for life.'

After the meal they walked leisurely back to the yacht. Jason ran his hands over the side before he got on. 'I know it's what we must do, but I will miss her,' he said.

Chapter 20

2030

Xen struggled over the assault course. He leaped to grab a thick rope and hauled himself up to the top of a tower, straddled the top then let himself drop into the netting ten feet below. He lay there briefly, wondering what he was doing, being put through this agony. For what? Then the sergeant's voice cut through his exhausted daze and he rolled onto his front, bounced his way to the edge of the netting and jumped down onto the ground.

It was the third day of gruelling exercises, and he hoped it was nearly over. The filthy, dishevelled group stood in a line waiting for the next trial and were dismayed to hear it was to be a five-mile march, carrying heavy packs, with a river crossing. Xen hoped the river would be slow moving. Swimming was not his strongest point.

They set off, in silence, listening to their own breathing and the clump of boots on earth and stones. They reached the river after three miles. It was wide, deep and dark in the shadows. He watched a leaf turn and glide along the surface, the flow smooth and steady. The sergeant asked for a strong swimmer to take a rope across to the other side.

Xen kept quiet.

'Number seven, what about you?' shouted the sergeant when there were no volunteers.

Xen shouted back, 'Not a strong swimmer, Sarge.'

'But you can swim?'

'Yes Sarge.'

'In that case you've just volunteered.'

The rope was tied around his waist. His pack was given to another man. Xen entered the water. The cold took his breath away. He began to swim, heading for a point on the other side where there was a large tree. He had to tie his end of the rope around it as a safety line for the others. He swam with a splashy crawl, but the tree failed to get closer. He was swimming against the flow, and it kept pulling him down stream. Xen turned to face up stream and increased his pace. It was working. The tree was getting closer, but he was tiring. He changed to breaststroke and pulled as strongly as he could. In two more strokes he was there. As he climbed up the muddy bank, he could hear cheers from the other men. A wave of pleasure coursed through him. When he'd tied the rope around the tree, he signalled it was ready.

Xen watched as one by one the other recruits slipped into the water and swam. There were some better swimmers than him but several struggled and had to use the rope to haul themselves across.

The sun was hot, and his clothes were beginning to dry by the time the last man was helped up the bank. Finally, the sergeant undid the rope at his side and swam strongly to join them.

Everyone walked the last two miles feeling tired and hungry. Xen was thinking of big fat sausages, and when he whispered it to number eight the response was, 'No, fish and chips.' Someone else said meat pie was best and another stated a preference for pizza. Eventually the sergeant put a stop to chatter and they finished the walk, in silence.

*

The last physical training day was a team challenge. There were three teams, each given a route, a compass, a tarpaulin, machetes and some rope. It was not a race. There were observers taking notes and marks were to be given for working as a team and using ingenuity to overcome obstacles. Members of the best team would earn commendations on their training certificate, and free beer that night.

Xen was teamed with four others and they moved swiftly along their route, only stopping to check their compass bearings. The first challenge was a gorge about three metres wide that had to be crossed. Everyone looked around for bridge-making materials – there were several saplings that looked as if they were long enough. While the others hacked down the trees Xen found some hefty stones that could be used to stop the logs from splaying, at least at this end. He also sorted out all the rope they had and decided it must be recoverable. There was no saying what the next challenge might be.

When the logs were assembled Xen explained his idea to save the rope. There was a general nodding and one man immediately began to tie the rope securely.

'Were you a boy scout?' Xen asked, watching the expert knotting.

'Yup, it's done.'

It took four people to lift the bridge into place and Xen offered to be the first one over and then hold it still on the other side. As soon as everyone had crossed, they put the rope in a rucksack and set off almost running to find their next challenge.

The second challenge was to light a fire and protect it from the rain. It was not raining so that was a bonus.

'Anyone ever lit a fire with just two sticks?' asked the man who was good at knots. It seemed nobody had.

'Let's erect a shelter and then we can all try it,' suggested Xen.

More saplings were cut and pushed into the ground and the tarpaulin tied over them. Xen cleared an area, placed kindling on it and everyone whittled sticks to make a fire from friction. It was easy to find dry grass and fluffy seed heads that they hoped to use to get a fire going. There was silence as everyone twizzled one stick in a hollow in another, trying to get it hot enough to cause a spark.

It was not working, so Xen got the first aid kit out of his pack and extracted some cotton wool. He placed that under his sharp stick and after a few moments of frantic twizzling a tiny flame appeared. He blew on it whilst the others watched the kindling catch light.

'Where did you learn that trick?' asked the knot man.

'We did it at forest school when I was a kid, only we used flints to make a spark,' said Xen.

There was only one challenge left, and when that had been successfully accomplished the group jogged to the rendezvous point. They were the first group finished and when the others arrived the observers went into a brief huddle. Xen's group won because they were the only team who had made fire. The others clapped him on the back, and he felt alive and happy. They relished the beer, their reward, and looked forward to going home the next morning.

When Xen went to bed that night he thought about the course. It had challenged him in many ways, but he'd overcome each difficulty and now he felt fit and confident. It was a long time since he'd felt like that. He might not fit the Secret Service spy stereotype, but he was now looking forward to his new job.

*

Back in Harrogate, he sent a text to Joanna saying he would come tomorrow and tell her about his training course. She replied,

Looking forward to seeing you and hearing all your news. Ruby shouted 'yay' when I said you were coming. XX

Chapter 21

July 2035

When Xen woke up on Joanna's couch it was all he could do to hold back from dashing into her bedroom and making love to her. Common sense prevailed and he looked at his watch – it was just after 6.30. He tried to close his eyes and have another hour of sleep but then he worried the timer might decide to send him back. He was also too excited. He was not only looking forward to being with Joanna and Ruby, he felt rejuvenated. It was the effect of the days of hard physical exercise plus the feel-good factor of achievement.

Having to keep quiet, Morgan came into his mind and his bald statement that he thought Xen was dead. Should he text Sonia and ask if she'd found out anything? Surely, if she had any news, she would have texted him. He would just have to be patient.

That brought him back to today and what they could do together. Perhaps they could take Ruby swimming. He would have to buy some swimming trunks first, but there was plenty of time to do that. He got up and went into the kitchen to make a cup of tea, doing everything as quietly as he could. Not quietly enough, however because Ruby heard him.

'Xen, Mummy said you'd be coming today. Can we go out somewhere? It's rained a lot and yesterday we didn't go anywhere.'

'I expect so,' said Xen opening the fridge door. 'Oh, there's no milk. I'll go to the corner shop and get some.' He went to look in the bread bin and saw Ruby shaking her head. 'OK I'll get some bread. Do we need jam?' She nodded. 'Bananas?' She nodded. 'Cereal?'

'No, we've got some. When we run out of everything else, we eat dry cereal or wet it with water. It's quite nice, but not as good for you as milk.'

Now it was Xen's turn to nod. She had already learned that life was not always easy, and she was only… five, six? Suddenly he worried he'd missed her birthday.

'When's your birthday?'

'It's the fourth of August and I'll be six. I'll be in the crèche that day because Mum will have started her new job. At the end of August Mummy gets paid a lot and then we won't run out of everything. Can I come with you to the shop?'

'You're not dressed, and Mum might wake up and get scared if you weren't here. I'll go on my own and be quick. I'll run all the way.' She was giggling as he went out of the door really fast but shut it quietly.

*

When Xen returned Joanna was awake and out of bed. Her fair hair was mussed up with sleep and her pyjamas were loose on her thin frame, but she smiled with delight at seeing him. When they'd hugged and kissed, they emptied the shopping bags. Joanna and Ruby wowed at treats such as cheese, ham and crusty bread that smelled so good they ate some straight away.

When breakfast was finished Xen asked Ruby if she had a swimming costume.

'Yes, Sonia bought me one when we stayed with her,'

'I haven't got a costume, but I'd really like to go swimming now my pot's off. I think the exercise would help get my strength back in this arm,' said Joanna.

'I haven't got one either, but we could go this morning and buy them then go on to the pool. Does that sound like a good idea?' Ruby jumped up and down then gave Xen a hug. She looked up at him with her big blue eyes and said, 'Will you teach me how to swim, please?'

'I'll do my best. Let's get ready then and go shopping.'

'You'll have to sub me, I've no money at all, sorry,' said Joanna, looking down.

'I know, Ruby told me. Don't worry, you start your new job soon and by September you'll get your first wage.'

'I'll pay you back then.'

'Please don't worry. I'm happy to help while things are tight and soon my pay will go up a lot too. Just humour me and let me treat you.'

Joanna smiled up at him and his heart fluttered. He kissed her and then there was organised action as they got dressed and found bags and towels.

*

While Xen was waiting for Joanna to try on a selection of costumes his phone pinged. It was from Sonia.

Hi, Xen didn't know how to ask Morgan about your death and then I realised I didn't have to. Looked you up in B.D. and M. Brace yourself. You died 1-9-2030. Got some help from a friend in the police and you were killed by an assassin, thought to be a member of a Chinese triad! Case was never solved. Not sure what time you're in now but worried about you.

Sonia

I've less than two months to live. What sort of computer job is this that in a month of starting it someone assassinates me? I thought I was just sitting in an office, not in the field like Sean. In that case why did I have to go through all that physical training? It would be good to speak to Sean, but I can hardly say I know when I'm going to die so please would you help me avoid it.

Joanna and Ruby came out of the changing room smiling and happy. He tried to smile back.

'What's up? Have you had some bad news?'

'No, not really, it seems my job is going to be more active than I thought, not all sitting in front of a computer screen. I hadn't expected that, and it might mean going abroad. Anyway, I assume you've chosen your costume, I've got mine, so when we've paid for them, we can go swimming.'

'Yay,' shouted Ruby offering him a high five. He responded, they all laughed and moved to the checkout.

*

The swimming trip was fun, although it was chilly standing in the shallow end, supporting Ruby as she kicked her legs and splashed a sort of crawl. Joanna suggested she might try swimming like a frog and demonstrated the leg action. This proved less splashy and Ruby began to gain in confidence. When Xen was almost turning blue, he asked if he could have a quick swim while they got out and dressed.

'We'll wait for you in the café,' said Joanna. Before they'd even reached the steps, Xen had done a length. He was swimming as fast as he could, needing the activity to warm himself and to help him cope with the fear of his imminent death.

It must feel like this when you're told you've got an incurable illness, he thought. But then you know what you're in for and can prepare. I wonder if Sonia's got any details, such as where and how? I hope it'll be something quick like being shot and not beaten up or tortured. He quashed visions of torture and strove even harder to exercise his anxiety away.

*

It was evening before Xen had the privacy, he needed to text Sonia back. While Joanna was in the bathroom getting ready to go to bed he quickly wrote,

Really shocked. Just over one month left to live! Please find details like when and where?
Xen

130

'Are you coming to bed? I've been reading for ages, and I miss you,' said Joanna.

'Yes, I'll probably go early in the morning to get packed and ready for my new job.' We're both starting new jobs, so let's make the most of our last night together for a while.'

Xen smiled and went into the bedroom, suddenly desperate for the warmth of her body and the comfort only she could give him.

*

Xen was in his own bed and it was nearly 8.00am. He was pleased to have this day to himself to pack clothes for London and to clean his flat.

After breakfast he cleaned everywhere and decided on food for the day, using up tomatoes and peppers so that his fridge could be left empty. He was not sure when he would be returning to it.

The rest of the morning he packed, did some washing, then went for a walk to Valley Gardens. He appreciated the trees and flowers all the more because he knew he would soon be living in the barren city.

By lunchtime he felt he had everything under control and sat in his armchair to relax and began to think. If he took the timer with him to London, he could visit Joanna on the weekend without coming back to the flat. He stood up to do that and realised how stupid it would be. If he picked it up to pack it, he might miss his first day at work.

His train to London was at 14.30 and he went to the station early. It seemed easier to wait on the platform than sitting, feeling anxious, at home.

*

Xen was pacing up and down the platform, when he got a text from Sonia.

Found out it was a shooting in Chinatown, your body found 11pm on 1/9. Please, please be careful, S.

So, all he had to do was to make sure he was not in Chinatown on the first of September. He smiled, bleakly, knowing that made it sound easy, but sometimes you had no choice.

His train arrived and he was in London in a couple of hours.

*

Xen opened the door to his new flat and dragged his case over the threshold. He left the case in the hall and explored. It didn't take long. There was a lounge with a kitchenette and small dining table at one end, a bedroom and a bathroom. It was purpose built for one person, although there were two armchairs and two kitchen chairs. The bedroom had hanging space, a chest of drawers and a double bed pushed against one wall. It was compact and basic but adequate.

He opened the fridge and was pleased to see a carton of milk. One of the high cupboards had a small jar of coffee, so he boiled the kettle while he was unpacking.

After resting and drinking his coffee Xen went out to find a supermarket and look at possible pubs or restaurants for his evening meal. There was a supermarket close by that stayed open late, so he deferred shopping until he'd eaten. The nearest pub offered a menu, so he tried it.

The barman was friendly and the atmosphere pleasant enough, but the prices were higher than he'd expected. He would need to cook from now on, at least until he received his first wage. Then it occurred to him he might not be alive to spend that wage, and he felt miserable and lonely. The thought reminded him he ought to reply to Sonia, so he wrote:

Thanks, Sonia, will try to avoid dying!! Taking up my new job in London tomorrow, Xen

Chapter 22

August 2035

Joanna and Ruby dressed as smartly as they could to go to the university for Joanna's first day. She had made a packed lunch for them both, grateful for Xen's thoughtfulness in stocking up the fridge.

They arrived ten minutes early, but it seemed most people came in early and it made her wonder if she was actually late. It was a while before she learnt that flexi time was an option and that many of the staff came early and went home early. She thought this could be useful when Ruby went to school, but that wasn't until September.

Maria Jones, Joanna's new supervisor, welcomed them and they went together to help Ruby settle at the crèche. This did not take long because Ruby began to play immediately with another girl, making models with Lego.

Maria then showed Joanna to her desk and sat down with her to begin the training process. It was quite complicated with data for each student to be entered and crosschecked, but she concentrated hard and was soon busy. Maria saw all was well and left her saying, 'Just ask if you're not sure. I'm happy to help.'

Joanna worked steadily and jumped when Maria put her hand on her shoulder and said, 'It's coffee time, and I forgot to show you the admin canteen and toilets. I'm sorry.'

'Don't worry I would've asked if I needed the loo.' They went together and Maria explained, 'You can buy sandwiches and drinks from the machines but it's also fine to eat your packed lunch in here. It only serves the offices.

You can go to the main canteen for the whole campus, but that's quite a walk away. They serve hot meals.'

'Oh, this is fine for me. I wouldn't want to go away from here in case Ruby needed me.'

Maria nodded. 'I'm going to get a coffee. Would you like one?'

'No thank you, I'll just have water for now.' She couldn't admit that she had no money to buy even a cup of coffee.

Before returning to the office she went to the toilet and checked her credit. She'd been paid her benefit, so was solvent for the next few weeks. She said a silent 'hooray'.

*

The day seemed to pass really quickly, and when Maria checked her work, she said it was fine. Joanna went to collect Ruby and was delighted to find her reluctant to leave.

'Come and see what Lisa and I made. Lisa's the same age as me. My birthday's in three days and hers is the day before. She'll be six too.'

Lisa was still working at their Lego model. It was, apparently, a town. It had some tiny houses, an office block and a bus. Lisa had fluffy black hair and the most dazzling smile. 'Tomorrow we're going to make a supermarket,' she said. Nat helped us with the bus.'

'That's wonderful, I'm glad you've both had a lovely day, but we must go now.' There was a chorus of 'byes' and Joanna thanked the two leaders for making Ruby's first day so enjoyable. As they walked to the bus stop Joanna said, 'Shall we bake some cakes for you to take to crèche on your birthday?'

'Yes please, but I thought we had no money.'

Joanna gave her a hug. 'I've got some now, so we might even run to a little present. What would you like?'

'How little? I'd really like some trainers like Lisa had. They sparkle in the light.'

134

'OK, we'll make it a proper birthday by shopping for the trainers and we'll make a jelly too.'

The bus arrived and they went home after buying cake ingredients at their local shop. Ruby wanted to make the cakes straight away, but Joanna said they must wait until the night before her birthday or they might go stale. They both went to bed looking forward to the next day.

2030

Xen arrived at the office and was surprised to see it had a proper front door with a name plate, C. Q. Associates, referred to, by those that worked there, as CQA. There were various security precautions such as a coded entry pad on the door and a scanning machine for brief cases or bags in the foyer. Finally, there was a fingerprint recognition pad on a tablet that allocated staff to a room and workstation. He was told, later, that this was because the office ran for 24 hours. It was a bit like being onboard a submarine – as someone got up another person used the bed.

Michelle Symonds greeted Xen with a smile and a firm handshake. She wore flat brogues with grey trousers, a white blouse and tweedy gilet. She was short, plump with greying long hair in a roll on the back of her head secured with a large silver clip.

'Come into my office first so we can get some paperwork out of the way and then I'll show you around. You must sign the Official Secrets Act, 2025, before we do anything else.'

Michelle gestured to Xen to sit opposite her, pushed the document in front of him and gave him a pen. 'Even with the most state-of-the-art technology this must still be done by hand and filed. Take your time, read it and sign when you're ready.' She busied herself at her computer and Xen tried to take in what he was reading but found it hard to concentrate. After getting the general gist he decided reading the entire document was not necessary and signed it. He pushed it across the desk, and she looked up smiling. 'I'll show you around now, starting with the gents.

He followed her out of the office, past the toilets, and she stopped with her hand on the drinks machine. 'You can help yourself, it's free, but an acquired taste.' She laughed as she strode into a large office space with booths and stopped at an empty one. There were two chairs at the desk, and she indicated he was to sit in the one opposite the computer while she sat beside him.

'Once you're sitting down each booth is sound proofed from the others, so we can talk freely here. Everyone has signed the Official Secrets Act but each member of staff doesn't know what the others are doing. Only a few people, like me, know who is working on what. So, I hope you understand, you don't share anything even with your co-workers.'

Xen nodded, but she waited and so he said, 'Yes I fully understand.'

'OK, but, having said that, you will be working with Mei Ling and you can share anything with her. You'll need her because you will be accessing information, much of which will be in Chinese.'

'So why does Mei Ling need me?'

'She's fluent in many languages but she's not a hacker. Your keyboard can translate what you type into Chinese characters if you need to communicate with someone. Mei Ling can check that there are no errors because this technology is new. Mei Ling is English but from Chinese parents. Her loyalties are to England, so don't worry if you discover something that will make China appear to be our enemy. It will not worry her. Now, this is how you get up the translator.'

Michelle typed in a simple code and then showed him a file where useful codes were to be found. 'We want you to begin by hacking into the Chinese Embassy here and then follow any interesting leads. If that's not productive then you can tackle their embassies in other countries and move on to the Chinese Government itself.'

'I thought the talks were going well with all the major countries agreeing about trade, weapons and the use of space technology,' said Xen.

Michelle grinned, 'All I can say is, don't believe everything you read in the papers. Right, I'll leave you to play for the rest of the morning and this afternoon I'll introduce you to Mei Ling.'

Xen got to work. Within minutes he'd found his way into the embassy in London and trawled around for something useful. There was a title to several messages that seemed to occur frequently, a possible code word. It was in Chinese, so he would have to wait for Mei Ling to find out what it meant. Meanwhile he copied the character carefully onto paper and continued to follow where its trail led him. There were not many references in the London embassy system, so he decided to look at another embassy and chose the one in Paris. There he found exactly the same. He was certain it meant something important, but he felt frustrated and suddenly his eyes were tired. It was nearly midday and he'd been working without a break for two hours. Now was the time to try that drinks machine.

Michelle was right – the taste was not quite of coffee as he knew it, but it was hot and as he sipped it his eyes began to feel better. Perhaps they lace it with extra caffeine or some eye-opening elixir, he thought. He was smiling at this idea as Michelle came up to him.

'Something's tickled you. Had a useful morning? Need anything?'

'Thanks Michelle, I'm fine but I need Mei Ling before I can do much more. What time is lunch, and where do people go?'

'Sorry I forgot to say that you can take a break of one hour whenever you want. There's no set time. Mei Ling will be here about 1.30, so now would be a good time. There's a sandwich bar around the corner to the left, all automated but fresh and tasty. You can bring whatever you get back and eat here, but there are tables there. In the other direction you'll find several fast food outlets. Go and explore.' She smiled and left him.

The sandwich bar had a great selection and even a cake or sweet biscuit machine. He chose tuna with tomato and looked longingly at the cakes.

'Go on treat yourself,' said a voice behind him. Xen turned and there was Sean. They were so pleased to see each other they hugged and laughed.

'I never thought we'd meet today, my first day. You knew. I bet you've been waiting for me,' said Xen.

'No, this is a real coincidence. I didn't realise it was your first day, or that you were working here. There are lots of offices, CQA being only one.' Sean chose a cheese and pickle sandwich and a chocolate brownie.

'How can you stay so athletic looking and eat so many cakes?' asked Xen.

'I've joined a gym here and I run every morning. You're looking trimmer too.'

'Thanks; I've been working on it. How much and where is the gym?'

Sean screwed up his face. If you haven't had your first wage you don't want to know. Look we've both got to go back to work. Let's meet tonight and eat together. I'll call for you. Send me your address. Must go, bye.'

When Sean had left Xen felt lonely. Everything was so new and seeing his friend made him almost hanker for the familiarity of the university. He sat and ate his sandwich and then went back to work.

A young woman, dark hair in a ponytail, slim with Chinese features and a beautiful smile, was waiting for him. She waved as he approached. 'You must be Xen. I'm Mei Ling, your interpreter.'

'Hi, Mei Ling, I've been looking forward to meeting you. Are you ready to start straight away?'

He showed her his sketch of the symbol 火and she said, 'It means fire.' He logged on to his computer, found it and asked her to read the word next to it – 龙.

'That means dragon. The code word then is Fire Dragon.' She read some more. 'Chinese ambassadors from many European countries are meeting for a seminar about it.'

'Have you got the date, time, place there?' asked Xen. When she nodded, he said, 'Write it down for me please. No, better not, I'm not sure how important this is, so just tell me.'

'It's here, in London at the Chinese embassy, 2pm tomorrow.'

'Thanks, Mei Ling. Stay here while I find Michelle.' Xen felt excited and scared. He had a strong feeling that this was important. Michelle thought so too and said he was to leave the matter to her now. She would find an agent to infiltrate the meeting. Xen wondered if Mei Ling was going to be asked, but decided to keep quiet, being unsure of the extent of her role.

By the end of the day Xen had a list of all the Chinese ambassadors in every country in the world. They were all invited to attend seminars at various locations on the same day. He wondered if he would be informed of any discovery the agent who infiltrated the London meeting made. He hoped so.

Chapter 23

2030

Sean buzzed the intercom at Xen's front door, and when he came in, he nodded approvingly. 'This is decent accommodation, actually better than mine. And it's closer to CQA. They must think you're valuable.'

'I hope so. I've enjoyed my first day, but I suppose we mustn't talk about it.'

'You're allowed to talk to people working on the same project, but I can't tell yet if we will be. Are you ready for something to eat?'

'Definitely, where are we going?'

'Wait and see,' said Sean with an enigmatic smile. 'It's a bit of a hike but worth it.' He led the way with long, confident strides.

He's at home here, in London, already, thought Xen. I hope I'll get used to it soon and walk like him with my head up and chest out. I'm almost jogging to keep up.

The pleasure of having Sean's company diminished slightly when they arrived in Chinatown. Sean looked at him. 'Are you ready for the best food in London?'

Xen managed a smile and nodded. The street was busy and noisy, everyone jostling to get to a favourite restaurant. Sean entered a nondescript door with a sign painted on it, no neon lights, lanterns or dragons. It seemed to be full, but they were shown to a table at the far end of the room. Xen found himself looking for fire exits. It was cramped, airless and he felt claustrophobic, but realised that was caused by fear.

'I know it's a bit hot, but just the fact that it's full of Chinese tells you the food is authentic,' said Sean.

'How did you find it? I'd have walked past thinking it was a private house.'

'I've made some friends at the gym and one of them is Chinese. She brought me the first time and we've been several times since. You'll like her, petite, sweet and really fit. She can out pace me on the running machine.'

'Is she your girlfriend? What's her name?' Xen waited to hear Mei Ling.

'Ho Chin, and she's not my *girl*friend, just a friend.' Sean picked up the tablet and looked at the menu.

Xen took this as a sign that he either wanted to eat or didn't want to talk about Ho Chin any more. He studied his menu, and they both keyed in their orders. The drinks arrived very quickly.

'Everything here is super-efficient. You'll find our food will come quickly too. It's the Chinese way not to linger in restaurants. Eat and go to make way for others.'

'That suits me,' said Xen. 'I'm hungry and tired. Starting a new job is stressful.'

Before Sean could comment their food arrived. They ate without talking apart from words of appreciation. As Xen became full, he sighed and left a few noodles on his plate, unable to eat any more. Sean cleared his and grinned at his friend, 'Pudding?'

'No, I'm bursting. It was not just excellent food but very generous portions.'

'I'm glad you liked it. We can come again another time, but it will have to be when I return. I'm going away for work. I'll be back on Monday, so I'll text you.' He stood up and Xen, feeling rushed, drained his drink and followed Sean out.

They stood briefly while Sean checked that Xen could find his way back to his flat. Then Sean strode away, and

Xen watched him go, feeling it had all been too fast and their leaving abrupt.

In different circumstances Xen would have enjoyed exploring Chinatown, but knowing it was to become a dangerous place for him he left quickly and concentrated on finding his way back. As he walked his thoughts, as usual, turned to Joanna and Ruby. He wished he'd managed, somehow, to bring the timer with him to London. It would be lovely to be at Joanna's on the morning of Ruby's birthday. He would just have to send her a text and buy her something on the weekend.

When he got back, he went to bed immediately, set his alarm, and slept deeply until morning.

*

4th August, 2035

Ruby ran into Joanna's bedroom and jumped up onto the bed. 'Wake up Mummy it's my birthday. I'm six.'

She bounced up and down and Joanna smiled, unable to play possum any longer. She gathered Ruby into her arms and said, 'You're my big girl now, my birthday girl. As it's still early we've time to have a special breakfast, what about pancakes?'

'Yummy, yummy, in my tummy; can I have jam on mine?'

'Yes, but we'll have to get up and dressed first and there's just a little gift waiting for you on the kitchen table.'

Ruby needed no more instructions – she slid off the bed and ran into the kitchen. Joanna followed her and filled the kettle to make tea.

'Can I open it?'

'Of course, you can but it's not much.'

Ruby pulled off the paper and squealed with delight.

'You like it?' asked Joanna.

'It's the best proper lunchbox ever. Can I take it to crèche today?'

142

'Yes, and we mustn't forget the cakes we made yesterday.'

When they were dressed and the lunchbox filled, they ate pancakes with jam and Joanna marvelled at Ruby's ability to be thrilled by such a paltry gift. Other children her age would have electronic gadgets or a whole set of clothes. Perhaps it was good sometimes to have limited funds so pleasure could be found in simple things.

Just before they left, Joanna got a text from Xen wishing Ruby a happy birthday and promising to see them on the weekend and go shopping for a present.

'You said you were going to buy me some trainers on Saturday. If Xen comes with us and he buys me a present that will be three presents I've had,' said Ruby.

'You're a lucky girl, Ruby. Come on we must go to work.' They walked along the street, Ruby swinging her lunchbox and Joanna clutching a bag with her lunch and the box of cakes.

When they got to the crèche they saw 'Happy Birthday Ruby' was written on the white board in thick pink writing. Ruby rushed to show her lunchbox and Joanna gave the helper the box of cakes. She was pleased to see Lisa admiring the lunchbox and not sneering at such a cheap present. She left the children to have a lovely day and went to her office.

It was beginning to feel familiar now and she looked forward to working there.

2030

Xen entered the CQA building hoping to hear something about the seminars. He'd found nothing new himself. Would Michelle let him know? It seemed she would, for, as he entered to go to his allotted booth, she called him into her office.

'Sit down Xen, in the armchair – might as well be comfortable. We infiltrated the meeting and it seems the Chinese are launching a special satellite carrying some sort of new ray. It will orbit the Earth zapping and reducing all space debris to dust. The seminar was to impart this news and to explain the plan. Next week they'll announce it to the world. It's, so they say, a benign useful tool and everyone will benefit from its mission. What's your thought on that?'

'I think it sounds like a clever, devious way of having a weapon of mass destruction in space. It could easily be pointed to earth and, if it's powerful enough, wipe out whole towns.'

Michelle nodded. 'I think you're right. I'm going to brief the government and hope the UN veto the project. Its unlikely China will be stopped, even if other powers object, so we need more information. I need you to hack into China's space development sites. Mei Ling will be with you all day, every day, until you find blueprints, reports, anything that will help. Xen it's vital we find out all we can about this weapon – if that's what it is.'

'I'll do my best, Michelle,' said Xen and left her office to make a start. He felt the weight of responsibility, especially as he had the knowledge that he was going to die, and therefore fail, resulting in devastation in five years. He comforted himself with the hope that the sand timer might help him change the future.

*

By the end of the day Xen and Mei Ling had found a likely site and hacked into it. Their work had found some technical reports that seemed to be about the satellite, so it was a good start. Before he left Michelle spoke to him again.

'You'll appreciate, I hope, that your work needs to continue over the weekend, but I'm not stopping you having the break. I'll share your work with another agent who will develop it further. When you come in on Monday, I'll update you, and then you go on from there. You've made an excellent start with us. Now go and enjoy your weekend.'

Xen left the building feeling elated. He'd been praised for his work and now he could catch the train to Yorkshire. Tomorrow he'd see Joanna and Ruby. He could hardly wait.

Chapter 24

2030

Xen arrived home and sank into his favourite armchair, exhausted. He wondered if Joanna had felt as tired after her first week in her new job. He asked Maizy for tea and she said, 'Welcome home Xen. Tea will be ready in four minutes.' It sounded like Maizy was pleased to have him home, as if a machine could have feelings.

He thought about the Chinese satellite, with its weapon aboard, and wished he could find out more about it.

Xen sipped his tea as he made a cheese sandwich from defrosted bread. He felt almost too tired to eat it. He still needed to wash some clothes, have a shower and change into 2035 gear before he could sleep.

Once his chores were done Xen turned the timer twice and lay on the bed.

*

2035

'Xen, wake up. I want to show you my birthday present. Mummy froze a cake so it wouldn't go stale.'

Xen opened his eyes, smiled at Ruby then hugged her to him. 'What did Mummy buy you?'

'Look.' She thrust the lunchbox into his hands. It was pink with pictures of 'Trinny Troll', the latest cartoon character, but neither he nor Ruby had ever seen the show. He opened it and saw two compartments. 'You can put a sandwich in this one and cake or fruit in that one, and there's space for a drink carton too. Lisa says it's better than hers.'

'Who's Lisa?'

'She's my best friend at crèche. I like Nat too, but he's only four. Can I wake Mummy now?'

'No need Ruby, I'm awake.' Joanna leant over the back of the settee and put her arms around Xen. 'I've missed you.'

'I missed you too,' he said, squirming around and kneeling up to kiss her. 'Any milk? I'd love a cup of tea.'

'Your romantic moments don't last long. Yes, we have milk and food too. I can even offer scrambled eggs for breakfast.

'Ruby get dressed now while I make tea, then we won't be fighting for the bathroom.'

Ruby laughed, making her hands into fists and shadow boxing as she ran back to her bedroom. As soon as she'd gone Xen stood and gave Joanna a proper kiss and held her tight. 'Have you had a good week? It seems fine by Ruby.'

'Yes,' she said pulling away from him to fill the kettle. 'I'm really enjoying my job and it's given me back my self-respect. In just three weeks I'll get paid and can get rid of this thing.' She waved her arm. 'I can access a bank account and use my solafone to pay for things, like everyone else. Anyway, before Ruby comes back, I know she would really like a scooter. Would that be too much money to spend?'

'I don't know what they cost but I'm going to be getting a better wage soon, so I'll buy it, whatever.'

Ruby came into the kitchen, 'Is breakfast ready?'

'Not quite. Xen would you make some toast, and Ruby will you get out some sauce and jam please?' They both did as she asked and were soon enjoying the meal and discussing the day ahead.

*

The shopping began in a shoe shop with Ruby trying on glittering trainers. Eventually she chose a pink pair, similar to Lisa's. When Joanna was sure they fitted properly, she paid for them and Ruby walked proudly out of the shop watching her feet sparkle, carrying her old shoes in a bag. Suddenly she turned and hugged her Mum's legs saying, 'Thank you, they're the best I've ever had.'

'So, onto the toy shop,' said Xen and Ruby cheered. She hopped and jumped between them and Xen wished they were a real family.

At the toy shop Ruby tried all the scooters with Xen and Joanna explaining that colour wasn't everything. Eventually they were all satisfied with a purple scooter with adjustable height handlebars. The saleswoman said she could use it until she was a teenager. Xen paid and Ruby hugged him with delight. 'I can't wait to tell Lisa about this.'

To finish off their trip they had a proper lunch with waitress service. Xen said Ruby could choose anything from the menu, as it was her special day. She chose fish and chips and they both joined her.

When Ruby had gone to bed, tired and happy, Joanna told Xen more about her job and the crèche, then asked about his job.

'It's all computer work but it's absorbing, and the day passes really quickly.'

'Are the people nice that you work with? I hope none of them are young and beautiful.'

'Don't worry, I only have eyes for you.' He kissed her and said, 'On my first day I met a friend in the sandwich shop that I used to work with in Leeds. He took me out to Chinatown, and we had a meal together. That was really good because I was feeling a bit lost and lonely. He'll be away for work next week, but I hope to see him again when he comes back.'

'That must have been lovely, Xen. What's his name? I'd like to meet him.'

'Sean, but as he lives in London now, I can't introduce you. Anyway, he's single, tall with thick blonde hair and very attractive so I definitely don't want you to meet him.'

This made Joanna smile. She hugged him. 'You're tall enough for me and I think you're handsome.'

They went to bed early and made love slowly, wishing it could go on forever. When it was time to settle to sleep Joanna said, 'Could you stay tomorrow?'

'I'd love to but tomorrow I have to travel back to London.'

'Well what time's your train? If it's in the afternoon we could have the morning together. Just seeing each other one day a week doesn't seem enough.'

Xen squirmed, hesitated and then said, 'I have to leave you early in the morning. I have to pack for the week and my train goes at 11am. I'm really sorry. Please kiss me one more time so it lasts until I can come back.'

Joanna turned and kissed him long and slow, then turned her back to him and went to sleep. Xen found it harder. He fell asleep wondering how to work it so they could be together more, when they lived in different time zones.

*

2030
Xen woke up to the alarm and quickly washed and breakfasted. He wanted to get to work early and see what had been achieved over the weekend. When he left the flat, he jogged, as he used to in Harrogate. He tried to think about work, but Joanna kept intruding. He decided to text Sonia and ask if she thought he could explain his situation to Joanna. This decision helped to push Joanna out of his mind, so that when he arrived, he was focused and keen to get started.

'You're early, Xen. That's good because I'd organised an hour's handover and Jake will be able to get away early. Come on, I'll introduce you.'

Jake was a proper geek, overweight, dark hair flopping over his smudged glasses. He needed a shave. His desk was littered with food wrappers and there were rings where drinks had been slopped on the surface. He rose, grunting, when they arrived, but smiled a welcome. 'Good to meet you, Xen, you've really opened a can of worms.'

'I'll leave you to it,' said Michelle. As she walked away Xen sat on the side chair with Jake at the computer. 'I've managed to find info about the satellite's computer. It's a very sophisticated system. I'll show you.' His pudgy fingers clattered over the keys and revealed a very clever, heavily encrypted system. 'Seems impossible, huh?'

Xen nodded, feeling certain Jake had found a way. More clattering of keys, which Xen followed carefully. He said, 'We're looking for the code name Fire Dragon, that's the name for the technology for destroying space debris – and possibly whole towns on Earth. When we've found out how it's controlled, we need to find a way of preventing it functioning, if that becomes necessary.'

'We also need to find more about the weapon itself, which seems to be some kind of ray, possibly a laser, and how it's powered,' Jake said. 'But I'll leave you to work on that. I'm off. Ah here comes the beautiful Mei Ling, you lucky boy.' With that he stood up and Xen did too, allowing him out of the booth taking his place at the keyboard.

Mei Ling smiled and sat beside him. They didn't bother with pleasantries but started work straight away.

*

It was a frustrating day. At the end of it, Xen felt he'd discovered very little to add to Jake's work. He had some more ideas but was too tired to try them. They would have to wait until tomorrow.

When he left to go back to his flat, he turned on his phone and saw he had two texts. He stopped walking to read them.

Hi Xen. If you are in your own time you will not have heard that more towns in Britain and other countries have been destroyed. Everyone's scared and China is being blamed by all the powers. There's talk of another world

war. Please let me know if you are getting anywhere near
preventing this mayhem. Sonia.

It was shocking to read her message and he felt totally
inadequate. How could he reply? He also felt sad because
he'd been thinking of writing to Sonia and asking her help
to reveal the truth to Joanna. Now he was not sure he
wanted to see Sonia in person until he had something
positive to report.

The second text was from Joanna.

I really miss you, Xen. I'm looking forward to seeing you
on Saturday but now Sonia has invited us to have a meal in
Leeds with Catherine, Jason and Andy, so we'll have
almost no time to ourselves. Please book a later train on
Sunday so we have at least the morning together. Joanna x

For a moment Xen felt like crying. He missed Joanna too
and she was adding to the pressure he already had from
work and from Sonia. He walked slowly the rest of the way
to the flat. When he got indoors, he realised he needed to
try to improve his mood, so he changed into his gym gear
and went for a serious run. At first, he felt unfit and
struggled, but then he felt a surge of energy and managed
to settle into a rhythm that felt right. He didn't think of
anything during the next thirty minutes. He concentrated on
breathing, where he was going and avoiding other people.

When he arrived back, he showered and cooked a pasta
dish, quick and easy. After eating he felt ready to look at
the texts again and reply to them.

Joanna, I'm sorry about not seeing you enough. I would
like to see Sonia and the others, and we will have the time
before the meal and afterwards together.
Give my love to Ruby. You already have mine, Xen xx

151

He knew this was not a satisfactory answer, but it was the best he could do. Somehow, he had to tell Joanna about his quest and ask Sonia to help convince her of the truth of it. That thought reminded him that he should text Sonia but decided not to. They would be meeting soon.

Chapter 25

2035

It was Friday night. Catherine, Jason and Andy were having a meal with Sonia and Roger. The wine was flowing freely because they were staying the night, so they were making the most of not having to drive home.

'That was totally delicious, Sonia. I love Moroccan food, the slow cooking in the tagine, then sweet and savoury together, perfect,' said Andy. He'd been making everyone laugh that evening, talking about his new job in medical research. He seemed to be working with an extraordinary set of characters, but Sonia thought there was a lot of embellishment. Still, it was a delight to see him happy for the first time since Isabelle had died.

'I think us men should show our appreciation by clearing up,' said Andy. Roger and Jason followed him to the kitchen each carrying plates or tureens.

When they were all in the kitchen Sonia turned to Catherine. 'While they're out of the way I want to tell you something about Xen, before we meet up tomorrow.'

'Has something happened to him? He hasn't fallen out with Joanna?'

'No, nothing like that. He has the sand-timer. The same one you used, but it projects him into the future. He lives in 2030 but when Harrogate was flattened, he found himself in our time. He didn't say anything because, naturally, he didn't think anyone would believe him.' Sonia watched Catherine's face as the shock of the news turned into hope.

'Do you think he's going to prevent Izzy's accident?'

'I think that's why he was projected into our time, but he is, at the moment, trying to prevent the disaster happening in the first place. It would have the same effect.'

'How did you find out?'

'You know I sometimes see auras around people, well I saw his and it was very odd. When I explained what I could see, he told me everything. He was surprised and pleased when I said I believed him.'

'Did you tell him about us, how Jason changed things in the past and prevented me from dying?'

'Yes, but not in a lot of detail because we didn't have much time. The thing is, I think we need to talk to him and see if there's anything we can do to help.'

'I'll need to tell Jason. We have to find a way to talk tomorrow without Andy, Roger and Joanna – they know nothing about it.'

The men came back in bearing hot drinks and chocolates, but as they settled to enjoy them Sonia felt her phone vibrate. She glanced at her wrist and saw it was Xen.

Sorry to interrupt your evening, Sonia, but I really need you to help me explain to Joanna why I can only see her on Saturdays. She's making things very difficult for me.

Thanks, Xen

'Have you got a message?' asked Roger.

'Yes, from Xen. He says he's looking forward to seeing us all tomorrow.' She hated lying to him, but she'd never told him about Jason's, Catherine's or Isabelle's, time travelling and didn't want to now. The problem was, how to chat to Joanna and Xen without Roger and Ruby. Perhaps after the meal they should to go to a playground again. Roger enjoyed pushing Ruby on the swing last time and it would give them some time together, though not, perhaps, enough.

*

154

2030

It was Friday, Xen was sitting in his booth, alone because Mei Ling had gone to fetch some coffee, when Sean slipped into the seat next to him.

'What are you doing here?' asked Xen. 'I thought you were away all week.'

'It seemed important, in the light of the launch of China's Space Clean satellite, to get back here and join you. I'm now part of your team.'

'Brilliant, welcome aboard, do you want a coffee? Mei Ling's just bringing ours and she'll get you one.'

'I'll get my own, leave you two to continue and we can have a professional chat at lunchtime. There are some things I need to sort out with Michelle. We need a larger booth to fit three, for a start.' Sean stood up, was introduced by Xen to Mei Ling, and then left.

'So, you haven't met Sean before,' said Xen.

'No, but you seemed happy to see him.'

'I've known him a long time and he's going to be joining us. His expertise is about satellites, their orbits and capabilities. We're having a meeting at lunchtime but for now I'd like to crack on looking for the weapon control system.' They had been looking for the control system for days, frustrated that they had, so far, been unable to find it.

By lunchtime Xen felt he'd plumbed the depths of the satellite's computer, but it seemed to be clean at every level. Could it really have just one mission? Might it be that there wasn't a hidden weapon at all? He stood up stiffly and rubbed his neck as Sean arrived.

'Hi both, Michelle's rustled up a lunch in the boardroom for us and the weekend people have come in especially.'

They followed Sean to the boardroom, and there was Jake and his interpreter who was introduced as Ho Chin. Xen noticed Sean giving her his brightest smile.

They helped themselves from the buffet, and when everyone was sat with food Michelle began the meeting.

'First I must thank Jake and Ho Chin for coming here during their break time. As you know China is launching their Space Clean satellite tomorrow and we all suspect it may carry a hidden weapon. Perhaps Xen could bring us up to date on his work on this.'

Xen squirmed with embarrassment, knowing he'd found no reference to any kind of weapon. 'Well we've accessed every section of their computer and have not found any instructions for a weapon. There are plenty of complex guidance systems governing every aspect of the command and control of the satellite, including a system to slow it down so it will enter the atmosphere and burn up. But no weapon controls that we can see.'

Michelle nodded and asked Jake if he had anything to add.

'I agree with Xen. I think we need more information on exactly how this machine destroys space debris. Does it zap a chunk with some kind of ray or laser that will break it into smaller pieces that are still a hazard?'

'They must know that to be truly useful it needs to hoover up the pieces, but then the satellite would gradually become full of debris. Presumably at that stage it would be commanded to enter the atmosphere and be destroyed,' said Xen.

'Now that's an expensive thing to do. I also fail to see how it can hoover debris up without chunks of debris destroying it. Don't forget they're moving incredibly fast,' said Sean.

'Could the debris be gathered in some kind of net?' asked Mei Ling. Everyone laughed and she coloured and looked down.

'Actually, that's not such an odd idea as it sounds. Like catching a fish, the act of netting slows the fish, bringing it under your control,' said Sean. Mei Ling gave him a grateful smile. 'But for now, I'd like to go back to the first idea of hoovering up debris until the satellite's full,' Sean continued. 'What if the satellite becomes too full to collect anymore, but stays in an orbit? Then, when China has a need of an orbital weapon, it directs the whole satellite to come down like a meteorite. It would work if it was shielded with tiles like the shuttle, or something more sophisticated like ceramic paint so it didn't burn up.'

'Well that would explain why we've found no reference to a weapon on the computer,' said Xen. He felt Sean had hit upon the truth, that the satellite itself would become the weapon, particularly if the zapping ray or laser was deployed just before impact.

Michelle stood up but motioned everyone to stay where they were. 'This has been a valuable discussion. I have another meeting to go to and I suggest you all stay and form a plan of action. Oh, and don't forget to watch the launch – the Chinese are giving it loads of hype.'

It occurred to Xen that he was unlikely to see it because he would be in the future. But he would be able to watch it on You Tube or catch up on Sunday. He was relieved that Jake would begin to implement any plan they made, and he could follow his lead next week. The plan was worked out with the action individuals had to take, and by the time they were satisfied it was time to go home.

'Does anyone fancy joining me for dinner tonight in Chinatown?' Sean asked. Ho Chin immediately said yes, and Jake and Mei Ling quickly followed her lead. Xen shook his head. 'Sorry I'm catching the train back to Yorkshire.'

Xen felt drained. It wasn't just the concentration and pressure of the job. The talk of a meal in Chinatown really scared him. It was getting closer to the date of his death. Would Sean invite him to another meal on that day? How could he refuse? Feign illness? He pushed the thoughts away and walked back to his flat.

The fresh air and activity improved his mood. When he got home, he collected the few things he needed to take with him and went to the station.

On the train he thought about Joanna. He wanted to tell her the truth, but would she end the relationship when she understood the problems? She deserved someone who could be with her all the time, but he knew he had to risk it.

*

2035

'I thought he was a regular bloke. Never suspected he was a time traveller,' said Jason.

'Nor did I, but you know Sonia – that sixth sense of hers made her suspicious. Anyway, Xen's trying to prevent the destruction that China's going to cause, before a war develops. If he manages that we'll get Izzy back.' Catherine's eyes brimmed with tears and Jason put his arms around her, although he felt just as emotional.

'So, what could we do to help? We don't have access to the timer, because it's wherever Xen lives five years ago. Perhaps he could contact us in his time? We were in Harrogate then and I was still working, but you, I remember, were a lady of leisure.' That made her smile and the mood lightened.

'Shall we suggest that? Even though he'll be a stranger, if he explains about the sand timer, we will believe him. We could even go to his house and see it. I've just had a thought. If we touched the timer we could go forward in time and meet ourselves!' They both laughed and agreed to wait and see what ensued the next day.

Chapter 26

2035

It was Saturday morning. Ruby discovered Xen, sound asleep, on the sofa. There was nothing sacred about sleep, as far as she was concerned, so she shook his shoulder and called his name.

'Oh, morning Ruby,' he said, rubbing his eyes and yawning. 'What's the time?'

'It says seven thirty-five, so it's OK to wake Mum. She says I must wait until it says seven-thirty, and its past that.'

'Before you do shall we make her a cup of tea? Is there milk?'

'Yes, but there's not a lot of food. Sometimes, Xen thought, she seemed very mature for a six-year-old. In a way it saddened him. His parents had not been rich but they both worked and there was never a time when food was scarce. 'I'll get up and make the tea then get some shopping.'

They went into the kitchen together and Xen shut the door so that their chatter and the clatter of crockery didn't wake Joanna. The tea was soon made, and Xen carried it into the bedroom with Ruby close behind him.

'Xen's here Mummy, wake up. He's got tea for you.' Joanna smiled sleepily and propped herself up on one arm. 'Tea in bed's a luxury I rarely get, thank you.' She sipped the tea and then put the mug down on the cabinet beside her and flopped her head back onto the pillow.

Xen leaned over her and kissed her on the cheek, enjoying the warm smell that was essentially her. 'I'm

159

taking orders for breakfast. Would you like an egg and bacon sandwich?'

'I would. I love egg and bacon sandwiches,' said Ruby, jumping onto the bed.

'Well it looks like that's settled. Thank you, Xen. We'll get washed and dressed before you get back.'

'No, you don't have to rush, we've plenty of time. Enjoy your tea and have breakfast in your PJs.' She gave him a lazy smile.

Xen picked up a couple of shopping bags and went to the corner shop. He'd forgotten to check what she needed so he decided to buy things that would help with packed lunches for next week and something she could use for a meal on Sunday. It was easy because none of them had any fads and seemed to eat anything.

He was walking back, weighed down with the bags, when it hit him again that he wouldn't be able to do this ever again if he was murdered. There was nothing he could do about it so he must make the most of every day, savour every minute.

'Hello, my two favourite ladies, are you up or still in bed?' said Xen as he walked through the door.

'I'm dressed, but it's my best skirt so I'm not to drop egg on it,' said Ruby.

'And I'm up but not dressed. I've got the frying pan out, oil, sauces and boiled the kettle again for coffee.'

'Excellent let's get cooking.' Soon the delicious smell of bacon rose from the pan. While Xen cooked, Ruby and Joanna unpacked the shopping bags commenting on his choices.

When they'd finished eating Joanna said, 'That was sheer heaven, thanks Xen. I'll make some coffee.'

The rest of the morning passed happily with them playing a game designed to help children calculate. Ruby won every time and was delighted to have trounced the adults. Then it was time to go out to meet everyone in a restaurant in town.

They caught a bus, which was slow with so much Saturday traffic but still arrived just before twelve o'clock. Sonia, Roger and Andy were there already and waved a welcome. Roger ordered some drinks for them. When Jason and Catherine came in, Ruby welcomed them by shouting, 'We're here by the window,' and everyone in the restaurant laughed. Catherine and Jason sat with them and Roger ordered more drinks.

'It's so lovely to see you all again,' said Sonia. 'I want to hear what you've all been doing. Three of you have new jobs so there must be loads to share.'

'We have some news too, we've sold the yacht; just heard this morning,' said Jason. 'It means we can buy a house and settle down in our old age.'

'Not so much of that, Jason, we're older than you two,' said Sonia. 'Will you be looking for somewhere near us? I do hope so.'

'Yes, we thought we would, because to live in any large town seems to make you a target for China. It's safer in a village, but I'd like to find one with a shop and a pub at least.' As she said that Catherine thought it would all be wasted if Xen managed to prevent the previous attack. Isabelle would still be alive, and everything would be different. She glanced at Xen and noticed how tired he looked. He had such a weight of responsibility on his shoulders.

The waiter, asking if they were ready to order, interrupted Catherine's reverie.

'No, sorry, we were too busy talking,' said Roger.

'No problem, sir, I'll come back.' He walked away and they picked up the menus to make their choices. Ruby found the children's menu and read it out loud. When she had read all the items, she asked, 'Do you think they'll have tomato sauce Mum?'

'Yes, I think so, but we can ask when you give your order.'

The waiter came back, orders were given, and the conversation turned to jobs. Andy said he really enjoyed his medical research work and was making friends with his new colleagues.

'I've made friends with Lisa and Nat at the crèche,' said Ruby. 'I go there when Mummy goes to work at the university, but soon I'll have to go to a new school.'

'Is Lisa going to the same school as you?' asked Catherine.

'I don't know; I hope so.'

'If we're all going to talk about our new jobs, I'm enjoying mine too, but my role will change when the autumn term starts. At the moment I'm helping students to find a course if they've not got their first option. Like Ruby I'm not sure how it will be in October. I think Xen should tell us about his now,' Joanna said, suspecting he would find it difficult.

Xen seemed unfazed as he explained. 'Well I work in London, for the government, and it's mostly computer work. They found me a flat, quite near and I'm getting used to living in a big city. But when I get on the train to come back to Yorkshire, I always feel a sense of relief. I like the pace of life here and I'm not sure I've found the job I'll want to do forever.' There were no questions as to the exact nature of what he did, much to his relief.

The food arrived, Ruby was given tomato sauce, and the conversation slowed as they ate. They finished with coffee and then Sonia went to the toilet and Joanna and Catherine went with her. Ruby was happy colouring in a picture the waiter had given her and said she didn't need to join them. Xen hoped they would talk to Joanna about his time travelling.

'The ladies have been a while,' said Roger ten minutes later.

162

'You know what women are like when they get together,' said Ruby. 'Natter, natter, natter.'

'You'll be a woman one day,' said Xen. 'Then you'll like a good natter too.' He could see Roger was beginning to worry, so Xen talked about going to the park when the women came back.

'That's OK by me,' said Roger. 'What about you Ruby?'

'Yay, yay, yay,' she said, waving both arms in the air.

'Well I'm afraid I can't,' said Andy. 'I'm meeting a friend from work for a game of tennis. Not the best thing to do after a big meal, but it'll take forty minutes to get there so it should have settled by then.' He looked at his watch. 'I really should go now. Ruby would you go to the Ladies and tell them I have to go, please?'

Ruby nodded and handed her picture to Xen. A few minutes later all the women returned, apologising for the time they'd taken. Andy settled his bill at the bar and there was a goodbye moment with handshakes and hugs. While this was going on Xen looked at Joanna and found her looking at him thoughtfully. He felt scared.

'Are we going to the park now?' asked Ruby. Roger nodded and requested the bill, which they divided into three, then they went to the park.

It was hot and humid, so everyone was walking slowly except Ruby, who ran ahead and back like an impatient puppy. When they got to the swings, as if primed, she asked Roger to push her. He obliged and the others sat on the grass close together.

'You know, don't you,' said Xen to Joanna, and she nodded.

'It takes a bit of believing, but Sonia and Catherine said it was true.'

'Well I can add something to that, Joanna,' said Jason, 'because I was the first one to find myself in a different time, after touching the sand timer. I went back to the 1920s. It felt weird and, like Xen, I was scared and daren't tell anyone. Now we're hoping he can stop that death ray or, whatever the Chinese weapon is, from happening. If he can we'll have Izzy back with us. Did the girls say that Roger and Andy are ignorant of all this?'

'Yes, I won't say anything because I don't want Ruby to know either. I think it might frighten her. At the moment I need to try and understand what it all means. Does everyone living now get transported back to that night when it happened? Then the attack doesn't happen, so we carry on as we were? I'd be out of work and wouldn't have met Xen. It would be lovely for you to have Izzy alive, but I'd be bereft.'

A breeze began to blow, and with it, rain. Just spots at first, but it quickly turned into a deluge. Joanna saw Roger running towards them holding Ruby's hand, and they all dashed for the bandstand. A lot of others had had the same idea and they could only stand crammed together on the periphery.

The rain continued to lash at them, and Xen shouted, 'I think this is the moment when we all go home,' They hugged each other and ran off in different directions, Xen, Joanna and Ruby to the nearest bus shelter.

Chapter 27

2030

Xen woke up in his own flat in Harrogate and lay in bed thinking about Joanna. She'd been upset when they got home, still damp from the downpour, but she'd hidden it well so that Ruby's day hadn't been spoiled. When Ruby had gone to bed, she let it all out. She was scared of going back to her days without a job and not knowing him. In amongst the tears she'd said she loved him. Xen hugged that thought.

By the time they went to bed she had calmed down, although he really hadn't been able to reassure her. They clung to each other and made love urgently, Xen in case it was his last chance ever and Joanna because she needed the comfort and release sex gave her.

*

2030

Xen had pack to go back to London, but before that he needed to watch the Chinese launch their satellite.

'Maizy, coffee please,' he instructed. 'Maizy, television on.' He fetched his coffee and sat down to watch the launch. He watched a rocket pushing its way up into space, and then explanations of how the satellite would clean up space debris. Mei Ling will be pleased, he thought, when the animation showed a robotic arm with a scoop attached. The satellite kept pace with the debris then small pieces were literally scooped up. Bigger pieces were hit at a careful angle by a laser to slow them down until they fell into the atmosphere and burnt up.

This last piece of information was exciting. He had found no weapon because laser communication was the norm. That same laser was being used as a weapon to knock chunks of debris out of their orbit. Could it also be powerful enough to destroy a town? He felt this was unlikely but wanted to talk about it when he got to work. The report on the launch continued saying this was just the first of a series of launches to orbit at different distances from Earth. It ended by mentioning that countries all over the world had congratulated China on the launch and its altruistic mission.

Xen stood to go into the kitchen and find something for breakfast, his mind buzzing with thoughts. Everyone was paying lip service to China, and he knew Britain couldn't be the only one spying and hacking their systems. Was it possible for another power to slow the satellite so it entered the atmosphere causing destruction just to discredit China?

As the toast popped up Xen's phone pinged with a message. He read it while eating.

Hi Xen, I hope Joanna recovered from her shock and you parted friends. When we ran from the rain Jason invited Roger and me back to their flat, and we had an idea. Why don't you visit Jason and Catherine this morning, in your time, and tell them about the timer? You could warn Isabelle to be away from Harrogate on the day of the destruction.
Love Sonia

The piece of toast was stationary in Xen's hand, forgotten, as he thought about the possibility. He could save Isabelle. Would his mission be complete? How would he know? Perhaps Jason might tell him what happened after he'd saved Catherine. He looked at his watch – it would be possible if he caught a later train.

He took a bite of the toast, which was now cold and limp, and wrote back.

166

Excellent idea, Sonia, please send their address. Xen

He cleared away his breakfast things, filled the washing machine with clothes, switched it on and went into the bathroom to shower.

When he was dressed, he checked his phone, and the address was there. It was not that close so he would have to use a taxi. It was now nine forty-five, not too uncivilised an hour on a Sunday morning. He asked Maizy to order the taxi, grabbed his wallet and keys and went outside to wait for it.

It was drizzling slightly but not cold. He had stood for only five minutes when the taxi arrived. He got in, the electronic voice checked the address was correct and when Xen confirmed, it set off.

Jason and Catherine had a lovely house, with a front garden vibrant with colour and a wisteria, laden with large purple flowers, growing up a trellis beside the door. As he rang the bell Xen felt worried they would be out, and equally worried they would be in.

Isabelle answered the door. 'Hello, can I help you?'

'I hope so; you see I went diving recently and found a sand timer. Since then my life has been crazy.'

He paused as her eyes opened wide with surprise and she said, 'How did you know to come to us?'

'It's a long story, but I know Sonia.' It seemed that was the magic word and she invited him in. She showed him into a comfortable lounge and as he went to sit down, he stood up again because Jason and Catherine came in.

'Isabelle says you've got the sand timer,' said Jason.

'Yes, it's from a ship called the *Daphne*. It's a long story, which I must share with you because Isabelle will, in a few years' time, be in mortal danger.'

'In a few years' time,' repeated Jason. 'So, you're from the future?'

'No, I normally live in this time, the same as you. The sand timer projected me five years into the future.'

'I went into the past and so did Isabelle.'

'I know, Sonia told me a little of what happened to you and it made me feel better. I thought I was having nightmares. But I must go to London this afternoon, so let me tell you what's going to happen.'

*

The family listened in silence until he got to the part where Isabelle died, and then there was a low groan from her parents and a gasp from her.

Xen finished his story by saying, 'Yesterday I went out to dinner, in Leeds, with Sonia, Roger and Andy. Then when I returned to my own time, this morning, Sonia texted me with the idea that I should tell you so you can make sure you're well away from Harrogate on that day.'

He sat back in his chair, and Catherine stood up abruptly, suddenly remembering her manners. 'Xen would you like a cup of tea or coffee. I know I need one and feel like it should be laced with something stronger.' They all smiled, and Xen said,

'Coffee would be lovely, thank you.' She left them to go into the kitchen and Isabelle followed her to help.

Xen turned to Jason. 'Can you tell me what happened when you'd completed your mission?'

'When I prevented Catherine from dying, I went back in time to that day. Sonia knew all about it and had a tough time reliving those months. She and I could remember what we'd done before, but other people behaved as normal. They didn't realise there'd been any change at all. It was different when Isabelle finished her mission. She had gone quite a long way back into the past. When she returned to her own time the sand timer had disappeared. I don't know where it went or how it ended up in the sea.'

'So, it seems if the mission is fully complete then the timer goes, so if it's still there when I get home, I have more to do.'

'Yes,' said Jason and stood up to take a tray from Catherine. She looked like she'd been crying. Isabelle's face was red and a little blotchy too. She was carrying a plate with some slices of fruitcake, which she offered to Xen.

'Oh, lovely, thank you. I usually refuse cake or biscuits, but this has been a... difficult experience.' It seemed bizarre to Xen that he was sitting with the same people as yesterday but that they saw him as a total stranger. 'If my mission isn't over, I could meet you again in the future. Then you'll remember this meeting, I think. It's a crazy situation.'

Jason sat back in his chair. 'Thank you for coming today, Xen; it's been unsettling news, but we appreciate the warning. I've written it down, the attack will be on the first of June 2035.'

'It's scary to think I might only have five more years to live,' said Isabelle.

'Well we can avoid it now so you will not die then, thanks to Xen. So, don't worry about it,' said Catherine.

Xen put down his cup and plate and stood. 'I need to go but here are my contact details.' He handed Jason a piece of paper. Jason shook his hand at the front door, and Xen walked along the road until he was well away from their house and then ordered a taxi.

When Xen opened his front door, he looked for the timer. It was still there so his mission was not complete. He looked at his watch and began to hurry. He pushed his damp washing into the dryer, packed clothes for the week and left to catch his train to London.

On the train he had time to think about the coming week. Fear seemed to catch in his throat and sweat formed on his brow. He went to the vending machines and pushed buttons for a bottle of cold water then stood, swaying with the movement of the train, and drank most of it before returning to his seat. Fear would stop him functioning and he needed to control it if he could.

*

Xen arrived at his flat in London later than usual and went through the motions of unpacking and then looked for something to eat. There was enough for breakfast but nothing to make an evening meal. He rang Sean and asked if he'd eaten. Sean said no and was happy to meet in a pub for a bar meal.

The pub was fairly quiet at half past eight on a Sunday and they were lucky to be able to order food as they stopped serving at nine. Sean ate with relish, but Xen slowly picked at his, deep in thought.

'Penny for them, Xen.'

'Oh, sorry Sean I was miles away. I was thinking about the launching of the satellite and if it was really a danger to us.'

'I have to say, it looked as if the system would work. No doubt Jake's been beavering over the weekend and we'll have an update in the morning. That's enough shop talk, tell me about this girl of yours.'

'She's called Joanna and I'm completely smitten. I adore her daughter, Ruby. The problem is she's working at our old university and I'm here all week. Not an ideal way for a new relationship to develop.'

'No, I can see that. Any chance she could move to London?'

'Not really, she's only just started her job and loves it. Anyway, it costs too much to live here. How are you and Ho Chin getting on?'

Sean looked embarrassed and hesitated before replying. 'I didn't tell you we were together, did I?'

'No but when we had that meeting last week, I saw you look at her, and I guessed. She's very attractive. Why does it need to be a secret?'

'I just don't think it'll be acceptable at work, so I'd be glad if you didn't say anything. She's really clever and has a great sense of humour. When we're together we seem to be constantly laughing. Ho Chin's family run the restaurant that we go to and they're comfortable with her going out with me. I'm taller than all of them and I felt concerned they might prefer her to have a Chinese partner. Ho Chin said they understood that the choice is limited, given they don't live in China, and they just want her to be happy. Another drink?'

'No, I should be going. It's been a long day and I need an early night.' They both stood and went outside. 'See you tomorrow,' said Xen. Sean smiled back and nodded as he turned to go.

Chapter 28

Michelle called a meeting with everyone and Morgan was there. The last time Xen had seen him was at his interview. 'You will all have seen China's satellite launch,' began Michelle. She looked around the room and saw them nodding before going on. 'Morgan has been in touch with the U.S Space Surveillance Network and can tell you what they've observed.' She turned towards Morgan and sat down as he stood up.

'Good morning everyone, it seems the satellite is doing what the Chinese promised. Most space junk is in low and medium orbits. Currently it's working in a low orbit circling the earth approximately every ninety minutes. So far, it's used the laser to slow ten large pieces of debris so that they've fallen into the atmosphere and burnt up. It's not quite so easy to see if it's also scooping smaller debris. We're hoping the manned space stations will be able to witness this when it comes into an orbit near them. It's changed course several times and we're interested in how long it can sustain this before its container becomes full.

'You've all been working on the computer system, but we need more information about the satellite itself, its fuel and it's exterior shielding. We still believe it to be dangerous when it becomes too full of junk. At this point we must use informants. Sean you will need to go to China. We'll talk details later. The rest of you must continue to monitor the Chinese government's systems.'

Xen walked back to his computer with Mei Ling and logged on. They both gasped as a hideous skull appeared with the words, 'YOU'RE GOING TO DIE!' emblazoned across the screen. The whole image then ran with blood. Xen stood up abruptly and Mei Ling joined him as they went back to Michelle's office. They knocked and went in without waiting. Morgan was still there.

'There's a death threat on my screen,' said Xen. Mei Ling began to cry. 'I think it's meant for me, not you, so don't cry,' Xen said.

As Mei Ling used the tissue Michelle handed her, she said, 'It was shocking, really horrible.'

Morgan and Michelle went to the computer, but the evidence had disappeared.

'Work as normal for the rest of the morning but log out when you go to lunch and call me when you log on again so I can see it for myself,' said Michelle. Morgan and I will discuss what we can do to protect you, so don't go out of the building.'

Xen nodded. He wanted to say there was no problem because he knew he was going to die soon. He sat at his station with Mei Ling and began to work but they both found it difficult to concentrate.

At coffee time Michelle called Xen back into her office, but it was Morgan who did the talking. 'If you want to go out at lunchtime you must wear this.' He held up a padded vest. 'It's stab and bullet proof, but obviously you're still vulnerable because you could be stabbed or shot in the head.'

Xen took it and said, 'I think the threat will have come from the Chinese. They've probably identified me from my modus operandi.

Morgan nodded. 'You can't go on working here, Xen. You'll need a new identity and it's not going to be any fun. You can't contact anybody you know, and it'll be very lonely.'

'But better than being dead,' said Xen. 'Can you organise that for me?'

'Give us until the end of the day and we'll be able to tell you more.' Morgan stood up and held out his hand. 'I'm sorry it has to end so soon, but you've done valuable work.

I'll say goodbye and Michelle will tell you this evening what has been arranged.'

Xen stood up, shook his hand and went to follow Morgan out, but Michelle called him back.

'Xen, you can't tell Mei Ling about this or Sean or anyone. The way it's normally done is that we fake the person's death. Your friends and relatives will be told of your demise and it'll be in the papers. If you want to go back to your home in Yorkshire today, I'll not stop you, but you'd be safer staying here.'

'What will happen to my personal effects, money in the bank?'

'All your assets will be frozen, and the normal probate will have to be gone through. We'll clear your flat here and your home in Yorkshire. You'll never see any of your personal things again.'

Xen bent over and held his head in his hands. There was silence as he considered the enormity of this new life.

Michelle stood and said, 'Stay here, I'll make us a drink and order some sandwiches for lunch.'

Xen barely heard her as he thought of questions he needed to ask. How would he earn his living? Would he have to live abroad? There was also a question he couldn't ask – what about the sand timer and Joanna?

When she came back Michelle was carrying a tray. 'I've added some rich fruit cake, the best thing for shock. Now I expect you've got some questions and I'll do my best to answer them.'

Xen asked his questions. Michelle said living abroad would be necessary and would be arranged for him as well as a new identity, passport and job. This was too much to take in and Xen lost his appetite. He just managed the fruit cake, encouraged by Michelle.

*

After lunch Michelle stood at Xen's workstation as he logged on and Mei Ling shut her eyes. Michelle's sharp intake of breath was enough to tell her the skull had appeared again. 'That's real enough. Come and see me before you go home, Xen.'

She left them and Mei Ling opened her eyes. 'Was it just the same?'

'Yes, nothing new. Let's have a look at the satellite again and see if we can find out what its protective shielding is made of.'

He found the site and Mei Ling read and translated. They became so involved in the task he almost forgot his predicament, but it hit him again when they had a tea break. He wanted, desperately, to return to Harrogate that night and spend a day sorting out his affairs. He wanted to withdraw his money, but cash was hardly used any more. Perhaps he could open an account in a different name? Then he realised he could simply transfer his money to Joanna's. She'd proudly opened an account to take her first wage from the university. He didn't know the details but was sure she'd tell him.

Xen took the drinks back to the computer and they sipped as they worked. The time went by quickly and he was surprised when Michelle came to ask him to come to her office. She told Mei Ling she could go home. He hadn't known her long, but Xen felt shocked and saddened, knowing he would never see her again.

'Here is everything you need to start a new life, Xen, or should I say Robert? You are now Robert Simms. You have a flight to Dubai and here is your passport, debit and credit cards, driving licence and details of a job with a company updating their systems. There will be enough money in your new account to tide you over until you get your first wage. Any questions?'

Xen looked at the ticket. The flight was on Wednesday from Manchester Airport. 'So, I still have one day as Xen? Can I go back to Yorkshire?'

'Going back to Yorkshire is your choice and a big risk if you do. We can give you a safe house for two nights, but if you go to Yorkshire, you're on your own. Your current identity will expire on Thursday, but by that time you will be out of the country and have disappeared. Good luck, Xen.'

They shook hands and he went back to his workstation for the last time to collect his jacket. Before he left the building, he put his bulletproof vest on, just in case, and went to his flat. He packed his belongings and got a taxi to the station.

On the train Xen could not relax. He studied everyone in his carriage, wondering if he or she was an assassin. There was one young man who looked tense. He kept glancing around, but as soon as the train moved away from the station, he settled in his seat and closed his eyes. Nothing happened on the train, but Xen only felt safe when he was in his flat in Harrogate with the door locked and bolted.

It was late and he was hungry and thirsty, so he checked the freezer and found a ready meal. While it was cooking, he sent a text to Joanna.

'I need your bank account details so I can pay some money in, will explain later,
Love you, xx'

The microwave pinged just as her answer came. He transferred the money then wiped his phone of all data so when they cleared his flat there was no information to be accessed. He opened a bottle of beer, sat in the living room and watched an old film that he'd seen before. It didn't matter; nothing mattered except Joanna and Ruby.

176

When the film finished, he stood up, yawning, and washed his plate. He showered, dressed in clothes for 2035 and turned the timer over. He fetched a T-shirt and carefully wrapped the timer to protect it and put it in his rucksack. All his cards, passport, phone and driving licence were placed beside the bed and his new cards and documents went into the rucksack.

Finally, he put the rucksack on, fastened it around the front and went to bed. It was uncomfortable, turning over difficult, so he thought he would never sleep but eventually he did.

Chapter 29

2035

Xen was woken by extreme discomfort. He cautiously opened his eyes and was relieved to find he was on the floor of Joanna's living room. The floor was hard and the timer in his rucksack was digging into his back.

He sat up, unclipped the rucksack and shrugged it off then pulled it towards him. He smiled with relief when he saw it had worked. The timer had transported him and itself into the future. He moved to the settee and looked at his watch. As he did so he heard Joanna's alarm ring. It was Tuesday, so she would be going to work.

'Xen, what a lovely surprise, has something happened?'

'Yes, but it's a long story....' He was interrupted by a squeal of excitement from Ruby who rushed to hug him. 'Hello, my favourite six-year-old,' he said. 'I'm afraid you have to go to crèche today, but I'll be here when you come back and I'll cook us a meal. What time do you get home?'

'About six and we're starving by then, so we get something quick like scrambled eggs or beans on toast. It's lovely to see you,' said Joanna.

'I'll make some tea if you want to get dressed. Is there cereal or something for breakfast?'

'Yes, we have food, thanks. Come on Ruby, let's start with you.'

Joanna went to Ruby's room and Xen went into the kitchen. He set out mugs, cereal bowls, and found fruit as well as milk in the fridge. He wasn't sure what she would make of his situation but wanted to tell her that evening, not while she was in a hurry to get to work. By the time breakfast was ready they were dressed.

'Well this is lovely,' said Joanna. 'I want to know what's happened to bring you here in the week, but can we chat tonight? You will be here tonight?'

'Yes, I'll be here, and we can chat then.' Ruby then monopolised the conversation telling Xen about a trip she'd been on the day before, organised by the crèche. They had been to a butterfly farm and then a picnic in the park. 'Today we're going to paint pictures of butterflies. They're symmetrical you know. That means one wing looks just like the other. People are symmetrical too.'

Xen smiled. 'Symmetrical is a great word, Ruby. The butterfly farm sounds lovely.'

'We must stop chatting now, Ruby. It's time to go. Give Xen a hug.'

Ruby threw herself at him and Xen's heart lurched with love. 'Have a good day both of you,' he said, and he kissed Joanna. They went out of the door, and suddenly it was too quiet, and Xen felt bleak. He made himself a cup of coffee and sat on the settee making plans for the day. It would help to make a list, so he found a notepad and wrote:

Find out what's in Robert Simms's account
Buy a solafone, assuming there's enough
Buy food for dinner tonight
What am I going to do for a job?
How can I make myself look different? Plain glass spectacles? Grow a beard / moustache? Dye my hair?

He finished his coffee and cleared away the breakfast dishes. When it was all tidy, he set off for the town centre. As he walked, he thought about his situation. He had wanted to be here, with Joanna, more than anything but now he realised he might meet people who knew him in the past who believed he'd died.

Should he have gone to Dubai? No, it was worth the risk to be with Joanna. Apart from Morgan and Isabelle, he'd not met anyone else from his past. Perhaps the problem was not as great as he thought. He would still grow a beard and buy the glasses just to make him feel like Robert, Rob, Bob? He thought he liked Rob best.

He went to a bank console to access his new account and was pleased to see not only had the government been very generous but there was also five years of interest on the money. It may have to last for a long time, because finding a job could be difficult. There was enough for him to buy a solafone so he would do that next.

The media store was an Aladdin's cave of new inventions. It was amazing what had changed in just five years. A solafone could now do everything making debit cards redundant completely. Cards could still be used but if you could afford a solafone you needed no other technology.

The salesman explained it could even monitor your health and warn you if there was a problem brewing. Rob was in the store for an hour browsing but eventually he settled on one and when it was on his wrist, he felt he'd truly arrived in 2035.

It was lunchtime so he had a sandwich and cold drink in a café. It was busy but he managed to find a seat, sharing a table with some students. He began using his solafone to find a job site when the young man sitting next to him spoke. 'That's a fancy piece of kit you've got there, looks new.'

'It is, I've just bought it, so I'm still learning. I'm looking for a job and not sure of the best site.'

The students looked at each other and then, almost in chorus they said, 'Posthaste.' They all laughed and then the man that had spoken first said, 'Posthaste reckon to find you something suitable within one week. You'll need some time on the site answering all their questions, but they're the best.'

'Thank you, I'll do it when I get home.' Rob had finished his lunch, so he thanked them again and left the café. He stood, irresolute for a moment, and then decided to buy a pair of reactive sunglasses. He could wear them all the time when he went outside and he would feel less exposed, should he meet anyone from the past.

On the way back to the Joanna's flat he bought salad, cheeses and large potatoes to bake in their skins. That would be much healthier than beans on toast, he thought.

Later that evening, having read her a story and kissed her good night, Rob shut the door of Ruby's bedroom. He found Joanna sitting with a glass of red wine poured for him. She had a glass of cola.

'Wine? Are we celebrating?' he asked.

'I'm not sure, but I thought whether it was good or bad news bringing you here, a glass of wine would help.'

'Thank you, here's to us.' They clinked glasses and Joanna said nothing, waiting for him. 'You know I've been working for the government and it was hush hush?'

She nodded.

'Well, I think I got too close to unearthing something very important, and I received a death threat.' He ignored her intake of breath and carried on. When he had told her all he could he sat back, aware of how tense he'd been.

'So, you're here to stay, you have no job and your name's now Robert Simms?'

'Yes.'

Joanna put her glass carefully on the coffee table and got up to sit on his lap. She put her arms around him and murmured. 'I'm so, so pleased. Oh my God I'm going to cry. I wanted us to be a normal family so much, but it seemed impossible. Now, suddenly, we can be together, properly.' She kissed him fiercely. 'Let's celebrate in bed.'

'That's a definite,' he said, 'but let's finish the wine first.'

She slid off his lap and took off her clothes, taking a sip or two of cola in between garments. When she was completely naked, she sat opposite him to finish her drink, teasing him, adopting a series of sexual poses until he could stand it no longer. He slurped the rest of his wine in one gulp, picked her up and carried her to bed.

Before they fell asleep, he said, 'It's wonderful to think I'll be here in the morning and not transported back. Will you marry me?'

'Yes of course I will, but you'd better get a job first.'

'He yawned, 'OK, I love you.' He just heard her saying the same back to him and then he slept.

It seemed he'd only just shut his eyes when Ruby came running in announcing it was morning. She snuggled in between them with Rob protesting at her bony elbows digging into him. Joanna's alarm went off and all three of them left the bed.

Over breakfast Rob said he was going to look for a job but would take care of any household tasks that needed doing. It took Joanna only a moment to fetch the notepad and write a list.

Rob read it and said, 'You'd better show me how to work the washing machine. It's completely different to mine.' Joanna gave him a quick lesson and then they left the house to go to work.

Rob made a cup of coffee, worked the washing machine and waited until it was whirring, steadily. He then sat down and sipped his coffee while looking at 'Posthaste'.

The site asked him to select all the types of jobs that he was qualified to do. He was aware his tech skills were out of date but had never worked in any other field unless he counted student jobs like labouring on a road building project and working in a quarry. Unsure what to do, he decided to lower his expectations and be prepared to do any job. Before applying for anything, though, he needed to set up an e-mail address.

He worked on the site for an hour and at the end of it he had two interviews lined up, one that afternoon and another the following day. He could see now why the students said it would find him work quickly. The first interview was for a person to work in a busy office as a computer technician. It paid considerably less than his previous jobs, but it was close enough to walk.

He finished the morning by drying the washing and while that was tumbling, he wrote to Sonia. Within minutes there was a ping announcing her reply.

Hello Rob and welcome to 2035. I must admit, as the date became closer, I was getting anxious. I'm not sure how to explain to the others your change of name. Any ideas? S.

Rob wrote back,

I think it would be possible to tell most of the truth. I was working for the Secret Service, had a death threat and was given a new ID.

Sonia wrote back saying she would do just that and, if he would send her his new e-mail address, she could pass it on to the others, along with his new phone number. Not long after that he received messages from Jason, Catherine and Andy saying they were glad he was safe.

He made himself a sandwich and a cup of tea and then dressed in the smartest clothes he had, for the interview.

*

It was not a high-tech company. Much of the equipment was familiar and Rob thought he'd convinced the panel of his competence. They asked for a reference and he had to admit he didn't have one

When he got home, he felt excited knowing he was going to be able to see Joanna and Ruby that night and every night. He just had time to begin cooking a meal when they arrived.

'Xen, sorry, Rob, I played outside all day today. Crèche has got a new climbing frame. We made it into a castle and then it was a ship. It has a net and I can climb to the top and over the other side.'

'That sounds great fun. I didn't realise you had an outside area.'

'It's really big and there's a cover so you can be out when it's raining. We have a sand tray and a water tray, and toys to ride on. I'm too big for the tractor but I use the scooters.'

'So, you had a lovely day.' Ruby nodded and he looked at Joanna. 'What about you?'

She smiled, at him and he noticed how tired she looked. 'It was difficult because they've put in a new computer system and we're all struggling to learn it. I'm getting better but have had to concentrate very hard. I was really ready to come home.'

Rob hugged her, kissed the top of her head and told her to sit in the living room, where he would bring her a cup of tea. When he brought the mug to her, she was asleep, so he put it down carefully and tiptoed out. Ruby was having her fruit juice in the kitchen, so he asked her to help him make the dinner, giving Joanna the peace, she needed.

They made a Bolognese sauce while the jacket potatoes were finishing in the oven. Ruby grated the cheese, eating a lot of it as she did so, and helped make a bowl of salad. When the meal was ready, they went to wake Joanna, but she already had her eyes open.

'I can't believe I fell asleep. I drank my tea and it was lukewarm.' She looked up at them, smiling. 'I think you'd better sit down for a minute.'

'No, we came to say dinner's ready and I'm hungry,' said Ruby.

'It won't take long, but I have to tell you both something important. I went to the doctor at lunch time and……. I'm going to have a baby.'

'Yay!' Ruby clapped her hands. 'Will it be a boy or a girl?'

'I don't know yet, Ruby. I have a scan booked next week and we should find out then. So, what do you think, Rob, about being a dad?'

Rob realised he was crying. He wiped the tears away, laughing and hugging her until she begged to be released. 'It's the best news ever. How long before he or she arrives?'

'The 4th of March is the due date but they're never very accurate. Ruby came two weeks late.' She stood up. 'Let's go and have this dinner. I'd like to celebrate with a bottle of wine but now I know for definite I'm pregnant, I can't.'

When the dinner was finished and they were relaxing in the living room Joanna said, 'I forgot to ask you about your job hunting.'

'It seems almost insignificant when you had such amazing news to tell us. I went for an interview in that large office block, Sheldon House, to be a computer technician. It doesn't pay much but it's better than nothing. I have another, similar job interview tomorrow. That will pay more but it's a bus ride away. I need to think about the money more than I used to because you and Ruby will be depending on my income once you give up work. How long away is that? I'm so ignorant of pregnancies.'

'When I was having Ruby, I kept working as long as I could and that was just over seven months. At that point I was very fat very heavy and constantly weary.'

'So, we're talking Christmas or early January?' said Rob looking at his solafone.

'You've bought a new solafone, very smart,' said Joanna.

'If I'd known your news, I'd have bought a second-hand one, but it's too late now. Ruby it's time for your shower and if you're very good I'll read you the rest of the story we began last night.'

'I'm always good,' said Ruby as she stood up.

'Yes, you're an angel, but I'll come and check you're properly dry and bring in your clean pyjamas,' said Joanna.

*

When Ruby was in bed Joanna and Rob snuggled on the settee and Joanna giggled. 'When I get enormous there won't be room for both of us on here. You know I keep thinking about the flat I had before it was destroyed. I had everything a baby would need there, cot, pram, highchair, toys. None of that mattered, until now. All those things cost a lot and I'm worried about the expense.'

Rob told her then about transferring all his money into her account before he was officially declared dead.

'That's a relief, but I don't want to think about that. This is our new life and I want us to look forwards not backwards.'

'Yes, I want to do the same, but I still have the sand timer so my mission is not finished.'

'Where is it?' asked Joanna.

'In my rucksack under our bed. As long as it's not touched nothing will happen.'

'What would happen if you did touch it?'

'I don't know, so I don't intend to do it. Anyway, enough talking. We must go to bed. I know you're worn out.'

Chapter 30

August 2035

Rob woke up and laid on his back thinking about Joanna and the prospect of being a father. Then he remembered he had another job interview that morning. He checked on his solafone for a message about the job he'd gone for yesterday but there was nothing.

It was nearly time for the alarm, so he slipped out of bed quietly and went into the kitchen. By the time the kettle was boiled Ruby and Joanna were up. Rob made the tea while the others got dressed and then he got dressed while they were having breakfast and making packed lunches.

Rob felt they'd scarcely had time to say hello to one another when Joanna and Ruby left. It was not enjoyable being a househusband and he hoped he would get one of the jobs. There was no time to muse because his appointment was at nine and he would have to walk some distance after the bus ride.

When he reached the bus stop there a queue and a bus was just pulling up. He hoped they would all get on, not having planned in a waiting time for the next one. By the time he was waving his solafone at the sensor it was standing room only, but he was aboard.

When Rob got off the bus, he realised he was now early, so he walked slowly, breathing in the moist air. He could remember when the air in Leeds was thick with engine fumes and he blessed the move to electric vehicles.

The company he was looking for was not smart like Sheldon House. Initially he walked past it because the sign was small. The unimpressive frontage reminded him of the entrance to the Secret Service and he had a moment of panic that he controlled by forcing himself to ring the bell. An electronic voice asked him to step back so he could be seen by the camera and to state his business. The door clicked open.

Rob walked forward slowly, fear mounting. The passageway ended in one, un-named door with no instructions, so he knocked and waited.

'Go in Mr Simms and take a seat,' said an electronic voice. Rob hesitated, his thoughts screaming don't do it, run outside where it's safe.

'Go in Mr Simms and take a seat,' repeated the electronic voice. Rob grasped the knob, turned it and pushed open the door. He was greatly relieved to see another man sitting, waiting.

'Hello, are you here for an interview too?' he asked. The man nodded but said nothing. They sat in silence for a few minutes, that seemed like an age, and then a door opened and there was Morgan.

'Mr Simms, please ……... Once again there were two armchairs, and Morgan indicated that he was to sit in one of them. A pot of tea and another of coffee were ready with mugs, side plates and doughnuts.

Rob sat, his heart thumping with anxiety. What was this job?

'So, we meet again, Mr er... Simms. I understand you managed to disappear effectively without taking up the post we organised for you in Dubai. Now you've surfaced back in your old stamping ground. Are you not afraid of being discovered and your life being threatened again? The

Chinese have very long memories, but of course, they believe you to be dead.'

He stopped talking and busied himself pouring tea then offered a doughnut. Rob took one, thinking he was going to need the sugar when he heard what Morgan was offering.

'You're right and I've been living here for some time and you are the only person to recognise me. But then you would have looked up all the applicants and know my history has been a blank for five years, when you invited me to come. So, is there a job on offer?'

Morgan delayed answering, biting into his doughnut with relish, chewing, swallowing and then sipping his tea. Finally, he leant forward and said, 'You signed the Official Secrets Act... as Xen Baxter. If you worked for us again you would have to sign it in your new status as Robert Simms. Only you and I know you are the same person.'

'What about Michelle? She gave me the passport, tickets etcetera.'

'You're right but she's moved on, been promoted to a different department. A lot can happen in five years. Which leads me to the crux of the matter. I want you to come and work for us again on one specific task, to stop the random destruction of cities all over the world and the appalling loss of life. I have several hackers, but, so far, they've not cracked the problem. You see, and here I'm really sticking my neck out, I don't believe China's behind this. My belief is that either the satellites have a fault which causes them to fall into the atmosphere, or, more likely, another power, Russia, North Korea or Saudi Arabia are deliberately bringing them down by sabotaging the computer system. This then discredits China.'

The long speech seemed to have tired him for Morgan sat back in his chair and Rob noticed he looked old and very pale.

'I don't understand why you think I can do any better than the others when I'm five years behind, technologically.' It's also a small salary for such an important task.'

'That was just the advert to encourage people with computer skills to apply. I hoped it would net you, but I wasn't sure. You can triple that figure if it will persuade you, after all you know it can be risky. The Chinese system was devised over five years ago and I believe not much has altered since your time.'

This was tempting, very tempting but Rob had another question. 'Would it be back in London?'

'No, we've moved some departments out, and this is one of them. It's here in this building and all new personnel, in case you were worrying about meeting Mei Ling, Sean, Ho Chin or Jake. They're all fit and well, by the way. We've had no more death threats. They just didn't want to move north, and Sean has married Ho Chin.'

Rob's smile increased to a broad grin. 'In that case I would be happy to sign up and help if I can.' They shook hands and Morgan said he would send details of when he was to start, an accurate salary, a time of the medical and so on. He thought the starting date would be in about a week's time.

Rob left the building feeling excited and nervous. The money would be superb, and he wouldn't have to be away from Joanna all week. It was also great news that Sean had married. His delight turned into action as he jogged along the street, passing bus stops until he was almost home. Then he stopped, took several deep breaths and walked the rest of the way. As he entered the flat, he decided to take Joanna and Ruby out for a meal to celebrate. They all liked pizza so he rang and booked a table for 6.30 at their favourite restaurant.

It was lunchtime. He made himself a healthy salad and mused as he ate, wondering what age he was now. When all the time travel started, he was thirty-two and his birthday was the 9th of September. Now he was Rob when was his birthday? He found his passport and noticed that Rob was thirty-seven with a birthday on, September ninth. At least that was easy to remember.

When lunch was cleared away Rob decided to text Sonia and Jason to arrange to meet them again. He wanted to tell them about the baby but thought Joanna might prefer to tell them when they met. That done, he plumped a cushion, lay down on the settee and was asleep in moments.

*

'Ruby be quiet Rob's asleep.' He heard her in the distance and opened his eyes.

'He's awake now, Mummy.'

'Are you ill? You never sleep during the day,' said Joanna.

'I'm fine, really. It's been a busy day and I've got a job. I've also booked a table to take us all out for a pizza at 6.30 so…' he looked at his solafone, 'we'd better move.'

'Pizza, I love pizza,' said Ruby and threw herself on Rob for a hug.

'That's great,' said Rob, 'but we'd better get ready quickly or we'll be late. I'll order a taxi.'

Joanna helped Ruby have a wash and change into a pretty dress. She adjusted her makeup and they were ready.

On the way there Joanna asked Rob about his interview. He told her about his surprise at meeting Morgan again and being offered a job in the Secret Service. She frowned, 'Isn't that dangerous and will you have to commute to London?'

'No, his department is now here in Leeds. There are no people I knew before, working there and the money is excellent. As for it being dangerous, they can hardly kill the same person twice.' Rob smiled as he saw her relax, knowing his comment was nonsense because he was no longer the same person.

'The money will be great, no more worries about giving up work when I have to. I'm looking forward to this meal out.'

*

When they got home, Ruby went straight to bed and was asleep in moments. Rob and Joanna put the television on and watched the first episode of a drama that they enjoyed. Then they went to bed and made love slowly, until Joanna could stand it no longer and urged him to speed up. They climaxed and laughed, as they lay entwined, at her impatience. They went to sleep feeling happy and contented.

They had a lazy start to the day on Saturday and, when eventually they were dressed, Joanna pointed out that they needed to go food shopping and there was cleaning and laundry to do.

'I'll go shopping,' said Rob. 'Do you want to come Ruby?'

'No, I want to stay with Mummy and help her or play.' Rob read out the shopping list he had on his solafone. 'Is there anything else?' Joanna added a couple of items and Rob left.

*

A little later Joanna said, 'I'm going to clean your room this morning so will you take something to play with into the living room or watch television for half an hour?'

Ruby nodded and collected her doll and tea set and took them to the living room. Joanna took down Ruby's curtains to wash and cleaned her window. While she was using the vacuum cleaner, she was oblivious to Ruby going into the master bedroom and pulling out the rucksack from under the bed. She had gone into the room to borrow one of her Mum's scarves to make a bed for her doll. The rucksack was sticking out, just a little, and caught her eye.

Ruby sat on the floor, undid the zip and pulled out the sand timer which was still wrapped in a T-shirt. When she had pulled the wrapping off, she gasped. The brass gleamed and she sat, mesmerised, as the sand trickled through. She wondered why something so lovely had been shoved under the bed and went to show it to Mummy.

Joanna was just coming out of Ruby's room and met her at the door. 'Put that down, now!' she shouted. Ruby put it on to the floor, shocked by her mother's reaction. Her face reddened and tears ran down her cheeks. 'It's dangerous, Ruby, and it belongs to Rob. You must never touch it again, understand? Now go into the living room.'

Ruby ran into the living room and slammed the door. Why was Mummy so cross? How could it be dangerous? Was Rob going to shout at her too when he came home? She began to cry squeezing her eyes shut, trying to stop. Suddenly she felt weird, there was a rushing noise and she felt herself moving then the movement was too fast. It was worse than any feeling she'd ever had.

Rob came home laden with bags of shopping but dropped them to the floor when he saw the timer glowing and Joanna on her knees looking at it.

'Don't touch it, he said. 'How did it get there?'

'Ruby found it. I thought she was in the living room, but she was in the bedroom, playing with it.' She looked up at him. 'Why is it glowing?'

'Where's Ruby?'

'I shouted at her and sent her into the living room.'

Rob looked into the room and, as he feared, she wasn't there.

Chapter 31

June 5th 2035

Ruby opened her eyes and began to cry. She was not in her soft bed at home but fully dressed on the hard floor of the café. She wanted her Mummy and sat up, sniffing. Mummy was sleeping just a little way away, with another little girl in her pyjamas. She sat up and knew she was ill because she felt nauseous. 'Mummy I feel sick,' she shouted.

'I'm coming Ruby.' Joanna sat up and saw Ruby still asleep next to her.

'Mummy.' Joanna looked around and there was another Ruby, needing her. She moved quietly to the girl's side and said, 'Would some fresh air help?'

Ruby nodded and Joanna helped her up. Other people were still asleep. They walked quietly past Isabelle, Andy and Morgan.

Outside the air was muggy, not fresh at all, as if a storm was brewing. 'Take some deep breaths.'

Ruby did so and nodded. 'I feel better now. Who's that little girl you were sleeping with? She looks like me. I've been here before, when everything was broken.'

'It still is broken,' said Joanna, trying to keep calm but not able to understand how her daughter could be here twice. 'How old are you, I've forgotten.'

'That's silly, Mummy, you know I'm six. Rob bought me a scooter and you gave me a lovely proper lunch box to take to crèche.' Joanna nodded as if she knew this all the time, but her mind was racing. Where was Xen? He'd know what this was all about.

'Shall we put the kettle on and make some tea for everyone?'

Ruby nodded and followed Joanna to the kitchen area. 'Is there any chocolate cake left?' Joanna watched her go directly to the tin just as 'her' Ruby would have done. They were both the same Ruby, but one had come, somehow, from a few months into the future.

When the tea was made Joanna carried the mugs into the area where everyone had been sleeping and found they were waking up. She almost wanted to laugh as their eyes moved from one Ruby to the next.

Morgan took a mug of tea mumbling something about seeing double and went outside. Isabelle moved towards them and took a mug for Andy and one for herself. 'Hello,' she said. 'My name's Isabelle.'

'I know,' said Ruby, and that's Andy and Morgan just went out. I think this is the day you and Andy go looking for Rob and you get caught in a storm and die.'

Isabelle gasped with shock.

'Who's Rob?' asked Joanna almost afraid of this doppelganger of her daughter.

'You know, Xen. He had to change his name so now he's Rob.'

'Talking of Xen,' said Andy. 'Where is he?'

'There he is,' said both girls simultaneously.

Xen was sitting, cradling his head in his hands, hunched with his feet drawn up.

'I think he feels yuck, like I did,' said Ruby going towards him. As she did so the younger Ruby confronted her. 'You look just like me. My name's Ruby.'

'I'm Ruby and that's my mummy.'

'She's my mummy, not yours.'

Xen stood up carefully almost staggering with his head swimming and said, 'You are the same little girl and Joanna is Mum to you both. This Ruby, who's six, has just travelled back a few months from the future. She has a special mission to save you, Isabelle, from dying tonight.'

'It must be the sand timer. Ruby's touched it,' said Isabelle.

'Yes, and Mummy shouted at me to put it down, so I did and then I went into the living room and I felt ill and I flew really, really fast and I had to shut my eyes. When I opened them I was here.'

Joanna sat down on a chair and Andy came to Isabelle's side. 'How do you know she'd been touching a sand timer?' Isabelle took a deep breath and looked straight into his eyes. 'It's a long story and I apologise for not telling you before, but I didn't think you would believe me. The short version is, my Dad bought a sand timer at an auction and when he touched it, he went back into the past. After many adventures he did something which changed the past and life carried on for everyone else as if nothing had happened.

'Years later, not knowing anything about its powers, I turned the sand timer and the same thing happened to me. I was stuck in the past, when you came looking for me, before we were even engaged. Do you remember? Sonia was in our house and she told you I was looking after a sick relative. You couldn't understand why I'd gone away without taking my phone.'

Andy dragged up a chair and sat on it heavily. 'That's quite a story. So, Xen and the second Ruby have come from the future?' He saw Xen nod. 'But I don't understand how you, arriving here from the future, will save Isabelle's life.'

196

'I was with you all, until this morning when I stayed in my own time. You and Andy went looking for me and got caught in a storm. You sheltered and during the night you went to relieve yourself, Isabelle, slipped and cut your head open. When Andy came looking for you, you had bled to death.' Isabelle covered her face with her hands and Andy put his arms around her.

'I know you all want to find your way out of here, but today you must stay put. If you walk towards Knaresborough tomorrow, you'll find a barrier and be rescued. You'll appreciate Morgan knows nothing of this and I really don't know how to explain two Rubies. Any ideas?'

Everybody looked blank.

'We could say we were twins,' said one of the girls.

'It would be a good idea, but he knows, until now, there's only been one of you.'

'Would it be possible to keep them apart, so he only ever sees one at a time?' said Joanna.

'OK, Andy will you go and find him, tell him we're resting today and moving on tomorrow, and I'll try to slip out with my older Ruby. We'll be in the car park area if you need us.'

Andy stood up to go out and the younger Ruby said, 'I wanted us to play together.'

'I'll pack us a picnic and bring it to the car park about lunchtime. I'm sure Morgan won't be bothered about joining us and then you can play,' said Joanna.

'Just one thing before I distract Morgan,' said Andy with a frown on his face. 'Morgan saw two Rubies before he went outside.'

'We'll all deny it and say he was mistaken,' said Rob. 'It's the best we can do.'

Andy went outside and saw Morgan well away from the café leaning over the rail looking at the river. 'Hi, are you feeling ill?' asked Andy, deliberately blocking Morgan's view of the café door.

'I've got a gyppy tummy, been sick twice. Even thought, I saw two little girls instead of one! Can't move from here at the moment.'

'It's not a problem. I really came out to say we've decided to stay here one more day and move on tomorrow. By the look of you I assume you're happy with the decision.'

Morgan nodded. Andy, hoping Rob and Ruby had gone, offered to get Morgan some water and a chair.

'That would be great, thanks.' Andy fetched water from the kitchen and a chair from the café.

Now that the coast was clear, the others came out to see what they could have for breakfast. They found some more bread buns, completely defrosted now. Joanna buttered two extra ones, glad that Morgan was not wanting to be anywhere near food and found a jug with a lid that she filled with water. Andy and Isabelle offered to take them to the car park.

'Just as long as you come back here afterwards and don't go wandering off and get caught in a storm,' said Joanna with a smile.

*

The day passed slowly with everyone, except Morgan, wanting to move on but accepting they must stay until the morning. The two girls met for the picnic and ran around the car park. They climbed the stumps of trees and balanced along broken walls. They played hide and seek and tired themselves out, so by the evening they were ready for a hot meal and sleep.

Rob was not sure what to do. Ruby and he probably needed to sleep in order to return to the future, but it was going to rain and there was nowhere to shelter except the café. Morgan might believe he'd seen double once, because he was ill, but would never believe it a second time.

Joanna walked with the younger Ruby back towards the café. On the way there was a flash followed quickly by a mighty clap of thunder. Ruby screamed and they both ran the last few steps, as the rain fell. When they arrived Morgan was sitting alone, looking miserable but looked up and managed a smile. 'Looks like we're going to have a storm,' he said.

'It's here already. Didn't you hear the thunder?' said Ruby, her voice louder than usual with excitement and fear.

'How are you feeling now?' asked Joanna.

'Much better, thank you. I've drunk some water, but I haven't eaten anything. I heard Isabelle say something about a curry. Would you tell her I'd prefer to have some bread and butter, please if there's any left?'

Joanna nodded and ran to the kitchen area. It was only a few steps, but she was quite wet when she got there. The smell of Indian spices was delightful. 'Hello, that smells delicious. I hate to sound like my daughter but is it nearly ready? Oh, and Morgan says he can't face curry but if there's any bread left, he could eat that.'

When the meal was ready Isabelle and Andy plated two extra servings and left them in the kitchen. The rest they took into the café and soon everyone was eating and talking. They were all glad they'd stayed another day, especially as they would have been caught out in the torrential rain that was still falling.

Ruby started to yawn, so Joanna suggested she got ready for bed. This was the signal for everyone else to clear away and wash up. That usually took twenty minutes, enough time for an exhausted child to snuggle into her sleeping bag and go to sleep.

Joanna had explained it was important not mention the other Ruby and she had managed to do so. She smiled looking down at her asleep and felt proud of her.

When the others came back into the café Morgan asked where Xen was, adding, 'He wasn't here for the meal. In fact, he's not been here at all.'

'He was at the picnic,' said Joanna, 'and when we came back, he said he wanted to go for a walk. He's probably found somewhere to shelter.'

'I plated him a meal, so I hope he'll come back for that,' said Isabelle.

*

In the car park there was no shelter and Ruby was frightened of the storm. It was too early to return to the café, so Rob picked her up and she clung to him, her face buried in his neck as the rain soaked them both. He began to shiver with the cold and wondered if hypothermia was possible in the middle of summer. He then remembered there had been toilets near the road. Would they be rubble, or could they provide shelter? He carried her there, his arms aching and found there was enough roof left for them to huddle under. He sat on the floor with Ruby on his lap and distracted her by telling her fairy stories.

When it got to 7pm he carried her towards the café. He asked her to be very quiet and they both crept into the kitchen. There was a strong smell of curry, but before they could eat, they had to get out of their wet clothes. Rob put the gas oven on and left the door open then draped Ruby's clothes on a stool in front of it. He wrapped her in a couple of towels and then he found their dinners in the fridge and warmed them on top of the stove over hot water. They spoke in whispers, but the rain was making so much noise he felt fairly safe.

When they'd finished eating Rob felt Ruby's clothes and they were dry, so she got dressed while he put his clothes by the oven.

'Where am I going to sleep, Rob? I want mummy to kiss me goodnight.'

'The walk-in larder is the best place, but we don't have any bedding. Perhaps there are enough towels and tea towels to make you comfortable.' He stood up, searched the drawers and found enough for her to lie on. When her bed was ready, he hoped she would lie down without any fuss, but she was tired and fractious. 'I need to clean my teeth and go to the toilet, and I want Mummy.'

'You can't clean your teeth because we haven't got a toothbrush and you can't go to the toilet in the café because we can't explain to Morgan about time travel. You'll have to pee in this bucket.'

He watched her struggle with her emotions, but eventually she used the bucket and went into the larder to sleep.

Rob sat in the doorway quietly and was relieved when he saw she was sound asleep. The others would be wondering where he was, so he needed to go into the café. He stood up and stretched, unwilling to leave Ruby. As he stood, looking down at her, she disappeared. 'Thank you, thank you sand timer,' he said aloud. He gathered up the towels and then went into the café.

'Where have you been?' asked Morgan.

'Getting thoroughly soaked, but I dried off in the kitchen and had the dinner someone had left me. It was delicious. The rain seems to be easing off so we should be able to leave tomorrow. I know it's early but I'm tired and ready to go to bed.'

'So am I,' said Morgan. Everyone else decided to join them. Rob closed his eyes, willing the sand timer to take him, but an hour later, when the others were all asleep, he was still awake. He got up quietly and went to the toilet but when he got back his sleeping bag was filled. He was looking down at his own sleeping body. There had been two Rubies and now there were two of him. He wondered how was he going to get back if he couldn't get to sleep?

Chapter 32

August 2035

Joanna backed away on her hands and knees from the glowing sand timer. Rob had phoned Catherine when Ruby disappeared, and she said if he touched it, he would join Ruby wherever she was.

'I should do it. She'll be frightened and I'm her mother,' she said.

'Yes, but I own the sand timer and I'm the one with the mission to save Isabelle. It must be me. Look, if you're anxious ring Catherine again and ask her to come over. Her, or Sonia.' Then, without another word he touched the timer, didn't lift it or turn it. One touch and he had gone.

Joanna thought people couldn't just disappear. Even conjurers used deceit and trick boxes. There was no real magic, but she'd just witnessed it. She bit her lip, frightened for Ruby but knowing she would be pleased to see Rob. In her mind Joanna saw Ruby running into his arms and holding him tight.

She walked into the kitchen and put the kettle on. If only she'd some idea of when they'd return; it might be possible, then, to feel calmer. The kettle boiled so she made a single mug of tea and took it into the sitting room. The television remote was by her chair, so she switched it on and then turned it off again. The tea was still very hot, but she sipped it feeling agitated and helpless. The phone rang.

'Hi Catherine. Yes, he's gone, just disappeared. I'm so worried and I've no idea when they'll come back.' She listened. 'I'd be really grateful for some company. That would be lovely.' Joanna turned the phone off and sat back, relieved. Catherine knew all about the power of the timer.

When Catherine arrived, it was mid-afternoon, and Joanna's stomach was growling. They hugged and Joanna found it hard to let go.

'We'd better be careful to skirt around that,' said Catherine, pointing to the still glowing timer. 'We don't want to all go whizzing off.' They went into the kitchen and Joanna put the kettle on. They sat at the table and Catherine noticed how pale and stressed she looked. 'Have you had any lunch?' Joanna shook her head. 'Right you sit there, and I'll make a sandwich.' Catherine opened the fridge and various cupboards until she'd assembled everything she needed. The kettle clicked off and Joanna began to stand to make the tea, but Catherine motioned her to stay put. 'I think you need fortifying and I noticed a bottle of rosé wine in the fridge. Let's open that instead.'

Joanna shook her head, 'No wine for me but please open it if you'd like some. I'd really prefer tea.'

Some colour returned to Joanna's face when she'd eaten and drunk most of her tea. Catherine topped up her glass, Joanna picked up her cup and they both moved into the living room. When they were settled in comfortable chairs Joanna said, 'Will you tell me about your adventures with the sand timer and explain to me why it happens?'

'I was in total ignorance of it for years. It seems, way back in Victorian times, the timer was commissioned for a ship owned by one of my relatives. When everyone directly descended from him died, the contents of the house were put up for auction and Jason bought the timer. At that time, he had a nautical collection of all sorts of things. He eventually discovered that the timer was trying to help women in my family to have a better life. It took him back in time and he made changes to the past, including saving me from dying. We tried to get rid of the timer by taking it to our sailing club. It sat there for years in a cabinet full of other nautical artefacts, but then Izzy, ignorant of its power, decided to clean it and the timer became active again. She disappeared, as Ruby has done. Jason eventually explained everything to me. Now I'm praying that Ruby and Rob are on a mission to save Izzy.'

'Thank you for telling me that. But if they're on this mission why is it taking so long?' Her voice rose in volume; almost whining with her anxiety. Catherine answered quietly and calmly. 'Well, when Izzy went out with Andy, they spent the night sheltering from the storm by a heap of rubble. It was the middle of the night when Izzy went out to go to the toilet.... You know all that but what I'm really trying to explain is we might have to wait until the middle of the night when her safety is assured. If that's the case, can I stay the night?'

'Of course, you can.'

Catherine offered Joanna another glass of wine, but she shook her head. 'Now let's change the subject and talk about you and Rob. Are you thinking of getting married?

'Definitely, when all this is over. I'd like this baby,' she stroked her tummy, 'to have a father that stays, and I know Rob will.'

'Pregnant? That's fantastic news. Congratulations! It doesn't show so it must only be two or three months. When's it due?'

'The fourth of March, so plenty of time yet.' She smiled at the thought, and, in the joy of sharing her news, momentarily forgot her anxiety about Ruby.

*

The afternoon slid into early evening and Joanna and Catherine made a salad that they ate in the kitchen. This time they drank tea and were sipping it when they heard a muffled thump. Joanna got up and went into Ruby's bedroom to find her asleep on the bed. It was hard not to wake her up and ask what had happened, but she gently undressed her to her underclothes and covered her up. Ruby must have been exhausted because she slept deeply throughout. Finally, Joanna kissed her forehead and crept out of the room, closing the door behind her.

Catherine was bending, putting plates into the dishwasher and looked up as Joanna entered. 'Are they back? What happened?'

'I'm sorry, I don't know yet. Ruby's come back but Rob's still there. Ruby was so deeply asleep I hadn't the heart to wake her.' She saw Catherine's face fall back into resignation and heard her sigh.

Joanna finished her tea and said, 'I was going to give you Ruby's bed, but now, I'm afraid, it's the sofa. I'll fetch a duvet and a pillow. Would you like to borrow some pyjamas? I have a spare toothbrush.'

'Yes please. I'm really tired now. I'm not sure I can sleep but I must close my eyes.'

They went to bed, both certain they couldn't sleep, but they did.

*

Catherine woke up in the car travelling to Harrogate. The car was on auto drive and Jason looked at her and grinned. 'We'll soon be there. We're so lucky that Isabelle and Andy survived when so many died.'

Catherine felt confused. She had gone to sleep on Joanna's sofa and woken up in the hire car. She looked at the date on her solafone. Xen/Rob must have done it. They were re-living the moment when they discovered Izzy had died, but this time she will have survived. She smiled back at him, wondering if he realised, they had done this journey before. She decided to keep quiet and see what happened. Inside she hugged the belief that everything would be fine.

They would have to sell the boat again and buy somewhere to live. If only the timer had transported them to before the destruction of Harrogate and could have prevented that.

*

Joanna and Ruby woke up in the café. This time there was only one Ruby and Rob was back being Xen.

Ruby woke up, climbed out of her sleeping bag and went to Joanna and Xen. 'Is there only one of me, now?'

'Yes, and, remember, you mustn't mention travelling through time. We'll be walking out of here soon,' said Xen.

'It won't be like last time,' whispered Joanna. 'Last time we did it without you and you caught up with us later, after we'd found Andy with Isabelle's body.'

'Yes, I remember. You told me it was all my fault. I'm really pleased it'll work out well this time.'

When they had eaten a hasty breakfast, they packed the rucksacks ready to leave. There was an air of expectation that this was the day they would be rescued.

Chapter 33

They were taken to hospital as before and Catherine only got a glimpse of Isabelle and Andy, through glass, but that was enough. She stood with Jason smiling and clinging on to his arm.

'We're so, so lucky to have her back.' She hugged him again and then hugged Sonia and Roger, who had stood back slightly from the close relatives. They didn't talk about the previous time they had been at the same point, but Catherine was sure Sonia would remember. They had a long hug and Sonia whispered, 'Second time lucky.'

*

That night, in the hospital, Xen was scared to go to sleep, but the strenuous walk through the mud to the meeting point, plus the emotional turmoil, finally overcame his resistance.

*

When Xen regained consciousness, he was reluctant to open his eyes. Was it 2035 or 2030? Eventually there was the sound of a tea trolley and he opened his eyes. He was still in the hospital and felt a mixture of emotions. The timer had obviously finished its task. He could be with Joanna and Ruby, but they had to start their new life again.

Last time he had commuted to London, using the timer to visit Joanna at the weekends. This time he had no job and no possessions. It was going to be hard, with no references, to explain a gap of five years. He could truthfully say he'd lost everything in the destruction of Harrogate and felt sure they would be relocated to a flat in Leeds. Would it be the same flat?

He was confused and he felt tired of it all. It was a relief to see an orderly bringing his tea and having to sit up in bed. When breakfast was over a doctor visited the survivors. She declared them contamination free and said they could leave the hospital.

'That's good news but we have nowhere to go, no home, nothing. What are we to do?' asked Xen.

'I believe Social Services and Leeds City Council, are sorting this out. Representatives will be holding a meeting at ten in the main canteen.'

*

Joanna, Ruby, Isabelle and Andy were already in the canteen when Xen arrived. Morgan had left earlier to stay with his daughter. Xen sat next to Joanna and Ruby snuggled onto his lap. 'I'm looking forward to going to our flat,' she said.

'Ruby it will probably be empty, and we'll have to buy lots of things, but it will be good to be settled.'

Xen watched Ruby processing what he had said and saw her face change from excitement to sadness. There was no easy way for her to realise that they truly had to start again.

Before they could say anything else several officials arrived with briefcases. In less than an hour they were being taken to see a flat. It was the same one as before and he could feel Ruby keyed with expectation. He knew she was anticipating seeing her bedroom with the cuddly toys and scooter. He anticipated her disappointment, but there was no choice. The flat was clean, tidy, with some basic furniture but empty of their personal possessions.

Ruby went into her bedroom and was silent. Xen went into their bedroom and looked under the bed for his rucksack. It was gone.

'It's a lovely flat isn't it,' said the woman from Social Services.

'Yes,' said Joanna, 'It's perfect and we're grateful.' She opened the fridge and there was some milk, bread and margarine. On the work surface the tea caddy was half full. 'That's kind of you, we can make a cup of tea before sorting out our bank accounts.'

'Don't worry. Everyone knows about you and I'm sure the banks in town will issue you with temporary cards or lend you some cash until your new cards arrive. Do you have solafones?'

Joanna shook her head.

'That's a pity because you could've used those. There's a corner shop just a short way away. Would you like to walk there with me, and we can sweet talk them into giving you a temporary tab?'

'That's a good idea, shall we all go?' said Xen and the miserable trio followed the social worker out into the street. It seemed impossible to Xen that the shopkeeper wouldn't recognise them after the months they had been going there. Moving back in time seemed more complicated than going forwards.

In the shop the manager was kind and soon they'd filled bags with basic essentials and bought Ruby a simple plastic toy and some sweets. The social worker left them outside the shop to walk back on their own, so at last they could talk freely.

'Let's go to the banks and the job centre this afternoon,' said Xen. We must be able to get at our accounts, and we must get jobs.'

'I no longer have an account, but I do still have my badge of shame on my arm, and that might have some money left.'

Xen noticed the change in her voice, and then she was crying. He stopped and gathered her into his arms. Ruby watched and then cried too so she was pulled in between them.

'There's nothing like a group hug to make us feel better. At least the timer's gone so I'm here with you for good now and won't have to commute on weekends. It could be worse. We did save Isabelle.'

'I did that,' said Ruby.

'Yes, we were so cross with you for touching the timer, but you definitely saved her, with Xen's help,' said Joanna.

209

The skip had come back into Ruby's step and they all felt a bit less depressed.

Back at the flat they made a simple sandwich lunch and then Joanna suggested Xen went to the bank and job centre on his own, knowing that the walk into the city centre was too far for Ruby. 'We'll make the beds and Ruby can play with her little toy.'

*

Once in the town Xen went straight to the bank and was surprised and pleased at his reception. He had to give details of his new address and then he was allowed to withdraw cash to keep him going until his new card arrived.

The job centre was less rewarding, but he was allowed to apply for one position while he was there, when he'd explained his circumstances. Life was difficult without any access to social media. He wanted, needed, a solafone, and wondered if shops sold them second-hand. The shop he'd been to before, when he bought a top of the range model, did have a small selection, so he invested some of his cash on one, feeling guilty as he did so. The phone was a start, but he had none of his contacts so he was still unable to phone anyone, but he could go back to the job centre and give them his number.

That done he went shopping in second-hand shops for clothes for Ruby, Joanna and himself. Finally, laden down with bags, he used the bus to go back home.

Ruby was delighted with her clothes, trying on the trousers, tops and admiring the underwear. Joanna was less impressed with his choices but pleased to have some clothes to change into. 'I've been a second-hand girl too long and I need a job so that I can hold my head up again. Tomorrow I'll go to the job centre,' she said.

*

The next day, before Joanna was ready to go out, they had a visitor, Sonia. She arrived with a basket of luxury food and a bottle of champagne. They were all delighted to see her but Ruby asked where Roger was.

'He's in town looking for places to buy. We're staying in the same hotel, by the way, so you can come and see us.'

'How did you know we were here?' asked Joanna.

'I just guessed that things would play out more or less as they did before. I'm glad I was right.'

'It's wonderful to see you and the first thing you must help me with is my phone contacts.'

'You could just wait long enough, Xen, to allow Sonia to get her breath. I'll make some coffee and we can eat some of those biscuits I can see in the basket.'

Sonia unpacked her basket and Ruby's eyes opened wide when she saw a chocolate cake. 'Mummy and I can bake chocolate cake, when we have all the things to make it with.'

'Well I don't know if this one will be as good as homemade but I'm sure it will do. Do you want to have this instead of a biscuit?' Ruby nodded fervently and then looked at Mum to see if it was allowed.

'We'll all have cake,' said Joanna. She got plates while Sonia opened the cake box and they all sat in the small kitchen talking about their current situation.

'I'm usually a person whose cup is half full,' said Sonia, 'but even I found myself miserable to be back at the hotel. We'll have to look for houses and when we buy the same one as before we'll have to decorate it, buy the same furniture. It's really hard because Roger has no idea we've done this before. Sorry, I know you're in a much worse position than us. Let's sort out your solafone, Xen.'

That took just a few minutes and then Sonia invited them to come to the hotel, for a meal, on Sunday, to celebrate their escape. 'I'll invite everyone, including Morgan and his daughter, but it will be a happier occasion, this time, because we'll have Isabelle too. I'm looking forward to it.'

'We'd love to come, thank you,' said Joanna.

'Can we go to the park again and will Roger push me on the swing?'

'Yes, if it's not raining.'

'It won't rain because it didn't rain when we did it before. That's right isn't it?' Ruby looked, pleadingly at Xen for confirmation.

'Definitely, as far as the weather is concerned, but we can change some other things.'

'What can we change?'

'Well you might want to order a different dinner or pudding or have a coke instead of lemonade.'

He saw Ruby absorbing this and then Sonia said what he was thinking.

'Roger knows nothing about time travel and I'm not sure Jason understands this is happening for the second time. So please be careful, Ruby, what you say.'

'I know, Xen already told me. I'm good at keeping secrets.' Everyone smiled.

'Talking of Roger,' Sonia said glancing at her solafone, 'It's time I left to meet him.'

When Sonia had gone, Xen stayed with Ruby while Joanna went to the job centre. He took Ruby to the corner shop and they bought ingredients for cake-baking, some crayons, a colouring book and a storybook for bedtime. When they got back, he made them some drinks and she begged him to read one of the stories to her. She snuggled up to him on the settee to look at the pictures, and before he'd finished the first page, she was asleep. Xen felt his own eyes closing and that was how Joanna found them when she returned home. She smiled and went into the kitchen to make a cup of tea.

'Wake up sleepy heads, here's tea and celebration cake.'

'Ruby, her hair tousled and eyes barely focussing, said, 'I like chocolate cake better than, celebration.' As her eyes focused, she looked at Joanna with a big smile. 'It is chocolate cake. Why did you call it that other name?'

'I said celebration because we are celebrating that I have a job, starting on Monday. How good is that?'

'Hooray!' Her shout brought Xen out of his deep sleep and seeing his family smiling he smiled too. 'You all seem happy, oh, tea and more cake. Thank you.' He rubbed his neck with a grimace and reached for the tea.

'We're celebrating,' said Ruby, Mummy's got a job.'

'That's excellent news. Tell me all about it.'

'I went to the job centre and I asked if there were any clerical vacancies at the Uni. The lady said she didn't think so but did a search on her computer and there it was, my job exactly as I had before. I said I really wanted it, so she rang, and they said I could come and have a chat. Needless to say, I was on the bus in seconds. I told them about being rescued from Harrogate, they said they recognised me from the media footage. They felt sorry for me, I guess, but who cares, I've got the job and a place in the crèche for Ruby.'

That prompted another hooray from Ruby, and Xen got up and gave her a kiss. 'Well done, now you're the bread winner and I'm the house husband.' His smile was rueful.

Chapter 34

Roger was in his element ordering champagne for the disaster survivors, and the hotel manager decided to put the second bottle on the house as his contribution to the celebration. Everyone was excited and chattering about their accommodation, what they hoped to do next and, obviously, the difficulties of losing everything and having to start again. They sat at one huge table. Isabelle was sandwiched between Andy and Catherine, with Jason, Sonia, Roger, Morgan, his daughter Kathy, Ruby, Xen and finally Joanna, who was next to Andy.

It was too big a group to be able to talk to anyone unless they were on one side of you. After the first course Roger went to the toilet and Morgan took that moment to casually move to Xen, lean close and whisper in his ear, 'Can we find a moment to talk?'

'Coffee will be offered in the lounge so that might be a good time,' said Xen.

Puddings were consumed with enthusiasm, particularly by Ruby who had chosen, death by chocolate and needed to be whisked to the ladies to be cleaned up after eating it. Finally, the waiter announced they should move to the lounge and he would come to take their coffee or tea orders.

Isabelle moved straight to Morgan's daughter. 'Hello, Kathy, I know you from somewhere but I'm not sure where.'

'I felt the same, but then I remembered. A year or so ago we both took an evening class in pencil sketching. I'm not sure we even spoke to each other because we were all concentrating so hard trying to make a good likeness. Do you remember when the teacher brought in that great big brass tuba? I got really lost trying to get all the pipes in the right place.' Isabelle grinned and said her problem had been making the tuba look as if it was shiny.

Kathy had Isabelle's attention and Morgan left her to speak to Xen. 'Can we go outside?'

In the front entrance of the hotel Morgan spoke. 'I interviewed you for a job, five years or so ago and then you had to be given a new identity and should have taken a job in Dubai. I was not too ill to see there were two Rubies and I had to admire your effort to keep her away from me, even staying out in that thunderstorm all that time. I was laughing to myself because I knew much more about you than you thought.'

Xen shifted from one foot to the other wondering what was coming next.

'You are currently repeating a few months because, for some reason, you went back in time to save Isabelle. What I'd like to know is where you've been for five years and why you've emerged, brazenly using your original name? Could be risky.'

Xen felt shocked and for a moment he said nothing. Then he looked at Morgan and said, 'I'd like to know how you think I could be travelling through time.'

'Touché,' said Morgan. 'You see you're not the only person who can do it. I can travel back in time too. I have a special place that's my secret portal. How do you think I had such a meteoric rise through the ranks? I just replayed events until I got the result I wanted.'

'I knew there was something different about you, but I would never have guessed you were a time lord.'

'Oh, I'm no Doctor Who! I'm mortal. I'm growing old and seldom feel the need to change something now.'

'If you're so powerful why didn't you sort out the Chinese satellites?'

Morgan shrugged. 'I didn't know the satellites were going to destroy towns anymore that you did.'

215

'Yes, well I did know. It was while I was working for you that I went forwards in time and rescued you all from the rubble.'

'Forwards? How did you do that?'

Before Xen could answer Ruby came up to them and said, 'Mummy says, are you coming in, because your coffee's getting cold?'

'Tell her I'm coming in very soon.' Xen waited until she'd gone and faced Morgan. 'We obviously have a lot to discuss. Could we meet tomorrow or Monday?'

Morgan nodded, 'Ten o'clock Monday morning,' and handed Xen a card. Xen pocketed it and they both went back to join the party.

A slightly misty morning had turned into a glorious sunny afternoon and Ruby was itching to go to the park. Finally, Joanna took pity on her and announced what they were going to do, if anyone wanted to join them. It seemed only Roger and Sonia wanted to go with them to the park, so they parted from the rest with hugs and agreements to meet up again in a few weeks.

When they reached the swings, Ruby demanded Roger should push her, and he happily obliged.

Sonia, Joanna and Xen sat on the grass.

'So, what did Morgan want? You were outside for ages,' said Joanna.

'I'd like to know that too,' said Sonia. 'He has a weird aura, like you. I don't know why I didn't pick up on it before. Perhaps it was because you were actually travelling in time so yours was really bright,' said Sonia.

'That's what we were talking about. He travels back in time through a portal somewhere. It's a place, not an object like the timer.'

'Wow, there's two of you. You're not so odd after all Xen.'

Sonia laughed at Joanna's words, but stopped when she saw Xen's worried frown.

'He can only go *back* in time so he's done it many times to promote his career, and, as he's a military man, I wonder if he may have been responsible for many deaths. I'm not comfortable with him, even wonder if he's evil. He wants me to meet him on Monday to have further discussions, and I don't know whether to go or not.'

'If he's got great powers then you may not be able to escape him for long,' said Sonia. 'I didn't think that he was wicked or cruel, and aura's do give you a feel for the person. You should keep the appointment.'

'He was kind to me, sorted out my broken arm and even gave me his old solafone, last time. I don't think he's evil at all,' said Joanna.

'So, you both think I should go?'

'Yes,' they chorused and laughed. Xen felt better, having the decision made for him, and the rest of the afternoon passed happily lazing in the sun.

*

Monday morning was chaotic as everyone wanted to go to the bathroom at the same time and all of them were anxious about the day ahead. Xen breathed a sigh of relief when Joanna and Ruby had left the house. He still had time to clear the breakfast debris before meeting Morgan.

When everything was tidy, he looked at the card Morgan had given him. The address was the one he'd been to before, the new headquarters of the intelligence section of the Secret Service.

The coffee and doughnuts were ready when he arrived, and Xen had such a feeling of déjà vu he could hardly believe he wasn't being interviewed for a job.

Morgan sat back in his chair, one leg crossed over the other, savouring his doughnut. Xen, determined not to be the first to speak, did the same. It was an impasse, so Morgan wiped the sugar off his hand with a napkin and began. 'There's still the issue of China's satellites to be resolved. I believe America is responsible. It makes political sense.

China is massive and has the ability to outstrip America with trade deals across the world. The President sees the threat and it's an excellent way to discredit China.'

'If that's true, have you found out how they're doing it?'

'Well, we're certain they command the onboard computer to abort the mission but we're having trouble proving it's coming from an American source. Once proved our government can expose America's dirty dealing.'

'That could upset our 'special' relationship with America.'

'Perhaps our government will be more subtle. I don't know, I'm not a politician.'

'I could offer to help but I'm not sure I have the skills, five years on.'

'What do you think about going back in time to when you first joined us, armed with the knowledge we have now? We could stop the first satellites falling.'

'Why talk to me about this? You could do it anyway.'

Morgan stood up and began to pace about, 'Getting stiff,' he said. 'If I did that you would have the ability to go forwards in time and could jeopardise my mission. I need you on my side to prevent the destruction of Harrogate and all the other towns.'

'I could get death threats again. Why should I help you? I need to think about it.'

Xen left the building and walked, then jogged in the direction of home. He wanted to talk to Joanna, but she was at work. Morgan's idea would put him right back in his flat, with the sand timer and he would not have met Joanna or any of the people he now considered as friends. Would any of them remember him? Ruby would be just under a year old. She had suffered enough not having her scooter and knowing she was five, not six. This was not fair. But if they succeeded, they would save many thousands of lives.

By the time Xen arrived at the flat he knew he would have to do it. He also knew Joanna would try to stop him. He sat in the living room on the settee, eating lunch but barely recalled doing it. He used his solafone and spoke to Morgan. 'I know it's the right thing to do, but can it wait until tomorrow?'

'It would have to be tomorrow anyway because my portal is not that close. I also need to download material from our current status so you can access it and continue from there. When you get to the office, after all the introductory stuff with Michelle, open the drawer in the desk and I will have left a memory stick there. I could probably be prosecuted for taking state secrets, but I don't know how else to do it. Once you've copied the material, please destroy the memory stick.' He breathed deeply as if the long speech had tired him, and then continued. 'The journey will take me about two hours and I'm slow to start in the mornings. I will send us all back to 2030, 11am tomorrow. Bye.'

*

When Joanna and Ruby arrived home, full of the enjoyment of their first day, Xen had cooked a meal and was ready for them. He had not anticipated how happy they would be.

'The others were really impressed by how quickly I understood the job and I wanted to laugh, knowing I'd done it before,' said Joanna.

'The helpers at the crèche showed me where the toilets were and introduced all the others to me and I felt the same,' said Ruby.

'So, going back and repeating a few months didn't feel as bad as you expected?' asked Xen.

They nodded and Ruby chattered about her friend Lisa and the fun they'd had. They ate their meal and Ruby was ready for bed not long after. Xen read her a story and kissed her goodnight, feeling sad to think he was going to lose her company. He had no idea how to treat a one-year-old Ruby.

When they were sitting in the living room with a cup of tea Joanna said, 'You'd better tell me about your meeting with Morgan. I've a feeling it's not good news.'

'He's going to take us back in time to 2030, when I first worked for him and was living in London. I've been thinking about it, and you and little Ruby must come and live in my flat there. I've promised him not to go back to my flat in Harrogate or to collect the timer. We've no choice, Joanna, please don't look like that.'

He moved close to her to hold her in his arms, but she shook him off. Her face was white, and her eyes shone with tears. 'We were so happy today, Ruby and I. How can we tell her we're going back to when she was one? It's too cruel.'

'We don't tell her. You both get up and go to work as usual tomorrow. Ruby will feel odd when it happens, but she won't remember any of this. If we don't mention time travel, she'll never know about it, so we will have no secret to keep. Apart from our feelings, it's almost certain we can prevent the satellite destruction of Harrogate and other cities. We can save all those people dying. I had to agree to it. I'm sorry.'

Joanna sat down again as she thought about it. 'I can see the reasoning and I know it's right but….'

'That's how I felt when Morgan proposed the idea to me.'

This time she allowed him to cuddle her and he felt her relaxing against his body. When she pulled away, they went to bed, but couldn't sleep.

'You will promise to collect us and take us to London. I hated living with no money in that tiny flat in Harrogate. I was so angry at having to cope on my own with a baby. Promise, Xen, please.'

'I promise. I love you both. I don't want to live without you. Now let's try to sleep.

Chapter 35

Before they parted that morning, Joanna gave Xen a long, passionate kiss and whispered, 'Remember your promise.'

Xen smiled and nodded, and then pulled Ruby into a hug and said, 'I'm going to miss you.'

She just grinned and said, 'See you tonight and I hope it's sausages for tea.'

He was still smiling when the front door closed, and he was alone. The smile faded as he sat in the kitchen wondering what, if anything, he should take with him into the past. The solafone on his wrist, but was there anything else?

There didn't seem to be anything, unless he took a sweater, but then he remembered he always packed to go to London so there should be clothes in his flat there.

What was he going to do until eleven o'clock? It seemed wrong to just sit and wait, but it seemed pointless to do much else. Eventually he tidied the kitchen of breakfast things and washed the dishes instead of putting them in the dishwasher. Then he took his wallet and set out to walk into the city centre. The plan was to be somewhere with a lovely frothy coffee in front of him when he travelled into the past. It was a better idea than just sitting around feeling increasingly anxious.

*

The plan worked and he'd almost finished his cappuccino when it happened. He suddenly felt disorientated as the room revolved and he was surrounded by a deafening rushing wind.

He closed his eyes, feeling nauseous from the spinning, and opened them only when the movement changed to a steady rocking with the sound of train wheels click clacking along at a fast rate. He opened his eyes cautiously, not moving anything else in case he felt sick. When he felt normal, he allowed himself to sit up and take note of his surroundings.

A glance at his solafone showed him it was late morning of the 31st of July 2030. The train began to slow down as he was arriving at King's Cross. He would begin his new job tomorrow, all over again.

He looked for his suitcase and saw it near the entrance to the carriage, along with several others. He collected it on his way out and stood on the platform allowing the crowds to flow around him as he thought about his new situation. Eventually, when it was quieter, he trundled his case to the exit and queued for a taxi to take him to his flat. The key was in his pocket and he noticed he was wearing different clothes to when he dressed that morning.

At the flat, he checked the fridge and found it was totally empty. Feeling desperate for a cup of tea, he went straight out to the nearest shop and bought sufficient to give him a meal that evening, as well as several breakfasts.

When the tea was ready, he sat down to text Joanna, but then he realised she had no solafone. Morgan hadn't given her his, this time around, and he had no way, now, of reassuring her of his good intentions. He felt very anxious and phoned Catherine, hoping she would remember him. She answered right away, and he said, 'Hi Catherine, this is Xen.'

'For goodness sake, Xen, what's just happened? We seem to have gone back to 2030!'

'I know, and I promised Joanna I would bring her to London to stay with me, but I can't phone her because in 2030 she had no phone of any kind. I have to go to work tomorrow and want her to pack everything and I will come back to Harrogate and collect her on the weekend. Can you go around and tell her?'

'Where does she live?' Xen gave her the address. 'OK, I've got that. I'll go right now; she's probably distraught. Bye.'

Xen felt happier after the conversation with Catherine and decided to buy Joanna a phone as soon as possible. It was appalling not to be able to communicate in 2030.

*

Joanna felt queasy and shut her eyes. When she opened them Ruby was crying, that baby cry she'd forgotten. 'I'm coming Ruby, Mummy's coming. Her eyes brimmed with tears too as she took in the flat with its shabby furniture. Had she had an amazing dream? Did Xen, Isabelle, Andy, Sonia, Roger and Morgan actually exist? She picked up Ruby and held her close, then noticed the time. Ruby would want food soon. She'd better look in the cupboards and fridge. Had she been away for months? If so, everything perishable would have gone mouldy.

The fridge revealed everything was fine. There was food for Ruby and she relaxed a little. When she did Ruby stopped crying and settled in her arms, finally going to sleep. Joanna put her in her cot and made herself a cup of tea.

She sat down with it and misery flooded over her. She'd been so happy, even when they had to start again in 2035 and she knew she was not pregnant anymore. Having a job had revived her self-respect. Being loved by Xen had made her feel attractive; had given her warmth and security. Now she was back in 2030, alone, coping, in this dingy flat that smelled of damp.

Tears welled again and she brushed them angrily away. There was nothing she could do. Where did Catherine and Jason live? Would they even know who she was if she could contact them? Her head thumped so she took the rest of her tea to the kitchen area and found some paracetamol.

She was just about to get food out for Ruby's lunch when the front doorbell rang. She unhooked the chain and opened it. There stood Catherine, smiling.

Joanna stepped towards her and they hugged on the threshold. 'I thought I'd dreamed it all and was devastated to be here. I've no solafone or anything. I felt so bleak. Sorry, please come into my hovel.' She managed to let go of Catherine and stepped inside, Catherine following.

'Oh my God, Joanna. You said it was awful and it really is. We must get you out of here as quick as possible. Xen was beside himself when he realised he couldn't contact you, and asked me to come round.'

'I'm so pleased you did. What are you doing?'

'I'm ringing Sonia. I always do in a crisis, and this is a crisis.'

Joanna heard her describing the appalling conditions Joanna and Ruby were living in, to Sonia. She finished the conversation and looked at Joanna, smiling.

Sonia says we must start packing everything you need to take with you and she's coming to take you to her hotel for the night. Come on, have you got a suitcase?' She noticed Joanna's face redden, about to cry again. 'No tears, we have work to do.'

*

Xen unpacked his clothes and cooked his evening meal, but he was going through the motions. He felt disorientated and angry. This situation was all wrong. He and Ruby had saved Isabelle and that should have been the end of it. What right had Morgan to spoil everything? Then he felt guilty for selfish thoughts and remembered all those who had died.

He started to get ready for bed and his solafone pinged. It was a text from Sonia.

Catherine went to see Joanna. She was so shocked at the conditions she's living in she phoned me. When I arrived,

*we packed everything in the taxi, and I found her a room in
my hotel. I intend to drive Joanna and baby Ruby to London
tomorrow. I know we cannot enter the city, but I'll get as
close as I can, park and get a taxi. Need your address. S*

Xen wrote back thanking her and giving her his address.
Then he added,

*Text me when you're in the taxi and I'll leave work and
be home to meet you. Thanks again, X*

They would be here tomorrow. He found he was smiling
at the thought, but then he worried about where Ruby would
sleep. Should he buy a cot? Sleep would only come once
he'd convinced himself to leave those problems to Joanna.

*

The next morning Xen's excitement about Joanna
completely eclipsed any nerves he had about starting his
job. He strode to the office with a confidence he didn't
possess the last time. There was nothing like adapting to
different times and places to help a man find his inner
strength, he thought.

Xen was introduced to Michelle and he had to remind
himself she could not remember him from before. It was
important to be quiet, listen to all the explanations and ask
where the toilet was when Michelle forgot to tell him. It
was difficult not to fidget with irritation at the careful
explanation of how everything worked, including how to
log on to his workstation. It was with considerable relief he
faced the computer, alone at last. He opened the drawer and
downloaded the memory stick to his computer, removed it
and put it into his pocket.

By lunchtime Xen, having examined all the new data,
felt he was making progress. He'd already seen the
engineering plans of the satellite and where the computer

was situated. He decided to think like a man who wanted to command the satellite to abort the mission.

The Chinese used Ada (2028) a universal computer language in the aeronautical industry, and eventually Xen found the command he was looking for. All he had to do was find a way to activate it, but that would be dangerous. A better plan would be to find a way to protect it, block a command from an unknown source.

After lunch Mei Ling arrived and she helped him translate Fire Dragon. He went through the same routine as before, feeling irritated. He was impatient to get on but realised he would have to take it steady. It would be completely crass to start some of the new things he wanted to work on before anyone knew China was going to send up a space cleaning satellite.

Xen was grateful when he got a message from Sonia. 'Sorry Mei Ling I have to go early because my girlfriend's coming to stay.' He stood up, collected his things and said goodbye, then went to see Michelle. He almost ran out of the building, desperate to get to the flat before Joanna did. He couldn't bear the idea of her standing, forlornly outside with baby, pushchair and cases.

He arrived just in time. Joanna leapt out of the taxi, hardly letting it come to a halt, and threw herself into his arms. 'I felt so desperate, so scared you wouldn't remember me.'

'I love you and Ruby. I was scared too, when I realised I couldn't phone you.' He kissed her, then turned to welcome Sonia, who was looking tired after her long drive. He hugged her, 'Thank you so much for bringing them, Sonia. They would have had to wait until the weekend if it hadn't been for you. You're a star and you deserve a cup of tea. Let's go in.'

Xen used the keypad to open the main door to the building and then his key to open his own front door. The two women went in and he began to empty the car. As he did so he heard a whimper, it was a tiny Ruby waking from a deep sleep.

'Hello Ruby, you're such a beautiful baby. Will you be happy for me to get you out of your seat?'

He fiddled with the harness and eventually undid it and lifted her out as if she was made of glass. He carried her, murmuring reassuringly, at least he hoped it was, into the flat and handed her to Joanna. 'We've just had a very one-sided conversation in which I introduced myself to her as Dad,' he said. 'I'll get the cases and boxes in now. Have you found the hot tap to make tea?'

'Yes, it'll be ready in a minute.' Xen went back to the taxi and when it was empty, told it to go. It glided away obediently. He found them in the kitchen. 'That's everything in but I've no idea where it's all going to go.'

'Don't worry I'll sort it when we've had our cup of tea. It's a lovely flat but only one bedroom so we'll be a bit on top of each other. It's so nice compared to what I've left.

'While you're unpacking, I'll go to the shop,' said Xen. He looked at Sonia. 'What are you doing tonight? I can offer you to share the bed with Joanna and I'll take the couch.'

'No, I've no intention of spoiling your first night together in 2030. I parked my car at Willesden, so I'll get a taxi, collect it and drive some of the way then I'll put up somewhere and do the rest tomorrow.' She hesitated and then said, 'Have you still got the sand timer? I can't feel it.'

'Yes and no, it's almost certainly in my flat in Harrogate, but I have agreed with Morgan not to go back to that flat or do any time travel while we work to prevent the Chinese satellites falling from space.'

Sonia nodded, finished her tea and stood up. 'Will you order me a taxi now and I'll use your bathroom then be on my way.' Xen did so and in five minutes Sonia had gone.

Ruby began to fidget and whimper. Xen frowned, 'What's wrong with her?'

'Well she could need a clean nappy, she might be hungry, thirsty or both. Babies can't tell you much, so it's trial and error. I'll put her on the floor, and she might kick and roll about a bit while I unpack her stuff. She has far more than me.' Joanna stood up and put Ruby gently on to the floor.

Xen stood too. 'Anything I can do before going to the shop? I feel a bit helpless with a child so young.'

'You and me both, but I've been practising for nearly two years, not forgetting the other five, so I'm getting better,' said Joanna, laughing. She picked up two cases and went into the bedroom.

Xen could hear her opening drawers and moving about. He looked down at Ruby with a slight feeling of shock. Ruby looked back at him and smiled. His heart gave a lurch and he smiled back, knelt down and played 'round and round the garden' on her tiny hand and tickled her under the arm. He was delighted when she squirmed and chuckled, and he began to feel less tense. There was an unpleasant aroma wafting up towards his nose, and he called out to Joanna. 'I think she's filled her nappy.'

'OK I've unpacked that stuff, so I'll give you a lesson.' She came in, grinning, with a bag containing disposable nappies, wipes and cream.

Ruby was wearing a summer dress, so Joanna lifted the back of it away and showed Xen how to undo the nappy. He recoiled at the mess and smell.

'It's no good backing away, Xen. A baby is totally reliant on us cleaning her bottom and putting cream on if she's sore. She can't do it herself, and until she's walking confidently, she can't be taught how to use a potty.'

'Ok, I'm listening and taking notes.' Joanna finished the nappy change and sat Ruby up with some cushions around her. Then she took the rubbish into the kitchen and put it in the waste disposal chute so that it would be instantly incinerated. 'It's your turn next. Every modern dad changes nappies. You just have to hope it's not as messy as that one.'

'Your mummy says I'm to change your nappy next time Ruby. What do you think of that?' Her reply was a series of nonsensical noises. He smiled and said something else, and she replied in the same manner. They were communicating, in a way, and he was enjoying himself.

'I thought you were going shopping while I unpacked. I've nearly finished.'

Xen stood up and went into the bedroom. She'd transformed it with a travel cot next to the chest of drawers and there were piles of baby clothes on the bed waiting for a home.

'We'd better make a list. What does Ruby eat? I've no idea.'

'Ok I'll finish this later and we'll make a list. She'll need to eat soon, so you'd better hurry. Make a list on your solafone as I think of things.' She began with essentials for Ruby and then added a bottle of red wine and something for dinner that evening. 'Oh, and anything else you think I might have forgotten but don't linger or Ruby will be screaming.' He collected a couple of bags and went out.

While he was out Joanna finished the unpacking, having found a place for everything then sat down in the living room with Ruby. She felt disorientated and exhausted. Xen's flat was lovely compared to the one she'd left but she had no knowledge of the area and very little money left on her wrist band. A feeling of misery was beginning to creep over her, so she went into the kitchen and put the kettle on again.

There was room to put a highchair, but she didn't have one. It was an essential now but too bulky to bring with her. She decided to ask Xen to order her one and hoped it would come quickly.

Xen arrived back as the kettle reached boiling point and Ruby began to cry. Joanna picked her up and she cried less, but then began working herself up to a full-blown bawl.

'Here, you hold her, and I'll get her food ready.' Joanna thrust the wriggling, irritable girl into his arms and he jiggled her up and down and began to sing, 'Here we go round the mulberry bush.' Joanna joined in as she was putting the final touches to the dinner and then motioned Xen to sit while she put a bib around Ruby's neck. He was fascinated to see Ruby behaving like a baby bird, opening her mouth as the spoon approached.

'When can she do this herself and eat proper food?'

'She can use a spoon, but you wouldn't want to be holding her when she does. The food goes everywhere while she tries to find her mouth. She can feed herself with little pieces of banana, that's less messy because she uses her fingers, and that's what she'll have for pudding. It would make feeding time much easier if we had a highchair. Would you order one for me?'

'Yes, I'll do it as soon as I can put Ruby down. I can see how hard it will be to do it on your own.'

Later that evening she asked Xen about his first day at work and he explained the difficulty he had of behaving as if he knew nothing and how frustrated he'd felt going through the early stages.

When he was undressing for bed Xen felt the memory stick in his trouser pocket. He took it out, went into the kitchen and threw it down the disposal chute. Now Morgan's secret was safe.

Chapter 36

The week seemed to rush by for Xen. When he stopped to think about it, he realised how much happier he was this time. He was not trying to court Joanna by visiting her every weekend. He was not confused or anxious about travelling forwards in time. It was 2030, and only a few months ago he had been working in the university, but his recent experiences had changed him. He felt so confident, and acutely aware of his responsibility for Joanna and Ruby.

Joanna spent the week getting to know the area she now lived in. She took Ruby in the pushchair up to the main street, went shopping for fresh food and explored. She found a park fifteen minutes' walk away. Ruby loved the baby swing and Joanna chatted with other mums. The devastation she'd felt at having to relive this period of time faded. She was no longer alone, trying to cope. This time she had Xen to rely on and she loved him. As she pushed the swing and Ruby chuckled Joanna wondered, again, if they could get married.

*

On the weekend Xen received a text from Sonia and read it aloud to Joanna.

'How's it going? Been chatting to Catherine and Isabelle and they'd like to meet up again, with you and Joanna. Would it be possible for you to travel to Leeds? Or what about us all meeting you halfway somewhere? That would mean staying in a hotel. Isabelle would like to tell Andy about time travel and could do with our support. Think about it and let us know.

S.'

'I'd really like to do that but it's a bit of an upheaval taking Ruby,' said Joanna.

'Yes, I'd like to see them all and ask how they're getting on going back five years. The only thing is, I did promise not to go back to my flat or use the timer.'

'Perhaps we could go back to the flat and just not touch the timer. Morgan would never know. The timer might not even be there, because we did save Isabelle.'

'I could certainly do with more clothes,' said Xen. 'We could be careful to avoid the timer and Ruby is only just walking so she wouldn't think to play with it like last time. Shall we go next weekend?'

Joanna agreed and Xen wrote back to Sonia asking where they could meet in Harrogate. Her reply came back quickly.

That's wonderful. I'll arrange it with the others and my choice of venue, (I'll foot the bill), is Betty's at Harlow Carr Gardens. What about meeting there at 12, before the rush? We can have a drink first and then lunch.
S.

'That sounds great,' said Xen smiling, but his smile was soon removed as Joanna said, 'I can't go to Betty's, I've nothing smart to wear and Ruby's bound to play up and scream the place down. I'll be evicted.'

'Trousers and a T-shirt will be fine,' said Xen. Joanna still looked uncertain and he hugged her to him. 'They want our money so they must accept us as we are.' He kissed the top of her head and added, 'I think you'd look elegant in a sack. Just walk with your head up high and be proud of how you look and how beautiful your daughter is. Don't forget, if Ruby does get irritable it isn't all down to you. I can take her out for a stroll in the woods nearby.' He felt her relax in his arms.

'Perhaps I could buy some smarter trousers this week before we go.'

'That's possible because you have the time, but we need to sort you out some money.'

'Let's go shopping, stock up on food, then we'll open a joint account and you'll have a card to buy things with. I suppose, as we're living together, you should inform Social Services.'

Joanna nodded and said she would contact the local office and talk to them about it.

*

Joanna was the proud owner of a debit card and Xen could see how it transformed her. When he got home from work there was a pair of smart trousers and a new blouse lying on the bed for him to admire, and Joanna was no longer wearing her hateful 'badge of shame'. Joanna's eyes sparkled and she happily put on her new clothes and did a twirl for him.

'You look lovely. It's perfect for lunch at Betty's.' He looked at her quizzically. Has something else happened?' She smiled and almost purred with happiness.

'I was chatting in the park and said I was looking for a nursery for Ruby and I was given the address of one called Tiny Tots and it's really close. I called in and while I chatted, I put Ruby on the floor. She went straight for the bright coloured toys and didn't look for me once. Marion, the lady in charge, said I should go away and come back in an hour and see how she reacts. When I came back, Marion had changed her nappy after giving her a drink of milk with the other children. Ruby was pleased to see me but hadn't cried once.'

'That's great, so are you signing up or whatever you do?'

'Yes, but just for two half days a week for now, and she suggested I built up the time as Ruby grows used to the routine. If she likes it, I might be able to get a part time job.'

Xen hugged her and stroked her hair, but any thoughts of a cuddle were blighted, as she pulled away saying Ruby needed her tea.

*

Later, when Ruby was asleep, Joanna asked if his job was going well. He nodded and said, 'I'd really like you to meet my friend Sean. We both worked at Leeds Uni and it was Sean who suggested I change jobs. He's now working in my department and has a Chinese girl friend called Ho Chin. Perhaps they could come around for drinks one night when Ruby's asleep? What do you think?'

'I'd like that. I remember you talking about him before but I lived in the future then so we couldn't meet. Let's do it on a Friday so no one has to go to work the next day, but not this weekend as we're going north.'

'I'm going to see if I can have this Friday as a day's holiday, then we'll have all day to get to Harrogate and not have to rush.'

*

Friday

Xen opened the door to his flat, put down his case and saw straight away the sand timer had gone.

He stood still and Joanna bumped his back with a holdall, 'Come on, let us in.'

'It's gone, Joanna, the timer's not here.'

'Well that's good isn't it?' she said, struggling to pull the pushchair over the threshold.

Xen went into the bedroom with the cases then came back to help her. 'I'm not sure if it's good or not. It probably means the task of saving Isabelle is done.'

'You know it is. I don't see the problem. Anyway, we can talk about it another time. Now we must unpack and feed Ruby. Is the kitchen through here?'

Xen nodded and picked up the bag of groceries they'd bought. He looked in the cupboards and found them well stocked with the basics. Then he went to the fridge, opened it and started back in disgust. 'Phew, what a stink!'

'Woah,' said Joanna, laughing. It was your fridge, so I think cleaning it is down to you.' Xen grinned, ruefully and began to look for the source of the smell. He picked out an open Camembert cheese and laughed. 'Everything's fine. It's just this,' he said holding up the cheese.

'Well if the smell still lingers after you've incinerated it, you'll have to wipe out the fridge.'

While he was doing that Joanna explored the rest of the flat then organised a bed for Ruby and unpacked their clothes. Ruby tottered around her, holding on to the open drawer and taking things out when Joanna put them in. 'You are being mummy's little helper, or should I say hindrance,' she said, smiling.

Ruby smiled back and said, 'Mummy.' For a moment Joanna wished Ruby was six again and they could hold a proper conversation. Then she felt guilty and told herself few people ever got the chance to have another go at parenting a small child. This Ruby would know Xen as her daddy and know nothing about time travel.

*

It was early evening when they decided to go for a walk before putting Ruby to bed. They headed for Valley Gardens, following the route they had taken when Harrogate was destroyed.

'It's lovely seeing everything as normal. I still have nightmares at being underground and then seeing all this area just a pile of rubble,' said Joanna.

They reached the wine bar where they'd sheltered after moving the dead bodies and she said, 'Morgan was very kind and gentle when he set my wrist. What's he like at work?'

'I don't really see much of him because he's the boss. I mostly deal with Michelle, who's very nice.' Xen pushed the pushchair up the slope into the gardens. The town noise diminished and the peace of the garden in the evening sunshine, was delightful. Joanna took Ruby out of the pushchair and they walked very slowly each holding one of her hands.

'This is such a beautiful place,' she said, 'peaceful even though there are other families, like us here. Aren't the flowerbeds lovely?' She watched a little girl riding her scooter and remembered Ruby's face when she got a scooter for her sixth birthday. 'I miss six-year-old Ruby, don't you?'

'Yes, but she'll grow to be six again and I'm really enjoying being part of her toddler stage. This must be easier for you than last time, no money problems for a start.'

'Yes, but the lack of money wasn't the worse thing. It was feeling so alone. I'm not alone, or lonely, now and I love being a proper family. This walk will tire Ruby out and she'll sleep well, but I think it's time we went back so she can sleep in her new bed and not in the pushchair.'

*

The following day was slow to start because Ruby woke up later than usual. Xen and Joanna enjoyed an hour's extra sleep. By the time breakfast was over and they were all dressed it was time to go out to lunch. Xen called a taxi and they waited a short while for it, standing outside with dark clouds looming overhead. 'I hope it comes soon or we're going to get wet,' said Joanna.

They settled into the taxi and before Xen had keyed in the address raindrops were spattering the windscreen. The taxi moved almost silently into the traffic. The journey took just ten minutes and when they pulled up outside the entrance it was raining hard. Joanna picked up Ruby and ran inside, leaving Xen to bring the push chair and changing bag. He was wet but laughing when he got inside. 'I don't know why I imagined today to be sunny and perfect. It must be because most times we've met with the others it has been. I wonder if they're here.'

Isabelle, Andy, Sonia and Roger were there with Jason and Catherine. It was almost a complete reunion, apart from Morgan. There was a flurry of welcoming hugs and kisses. Everyone chatted about the weather and then they admired Ruby, who was looking so gorgeous in her little dungarees and T-shirt. There was great care taken not to talk about time travel, at least to start with.

The menu was perused, the food ordered, and the waitress brought water to the table. Then Isabelle began. 'Andy is feeling completely out of his depth because we all know each other, and he doesn't understand how.'

'He's not the only one,' said Roger. 'Sonia's been talking about you all as if she's known you for years. Granted we know Jason, Catherine and family, but Xen, Joanna, and baby what's her name…'

'Ruby,' said Joanna, 'and when we met Isabelle and Andy, Ruby was nearly six years old.'

That statement was met first by silence, and then a snort from Roger. 'Sorry I think I misheard you. Six months was it?'

'No, six years,' said Xen. 'This is going to be hard to grasp, but we have all been time travelling.'

'Total twaddle,' said Roger.

'You say that, Roger,' said Andy, 'but I've been having really weird flashes of what seem like memories. And then there's the nightmare; I dream over and over that Isabelle is dead, her head covered in blood and she's laying on a heap of rubble. I wake up sweating and can't understand why my mind fixes on something so appalling.' He looked at Xen. 'I've actually been through some awful experience like that, have I?'

Isabelle held his hand and said, 'Five years into the future there will be a cataclysmic destruction of Harrogate. We were there and Xen rescued us. Unfortunately, you and

I went walking and there was a storm and we sheltered under that rubble that you've dreamt about. In the night I needed to pee, so I went around the edge of the rubble but coming back I slipped and cracked my head. By the time you woke up I was dead. The whole story is complicated, but we have all gone back in time now five years. Now we must avoid Harrogate in the summer of 2035.'

Roger had listened carefully and seemed less sceptical when he said, 'I seem to remember pushing a little girl on a swing. I've never had children and I really enjoyed being with her. Was that Ruby? Did I really do it?'

Now it was Sonia's turn to explain. 'Yes, we all met up, after that awful event, in Leeds. We had a meal together, just like this, and you did push Ruby on a swing.' Roger breathed in to ask something else but left it unsaid because their meals arrived.

Chapter 37

Morgan sat before the consultant feeling anxious. 'I'm afraid it's not good news. The cancer has spread remarkably quickly in just a few months. There's no treatment now that will stop it.'

Morgan sucked in a deep breath. He was not surprised but it was still a shock. 'So how long have I got?'

'Two, maybe three months; I'm really sorry we can't help you. We'll put in place a care package for you when you feel you need it. Do you have relatives who can help?'

'Yes, my daughter, but first I've got to tell her. I'm not looking forward to doing that.'

Morgan asked a few more questions and was given a leaflet to explain palliative care packages then stood up and shook the consultant's hand, before leaving the room.

As he walked down the corridor, he wished he could have explained to the consultant that the cancer had spread slowly, giving him an extra five years, not just a few months. He should have had something done about it before, but he was busy and had thrust the whole thing to the back of his mind, in denial. Then, after his latest travel back in time, he had realised how tired he was and how haggard he looked in the mirror.

Now it was too late. He didn't dwell on the consultant's prognosis, knowing he could do nothing to change the outcome, but he needed to put his affairs in order. First, when he got home, he must re-read his will and check the small print. He would need to go and see Kathy to break the news, as gently as he could. Then there was the secret of the portal. Should he let it die with him or should he pass it on to someone responsible? Who would he tell? Kathy would think he was crazy, and she had enough to worry about with his imminent death. Her husband was a lovely, kind man, but unimaginative.

Xen, it had to be him. Morgan got home, made a coffee with a whiskey on the side and sent a text.

I need to see you, something personal, not work related. When can we meet (not at work),
Morgan

Xen read it when he went to the toilet at Betty's and was very curious. He wrote back:

I'm in Harrogate, reunion lunch with Isabelle and family.
Can I see you on Monday after work? We could go for a drink.
Xen

Morgan's reply came before he reached the dining table and he read it quickly before joining the others.

I'm coming to Harrogate. Can you meet me tomorrow morning before you set off for London? Or late tonight, say 9pm?
Morgan

Xen arranged to meet him that evening, and Morgan sank back into his chair sighing with relief. Then he organised his journey.

*

Morgan stepped off the train at 8pm, having had nothing to eat, and he was feeling lightheaded. He used a taxi to take him to a pub close to Xen's flat and ordered meat pie and chips. It wasn't a healthy option but that no longer seemed to matter. He'd just finished and was wiping his mouth after a swig of beer when Xen arrived. He stood up, a little unsteadily, and they shook hands.

'Would you like another?' asked Xen. Morgan shook his head and Xen ordered himself one using the table's tablet. 'You don't look well Morgan. What was so important you had to rush up here? I could've seen you on Monday.'

Morgan took a deep breath but said nothing as Xen's drink was arriving. When Xen had taken a sip and set the glass back on the table, he looked at Morgan, eyebrows raised, and waited for him to speak.

'I found out from my oncologist this morning that I have only two or three months left to live.' He saw Xen about to speak and held up a hand. 'Don't say anything, please, just listen. I don't want the secret of my time travel portal to die with me. I want to tell you where it is and how to make it work. You see it's in Brimham Rocks, so I had to travel here to show you. Can we meet early tomorrow and get there before your train? The other possibility is for you to postpone your train until Monday and then there'd be no rush. I can obviously explain your extra day to Michelle, so there's no problem there.'

'I'm really sorry about your cancer and the prognosis, Morgan. I can see why you want to show me the portal but I'm not sure I'll ever want to use it.' He picked up his glass and had a drink to give him time to think. 'My train's booked for 11am and to get to Brimham Rocks before that would be a push, so I think the travel home on Monday idea would be better. Joanna and Ruby are with me and she's enjoying being in Harrogate again. So, let's have a civilised trip to Brimham, say meet at the car park at eleven?'

Morgan nodded, finished his drink and stood up. 'I must go, Xen, I'm exhausted. I'll see you tomorrow. Give my love to Joanna.'

Xen stood when Morgan did and watched the older man make his slow way to the door. He sat down, heavily, to finish his drink feeling a mixture of emotions. He felt upset

241

by Morgan's news but flattered that Morgan wanted to share his secret. The sand timer had been confusing enough. Did he really want to have this knowledge?

*

Joanna cried when Xen told her about Morgan. She was also uncertain about Xen having the secret of turning back time. 'Why would you want to do it?'

Xen shrugged, 'I don't know, but Morgan's used it several times in his life. I don't have to use the power, but I've agreed to be shown the secret tomorrow, so I must meet him. Do you want to come? You can have a walk while we're having our meeting.'

'No, I think it's better for you to go on your own. I'll be happy walking around the town, shopping and having a coffee.'

*

Sunday was grey and drizzly, but not cold. The family had breakfast together, with Ruby feeding herself and making a mess. Xen enjoyed watching her clumsy efforts, and even offered to change her nappy afterwards and get her dressed. Joanna took the opportunity to have a shower and dress herself. When Ruby was dressed and playing happily, Xen phoned Morgan and offered to collect him. They could go to Brimham Rocks together. Morgan agreed.

It was raining quite hard, when they arrived, so the car park was nearly empty. While Morgan was getting slowly out, Xen looked up at the amazing rock formations and remembered climbing them and squirming through little tunnels as a child. He imagined bringing Ruby, when she was bigger, and found he liked the idea of teaching her how to climb safely. The taxi slid away and he noticed that Morgan was using a walking stick.

Morgan grimaced at the rain. 'I should've brought a brolly, not a stick.' He turned up the collar of his raincoat and set off slowly up the main path. The slight hill made him breathe heavily and he began to wheeze. After a few

242

minutes he gasped, 'I need to stop for a minute, catch my breath.' He grinned ruefully, 'It's good we're doing this today; not sure I'd be capable next week.' They stood silent for a moment and then Morgan set off again saying, 'Come on let's do it.'

They stopped at an unimpressive flat rock right at the edge of the escarpment. The view looking down the valley with green, undulating hills and fields bordered by dry-stone walls was lovely, even in the rain.

'Are we here?' asked Xen. He could see no obvious portal, but then if it was obvious anyone could find it.

'It's actually underneath this rock,' said Morgan. 'You must climb down and then look up at the rock. You'll see two shallow indentations along its edge. Don't do what I tell you next or we'll be transported again. When you need to, put a hand in each indentation, press hard as if trying to lift the rock and say the date you wish to go back to. If you're successful you'll feel the rock vibrate, then it's done.'

Xen climbed down slowly taking extra care because everything was so wet and slippery. He saw where to put his hands but resisted the temptation. When he was safely back with Morgan he said, 'How did you find out about it?'

'The same way as you, someone showed me. It was actually my father. I'd like to have handed it on to my son, but I had a daughter. Kathy's lovely but not ambitious, just contented to be a wife and mother. She would never see a reason to use it.' He turned to move and let Xen help him step off the rock. Then he straightened his back and set off saying, 'Call the taxi now, will you, and we'll have less wait when we get back to the carpark.'

Xen did as he was asked and then caught Morgan up. They walked in silence and Xen's thoughts were muddled. Perhaps he was feeling a sense of anti-climax. There had been no runes or symbols of any kind on the rock; no indication it held any power at all. 'You say it will only go back in time, never forward?'

Morgan nodded. His voice was breathy as he replied. 'I tried it, but it didn't seem to register. If it has that power, there must be another trick that I don't know.'

Xen was pleased when he saw the taxi coming down the lane as they reached the carpark. He was worried about Morgan; whose face was now ashen. He thought it might be wise to get the taxi to take him to hospital. He suggested it, but Morgan shook his head. 'I'm exhausted. I just need to rest. Just take me to my flat and I'll be fine after a rest.'

Later, when he was getting out of the taxi, Morgan said, 'I'll tell Michelle about your extra day and see you on Tuesday at work, I hope.'

*

Joanna and Ruby had returned from their morning outing and boxes and bags were piled in the flat. Joanna was kneeling in the midst of it all changing Ruby's nappy. She looked up at Xen and grinned. 'I think I'm becoming a shopaholic. You'd better give me an allowance, so I don't do what I just did again. I'll show you later what I've bought. Hold Ruby for me a moment and I'll make a cup of tea and then you can tell me about your trip.'

Xen explained what had happened, and then he said, 'I don't think he'll come back to work. I wanted to take him to hospital, but he wouldn't let me. It's been an interesting but sad morning for me. Let's see what you've bought; I need cheering up.'

She fetched a summer dress, two pairs of casual trousers and two tops. Xen dutifully admired them, and she went back into the lounge and came back with a large bag full of clothes for Ruby. 'I bought a couple of dresses for her which cost a lot. Then I found a charity shop that was open

244

and got all of these for less than the price of the dresses. A real bargain.'

'They look perfect to me. Is that everything?'

'Nearly, just two more bags.' She brought them in, placed them beside him and held out her arms for Ruby. She sat Ruby on the floor and gave her a wooden spoon and a saucepan to play with. Then turned to look at Xen with an air of anticipation. 'Open the bags, I bought them for you.'

Xen smiled and pulled out a short sleeved smart shirt and a casual top.

'They're perfect, the right size and everything. Thank you for thinking of me.' He stood up and gave her a kiss. Then he felt it almost impossible to let her go. 'I love Ruby to bits, but she does limit the possibilities for spontaneous sex.'

'Well, I'll see if Ruby will have a drink of milk and then sleep for an hour or so. She had her lunch before you came in and she should be tired enough.' They looked at each other grinning.

The enforced wait was enhancing their desire and at last Joanna was able to put Ruby in her makeshift cot. She gave her a kiss and whispered, 'Go to sleep my lovely girl so Mummy and Daddy can have a cuddle.' She crept out of the bedroom and Xen gathered her up in his arms. 'Who needs a bed, the floor will do,' and they stood, giggling like naughty children, taking their clothes off and then snuggling onto the carpet.

Chapter 38

Two weeks later

They were having breakfast together before Xen went to work and Joanna took Ruby for her first full morning at Tiny Tots. 'You know I missed Harrogate when we first came here and I really enjoyed being there again,' said Joanna between mouthfuls of toast. Perhaps we'll go back there again in 2035 when you go to work in Leeds.'

'I don't know if that'll happen. Morgan is not going to be around by then and, if you remember, I ran away from a death threat. That hasn't happened yet, and it might not. Going back in time doesn't mean repeating exactly what happened before. Anyway, I must go. I hope Ruby enjoys Tiny Tots, see you later.'

Xen left the flat and jogged part of the way to work, then stopped because it was too soon after breakfast and running was giving him indigestion.

When he'd gone through security Michelle was waiting for him. 'Morning Xen, can you come to my office for a moment?' Xen nodded and followed her, wondering if he'd done something wrong.

'Take the easy chair, would you like a coffee?'

'Yes, thank you, milk no sugar.'

'I know how you take it, Xen.' When the serving of coffee was done, he asked. 'Is there a problem Michelle?'

'Not exactly, just something I want to run by you. When you were in Harrogate a couple of weeks ago, I know you met Morgan and he told you about his cancer. It's progressing very quickly, so I need to tell you he's given in his notice. There will be a vacancy to fill and I'm going to apply for it. If I'm successful there will be a vacancy here. I think you should apply, if it all goes to plan.'

'But compared to Jake I'm a beginner and what about Sean?'

'Jake's an excellent hacker but lacks leadership skills. People like you and Sean, who've been lecturers, would fit better into a managerial role.'

'So, you will be speaking to Sean too, and we'll be rivals for the position?'

Michelle nodded. 'I suspect he'll refuse because he really likes the action of being in the field. I've noticed he gets frustrated when tied to a desk for too long. There are suitable people in other departments too, so the list of applicants is longer than just you and Sean. It's all supposition at this stage anyway, because I may not get Morgan's job. That's all I've got to say at the moment so, if you've finished your coffee, I suggest we get some work done. You'll be interested in Jake's handover report.'

Xen stood up, placed his cup on the tray, and went back to his workstation. Should he apply for Michelle's job? He really had to, what with Joanna enjoying his money so much.

He realised he was smiling, remembering her delight in shopping. He'd never been all that ambitious, but having responsibilities changed everything. If Michelle moved up, he would apply. Xen's thoughts turned to Morgan, and he wondered if he would stay in Harrogate to be near his daughter.

'Penny for them Xen, did your weekend go well?'

'Oh, sorry Mei Ling, I didn't hear you arrive. Yes, it was fine. What about you?'

'My weekends are always busy. I help in Ho Chin's restaurant. It's very popular.'

At the mention of the Chinese restaurant Xen felt a surge of fear but he managed to smile and said, 'We really must get started.'

He opened Jake's handover file and read what his colleague had been doing over the weekend, then he whistled, quietly.

'Has Jake found something?' asked Mei Ling.

'Yes, I think he's cracked it. He's discovered how another power, like America, could give the satellite the order to self-destruct. That would bring it down like a huge bomb. I need to speak to Michelle.' He stood up quickly, energised by the breakthrough.

Michelle nodded. 'I was working yesterday, and Jake explained it to me then but now I'd like to call Sean in, and you can explain it to him. When Sean came into her office Michelle motioned them both to sit down. 'Sorry Xen, say it all again – Sean needs to understand how it's done.'

Xen repeated Jake's find and then Sean turned to Michelle. 'So, we need to warn the Chinese space scientists?'

'Yes, they must be given the opportunity to understand this weakness and change it. This will be your task Sean but Xen or Jake must go with you so they can show where the problem is. Do you want a trip to China, Xen?'

'It's tempting but Jake deserves to go because it was his discovery. I think you should ask him and if he doesn't want to go then count me in.'

Michelle nodded. 'I'll ring him and let you know. Sean, will you contact our agent in Beijing and fix a meeting for the beginning of next week. That should give him time to contact the Chinese National Space Administration. You will also have to make contact with the British embassy there and let them know you're coming on a scientific mission.'

'Are they going to be angry when they know we've been hacking their computers?' asked Xen.

'I doubt it,' said Sean. 'They're probably doing the same thing to us. Everyone spies on everyone else, although the space scientists do share a lot of information. I'm looking forward to this trip.'

*

When it was time to go home Michelle told Xen that Jake had jumped at the chance to go to China. This was both good and bad news. Xen would have liked the opportunity but didn't want to leave Joanna and Ruby for an indefinite length of time. He felt elated with their achievement and hoped Michelle would tell Morgan. It would please him to know his last time travel had proved so successful.

*

The feeling of euphoria stayed with Xen as he walked home. He felt confidant and successful and that made him want to share the news with Joanna. His thoughts turned to her and Ruby and by the time he arrived at the flat he had decided to ask Joanna to marry him. Should he cook a special dinner or take her out?

'Hi Daddy, we've had a lovely day. Ruby stayed all morning at Tiny Tots and didn't cry for me once. She had milk and a snack and played with the toys that made a lot of noise and are covered in flashing lights. I brought her home and after lunch she went to sleep for nearly two hours!'

While Joanna was talking, he was watching her animated face and knew he loved her more than anything. He took her in his arms and kissed her for a long time. She pushed him away to breathe and said, 'That was lovely. Are you OK?'

'I'm fine, I've had a good day too and I love you to bits. Let's get married soon.' He laughed, ruefully. 'I was going to find a special occasion to ask you, but I just blurted it out standing here in the kitchen. I get no marks for romanticism.'

'I think this is better than creating an occasion. I'd have only become suspicious if you'd taken us out somewhere

249

posh. What about late September?' Xen nodded grinning widely as she continued.

'Shall we arrange it in Harrogate so we can invite our friends? Perhaps Sean will come too with Ho Chin. Let's see, what date's the last Saturday in September? I'll find a hotel to do us a meal.'

Xen hugged her to him, kissed her, and said, 'I'd open a bottle of the finest Champagne, but, as we haven't any, shall we celebrate with a cup of tea?'

About the Author

I was born in London in 1946, the middle child of three. The family moved to Harlow in Essex when it was a very small, new town with an enthusiastic community spirit.

I went to S. Martin's College of education and became a primary school teacher, returning to Harlow for my first job. The following year I married John, we moved to Biggleswade in Bedfordshire and, during the next seven years, our two children were born. During this time, I studied with the Open University and gained a BA.

John was offered a promotion if he would move to North Yorkshire. He accepted with pleasure, having had many camping holidays in the area. The gentler pace of life was good for growing children and for a writer.

Writing has always been something I enjoyed, poems, stories and holiday diaries but, when I took early retirement, I went to a creative writing class. Out of that a self-help group was formed called The Next Chapter. We wrote stories and poems but were all excited when a local author suggested a course called, 'Write a book in a Year'. I wrote my first novel, 'Forced to Flee' about the ethnic cleansing of Albanians in Kosovo, during the collapse of Yugoslavia.

There was still a need to write and, as I have enjoyed many fantasy stories, 'Pathway Back' became my next project. The idea for the sequel, 'The Pathway Forward', was forming as I wrote it.

Whilst writing all three novels I have been creating a memoir, so keep an eye open for, 'When Life throws you a Lemon.'

Printed in Great Britain
by Amazon

65777638R00149